THE DAYS

of

SOLOMON KAHN

THE DAYS

of

SOLOMON KAHN

a journal

Translated and Edited by

Martin Itzkowitz

For My Grandchildren and Theirs

CONTENTS

FOREWORD

In the summer of 1996, while cleaning out the home of my late parents, Max and Esther Rothstein, I came across some books and papers of my grandfather, Solomon Kahn. I was pleasantly surprised to find the five or six books, a small fraction of those he had owned. They evoked memories of my childhood, part of which was spent in study with him out of some of these very texts. But finding the papers, which I hardly remembered existed until its closing entry hit me with full force, was overwhelming.

However literate an often-impoverished working man might be, he is not likely to keep even the irregular journal that my grandfather had kept. I say irregular, because consecutive pages, identifiable because they were still held together by the glue of the now absent binding and bore no evidence of intervening leaves having been removed, often have widely disparate dates. But the entries were more frequent than the papers I found suggested. First, in many other instances there was clear evidence of pages having been torn out. Second, the entries seemed to focus dispro-portionately on my family of origin. But my grandfather had had six surviving children. Why would he attend to the life of one of them to the relative exclusion of the others?

I surmised that when my grandparents were institutionalized in old age, the journal, like the books, had been divided among their children. Done in haste, the division had been imperfect, and so several entries not pertaining to the Rothstein branch were retained in my mother's portion. Calls to my then surviving aunt and uncle, Claire Wexler and Abraham Kahn, confirmed this had been the case. What remained of their pages also included material concerning family branches other than their own. Unfortunately, they had retained far fewer entries than my mother had, and my cousins, if they had saved any at all in their inheritances, fewer still.

Three items bear special comment. Appendix A, my grandfather's ethical will, was a document separate from the journal papers. Here, it is a slightly revised version of a translation made just after his death by his son, the late Rabbi Ruven Kahn, and me. The last two journal entries, the final one an absolute impossibility in any case, could not have been in my grandfather's hand. They are, in fact, in mine.

I had written the first of these—in halting Yiddish no less—shortly before my grandfather's death, and long after he had grown so incoherent that I had stopped visiting. It was, I suppose, a way of maintaining contact, and also of atoning for having disappointed him with my increasingly secular ways. And it was finding this entry, bundled somehow with the others, that brought the journal home like a thunderbolt.

The second, written in English, is an homage of another, more reflective sort, composed after a visit to the Kahn family plot once my house cleaning task was completed. These last two passages are included here in the belief that they share the spirit of those entries that are truly Solomon Kahn's.

Though in a sense incomplete, *The Days of Solomon Kahn* is full enough, I hope, to depict the man who lived them—his character, his concerns, his time and place, all of which are no more. It is this passing of an era that has prompted me, however belatedly, to place the journal beyond the purview of the personal and familial. Begun as one man's recreation, it is now something of an historical document—albeit one that entertains as it enlightens—and so should be made part of the public record. The simplicity and occasional eloquence of my grandfather's Yiddish, captured so faithfully by Martin Itzkowitz, is no less than a fanfare for the ordinary person in prose.

Allan Redstone
Columbus, Ohio

PREFACE

The Days of Solomon Kahn is a sporadic journal that covers, roughly, the last two thirds of the title figure's life. But references within the record give hints and sometimes details of events in the first third of that life as well.

Among the youngest of twelve sons, Solomon Kahn (SK), was born in czarist Russia about 1870 and grew up in or near Minsk in what is now Belarus. Beyond the fact that they were observant Jews, little else about the family is revealed here or otherwise known. It is clear that they raised a few garden crops and kept chickens. Since Kahn refers to his work as a blacksmith with fair frequency, it is possible that his father was a smith as well. If so, the smithy would have likely been in close proximity to the living quarters, perhaps adjoining them. Obviously, Kahn was familiar with prayer book and biblical Hebrew and was fully literate in Yiddish. His brothers very likely shared his knowledge of Hebrew and, given their exchange of letters, undoubtedly shared his Yiddish literacy.

Having served in the czar's army, married, and begun raising a family of his own, Kahn came to America in 1902. His wife and three children, one of whom he had never seen, followed two years later. It is precisely at this point that the journal, as we have it, begins.

Perhaps the most startling thing about the journal is that it was kept at all. Men and women of Kahn's time, place, and social condition simply did not do such things. It was a time-consuming activity, secular besides, and generally what Kahn himself might have called a *narishkayt*—a bit of foolishness. He appears to have been quite conscious a writer to boot. He several times refers to the fact that he is writing and, on occasion, follows up the theme of a particular entry with further discussion or commentary in another entry a day or two later.

In addition, if he began keeping the journal before his family's arrival in America, it might have been a way of coping with the pain of their absence and with his own relative isolation as a recent immigrant himself. However, since the journal includes no entry prior to November 8, 1904, such suggestions are merely speculation.

Why, then? One might suggest that for him it was a creative release—perhaps as much in the physical act of writing itself as in the formulation of phrases and ideas. Patient teacher though he turned out to be, Kahn had always worked with his hands. We have glimpses of him shoeing horses, repairing pushcarts, cobbling the family shoes, making a bench, fitting new handles to knives. Perhaps his principal occupation, sewing machine operator, was too mechanical, repetitive, and enervating to be a source of satisfaction.

Readers will note that entries grow more abundant from the late 1930's on. Someone at work up to sixty hours a week is likely to have little more than sleep for diversion. In retirement, however, Kahn had far more leisure to observe, think, write and reflect on what he had written. Still, this leaves the earliest entries unexplained.

At least equally puzzling is Kahn's intermittent literary flair. We have sporadic passages that range from well-turned to eloquent. In addition, several of the entries are written in present tense, as if Kahn appreciated the sense of immediacy such a choice could create. He has an ear (and memory) for dialogue as well. However, since Kahn nowhere pretends to literature, his choice is far likely to have been—like that of other true primitives—more intuitive than deliberate. Lacking full or satisfactory explanations, then, let us simply be grateful for such anomalies.

We have in *Days* both the record of an individual life and the age in which that life was lived. But gaps in the journal in its present state also create gaps in the historical record. World War I, for example, seems hardly to have occurred, and even World War II, with which Kahn, a soldier's father, was more intimately involved, is scarcely presented as a blow-by-blow account. Less global events, such as the Triangle fire or the murder conviction of Louis "Lepke" Buchalter, are dealt with only sporadically. Still, in these hundred-odd days one finds hints and more of the major concerns of the first half of the last century—immigrant poverty, the rise of labor unions, the Depression, warfare, Nazism and the Holocaust, assimilation, racial and ethnic prejudice.

As representative of the lives of many immigrants who arrived during the "great wave" after 1880, and of Jews from Eastern Europe especially, the journal is more fully articulate. But it is also somewhat atypical in its conservatism. For Kahn, America was a land of freedom and (perhaps) opportunity but no less a place of danger that threatened the practice, values, and culture of Jewish orthodoxy, all of which he strove to maintain and perpetuate. On the one hand, he attends night school and, bearing his framed citizenship certificate, proudly has his grandsons accompany him to the polling place. On the other, his essential quietism is offended and challenged by America's aggressive materialism that leads one of his sons to arrest on a gambling violation and a neighborhood landlord to turn beggar (without need) during the Depression. Even amid America's virtues, Kahn remains essentially in exile.

Beyond a staunch commitment to Zionism, his politics, to the extent that he can be said to have had any, are similarly restrained and for similar reasons. He has no use for the socialists (communists are beneath discussion), principally because their avowed secularism violates his fundamental faith, but also because he does not accept the world view of class struggle between the haves and have-nots any more than he accepts a son-in-law's division of the world into bastards and fools. His dogma are the commandments and rabbinical teachings; his ethic, *mentshlikhkayt*,[1] which can be applied to dealings with even bosses and landlords.

However, to emphasize the politics or historical events as recorded in *Days*, is to ignore the cake for the frosting. The essential charm of the journal, even in its rare insensitive passages, lies in its utter domesticity—the liveliness of Friday night gatherings, the competition between two of Kahn's daughters, his wife Rivke's colorful nicknames for friend and foe alike, his method of teaching his grandsons or how he inadvertently gets them drunk, observations on the sexual prowess of a neighborhood dog. Not that all is comedy. The shadow of Hitler is cast over many pages, as are those of poverty, illness, the deaths of children, fleeting time, and final dementia. As far as he can, given the limits of his education and experience, Kahn sees life whole.

Rendering Kahn's vision into English has posed some stylistic problems. The entries themselves are uneven, unpolished, and their language not usually remarkable. Yet there are phrases, sentences, paragraphs that glow brilliantly. How, then, to present these and yet create the sense of a unified whole? One might be tempted to say that I have recognized this difficulty without confronting it. Almost without exception, I have allowed such inconsistencies to stand, believing that in due course, readers will recognize them as idiosyncratic and so characteristic of the journal's style.

Another difficulty is that some of Kahn's phrasing is mannered and repetitive. Here, I have attempted to include enough instances of a formulated phrase (e. g., "thank God") to suggest the stylistic quirk but have varied it frequently, at times retaining the Yiddish original, in order to avoid any hint of monotony. At other times, in the case of the word *take*, for example, I have generally allowed the Yiddish to stand, and only occasionally translated it as "truly" or the equivalent.

The effect in such cases, I hope, is English as one of Kahn's children might have spoken it, on occasion deviating from standard grammar and unabashed by incorporation of some (occasionally anglicized) Yiddish vocabulary and phrasing. Such a speaker was more apt to say, for example, "It's a long time, *take*, since they came to visit" than "It's certainly been a long time since . . ." or some other "Yankee" equivalent, which would have conveyed the prose sense of the original expression but not its flavor. In instances like this, *take* serves as a cultural marker. I have, however, scrupulously tried to avoid caricature, which is the risk attendant on such an approach. The reader will decide with what success.

Kahn's use of names presents a minor problem in regard to consistency. For his children, their spouses, and people of his own generation he uses Hebrew or Yiddish names almost exclusively.

Max, for one of his sons-in-law, is an exception, and *Essie*, for his daughter Esther, might be another, perhaps influenced by English usage.[2] With his grandchildren's names, however, he is less consistent, in some cases—most prominently *Ari/Allan* and *Yoyne/Jerry*—using Hebrew (or Yiddish) and English interchangeably, rarely, however, in the same entry. Particularly because such usage suggests something of the degree to which Kahn assimilated, I have not attempted to alter his practice in the version presented here. However, to resolve any possible confusion, Professor Allan Redstone, grandson of Solomon Kahn, has graciously supplied a table of names that appears as an appendix.

My most flagrant emendation is the substitution of Gregorian dating for Jewish. Since Kahn wrote in the evening almost exclusively, and because Jewish days begin at sundown, his dates would have corresponded in the secular calendar to those beginning after midnight. Here, however, the dates are those upon which, again according to the secular calendar, the entries were actually composed. With one noted (and notable) exception, if Kahn appears to have written upon days when such activity is traditionally forbidden, he has done so only after the Sabbath or festival has ended. For the most part, occasional errors, omissions, or obscurities have been emended silently when incidental to the entries in which they occur.

As indicated above, a considerable number of Yiddish words and expressions have been retained. These are italicized, translated, and often explained in a note at their first use and, if repeated (sans italics) in subsequent entries, listed in the appended glossary. If appropriate, such notes will also include variant singular or plural forms that appear later in the text.

Two words, however, have been italicized throughout the journal proper: *take* to avoid possible confusion with English "take" and *sider* (prayer book) to avoid confusion with English pronunciation, as in "outsider."

Explanatory notes to establish context for journal content have also been provided. In the main, these deal with living or working conditions, religious practice, and persons or events referred to in the entries. Of course, readers familiar with either the language or historical background for which there are annotations need simply read on.

I am grateful to have had the opportunity to work with the journal, principally to have made the acquaintance of Solomon Kahn throughout the joyful labor. I am, of course, most profoundly indebted to Professor Allan Redstone for bringing his grandfather's verbal legacy to my attention and entrusting it to me. I am thankful as well for the information and insights provided by Solomon Kahn's other grandchildren, most especially the late Jerome Wexler. Thanks (at least) are also due my wife, Ann, for distinguishing carefully between desertion and my years before the twin masts of the library and computer screen.

A NOTE ON TRANSLITERATION

Transliterations of Yiddish in the text, with few exceptions, follow the method advanced by the YIVO Institute for Jewish Research, one that has by now been generally adopted by Yiddish scholars. Such exceptions that occur primarily involve words from Hebrew, including some that refer to religious observances or practices that have become especially familiar to English speaking readers in other forms. But I have treated such words on a case-by-case basis, using, for example, *Bar Mitsve* and *Toyre* instead of *Bar Mitzvah* and *Torah* to help establish the writer's voice while preserving essential clarity.

Editorial comments in the notes, however, do not necessarily conform to the YIVO pattern. Nor do the YIVO transliterations proper necessarily reflect the usage of a particular dialect, although Solomon Kahn himself would have spoken the one known as Litvish (Lithuanian) or Northeastern.

KEY TO PRONUNCIATION

Vowels

a=the vowel in *far*, *fog*

e=the vowel in *bet*, *wren*

i=ranges from the vowel in *fish* to that of *feet*

o=the vowel in *hub*, *hovel*

u=ranges from the vowel in *put* to the vowel *in soon*

Diphthongs

ay=the diphthong in *mild*, *shy*

ey=the diphthong in *shade*, *convey*

oy=the diphthong in *coil*, *joy*, (approximate)

Consonants

Consonants are typically pronounced as they are in English. However, *g* is restricted to its "hard" form as in *go* and *gag* and the letters *c, j, q, w*, and *x* are never used.

kh=the consonant cluster in *Bach*

dzh=the *g* in *gem*

ts=the consonant cluster in *cats*, *blitz*

tsh=the consonant cluster in *chip*, *watch*

zh=the *s* in *pleasure*

Note: Final letters of some clusters, as in *kugl* (pudding) and *mameloshn*, (mother tongue, i.e., Yiddish) have syllabic value.

Solomon Kahn's Journal

NOVEMBER 8, 1904

A t last, they are with me—Rivke and the children, three of them now. It is more than two years since I left them at home—in the old home—to come here. More than two years working, saving to send for them.

Last night I couldn't sleep, so early this morning, even before the sun, I went to Battery Park.[1] It would be hours until the first boat from Ellis Island, but other people were already waiting. When it came, there was a nice competition between the engines and the pounding in my chest. I could hardly see the passengers through the crowd, so many as they were and as short as I am. But no Rivke, no children. All around me people running, shouting, crying, falling into each other's arms, making me feel even more alone than I had been for all the long months.

So it went all morning and into the afternoon. By three o'clock, I almost gave up hope. But the next boat soon emptied and I finally saw them, almost the last to leave. Then I was the one who ran and shouted. Then it was the two of us, Rivke and me, who wept and embraced. She held me for a long time. Her warm tears wet my neck inside the collar of my overcoat. After a few minutes, I stepped back to look at her, still holding her by the arms. The same, thank God, the same dark eyes, dark hair braided and coiled, the pale, smooth face—only a little tired. Who could blame her?

And the children. Here was Reyzl, maybe seven now, smiling shyly, because she knew who I was. And there was Asher, three or four years old, who did not, hiding behind his mother.

"That's your father," Rivke told him.

He buried his head in her skirt. Our first laughter together again.

"Reyzl," I said, bending toward her, "can you give your father a kiss?"

She came to me slowly, and I took her in my arms.

"*Tate, oy Tate*,"[2] she whispered, then suddenly kissed me on the mouth.

"Not on the lips," Rivke scolded.

I waved a hand for her to let it pass as I set the child down.

Then, standing before me, I noticed little Ruven for the first time. He had waddled to Rivke from behind a bundle when his sister let go of his hand. The child I had never seen. Rivke was pregnant not more than two months when I left. If I had known, who knows if I would have.

"A beautiful boy, Rivke," I said.

"A smart one too," she answered.

I lifted him to me. He did not pull away, but put his fingers through my beard and into my nose. I pressed my forehead against his.

"I'm your *tate*," I told him, "your *tate*."

He shook his head and kept poking at my face.

But something was happening with Asher.

"*Tate*?" he asked, looking from behind Rivke.

I smiled.

"*Tate!*" he shouted.

Leaving his mother, he rushed toward me. I took him up with my free arm.

Later, as we walked to the car stop, I couldn't tell whether the eyes were open wider or the mouth. Such buildings! So many! And the machines[3]—with such a noise—and so fast! By the streetcars, they were startled again. Which of them, after all, had ever seen such a carriage, moving as if by itself? I am sure they would have refused to get on. But lucky for us, ours was a horse car.[4] So onto this the five of us climbed with all our bundles, and by the time we got off, Rivke and the children had almost calmed down.

But walking from the car stop to our building they were again amazed. So many people! Not at all like us, many of them! Not like the peasants we are used to either. And such sounds with such smells!

"*Tate, Mame*, look over there!" Reyzl called. "That man was black!"

For me, of course, who had seen every kind and color, this was nothing new.

As we walked up the five flights of stairs, I explained to Rivke about the apartment.

"We have three rooms, but the rent is a little less than on the lower floors The children will have one room, we another. And in the kitchen all of us can eat together or, if we have sometimes a guest, sit around the table with our tea. About a boarder we'll talk later. The toilet[5] is in the hall," I went on, "but running water for washing and cooking we have inside."

Once we were in the apartment, I showed her exact. "Here's the sink; here's the stove; the coal bin I just filled. We have a back, so there will not be much light.[6] The new paint is maybe four months old. When they need to paint again—who knows in how many years—we'll maybe move."[7]

Rivke did not say a word through all this; the children were not so quiet, jumping on the bed, pulling drawers and banging them shut. But soon it grew dark, and when I lit the gas lamp, for maybe the tenth time this day everyone gasped. Rivke stood in the shadows, still trying to understand it all. Sounds of traffic, children playing, angry husbands and wives, coarse workmen— came in from the halls, through the windows and even the walls themselves. Smells of cooking, garbage piled up in the alleys, standing drains joined them. Lamps from the next street glared through our bare windows; a mouse peeked through a gap in the floorboards then disappeared.

Rivke turned to me. "Amerike," she said. It was half a question—a little wonder, a little fear.

"Amerike," I nodded. Half an answer; the tone of my voice was an echo of her own.

OCTOBER 16, 1906

When the telegram came from Baltimore yesterday morning we knew it must be bad news. It was from Rivke's sister Rokhl. Their mother was dead. From pneumonia. In just four days. They would wait until two o'clock today to bury her in case Rivke and Hinde could come.

To go to Baltimore was out of the question. Where would we have money for tickets? And even if we tried to borrow, who knows if we could get the money in time? And how could we send two women who had never been out of New York to a strange city to arrive maybe in the middle of the night? And both of them pregnant on top of everything else.

So we sent a telegram to Rokhl and the others in Baltimore, telling them their two sisters could not come, that they should all be strong, and that they should not hire someone to say *Kadish*.[1] I would say it myself.

From then until this afternoon Rivke and Hinde were crying in each other's arms. Usually, they are not the closest of sisters, but such a grief they could share without the quarrels and grudges between them getting in the way. But after 2:30, when they thought the funeral was over, they started the *shive*,[2] each in her own apartment. For the rest of the week the neighbors and cousins nearby would help with the cooking and the little ones and bring what comfort they could. They also understood very well that I and Hinde's Motl could not afford to lose yet another day's pay.

When I came back from *shul*[3] this evening, a meal was on the table, but everyone had left to take care of their own families a few hours. The children, already finished with supper, understood how things were and worked at their lessons quietly. Once in a while, Reyzl would blow the nose or whimper softly like a little cat. The oldest of the three, she remembered her *bobe*[4] the best. A couple times she made a noise, I took her face in both hands, wiped away the tears with the thumbs, and gave a kiss on the forehead.

Rivke, I am sure, had not eaten a thing. She sat by herself and rocked back and forth on her low stool.[5] "A pregnant woman does not have to sit in such a way," I told her, but, of course, she would not listen. Over and over, she stroked her swollen belly, repeating her mother's name, Esther—Esther, again and again.

Death is a fearful thing, even more in a strange place—how long have we been here after all—and when the living are scattered. And this is the first time in America that death has touched us. But in both Hinde and Rivke there is already new life. And with His help, Esther's name will surely be preserved.[6]

APRIL 4, 1910

Tomorrow they are coming to take the farm away—the bank and the policemen.[1] Six months we couldn't pay. The man from the society[2] saw how it was and wouldn't give more help—who can blame him? So there is no surprise.

We tried, my brother Borukh and I. But what did we know about farming? Whoever had a farm? A goat, yes. Some chickens. Onions and potatoes out back. And I could shoe horses. But this was not fields and plows, with cattle and hay, and milking for an hour day and night and then dealing with the dairy.

And Borukh, who knows everything, of course, is not so easy to get along with, even if you give in all the time. He's older, so he's smarter. I don't know where such a thing is written. Not in any part of the Talmud I know. "The future is tomatoes." How often did we ever see a tomato before New York? But we planted them. For the worms—at least they enjoyed. Then it was "Green peppers will save us." They didn't. So much for Borukh Ha-Novi.[3]

And with Rivke he didn't get along better than by the vegetables. The two of them so much alike. It's a good thing he has his Dina, who seems to say only "hello," "goodbye," and "yes"—and that Rivke has me—even if I say more.

But tomorrow is the end of the farm. The end of Connecticut

and the *shlep*[4]—more than a mile—to the room we use for a shul; no more davening on *Shabes*[5] without a *minyen*.[6] And in the city, at least, there will be a rabbi and a people to study with who live nearby.

We are taking with us the lesson of a bad experience and a couple dollars to start again. Also one or two little stories that could make us laugh when we remember. Reyzl reaching for a coil of dough and finding a snake that chased her from the shed—not so funny when it happened, and little Essie falling in the manure pile almost every other week. Borukh would yell at her for spoiling the dung and making the crops fail. And Rivke would scrub the child half raw with a floor brush, relieving herself with a mother's curses all the while.

Let us hope for better times in Newark.

MARCH 27, 1911

A terrible fire late Shabes afternoon. I could see from outside the shul a cloud of smoke above the buildings. This was not the cloud of the Lord.[1] Something, I knew, must be burning. I did not know that it was people.

Terrible, terrible the loss of life. The dead, they say now, more than a hundred forty. Women mostly, some of them not more than girls. Burnt to death, choked to death by the smoke, smashed and broken from jumping out of windows—like candles some of them, their hair flaming like wicks—because no water could reach the fire and no fireman could reach them. In one disaster so many ways to die.[2]

Poor, all of them. Who but the poor work in such a place as a shirtwaist factory? So all over the neighborhoods where they lived, and more, there has been nothing but cries of pain and tears enough almost to have put out even such a fire as this. By Jew and by gentile the same.

We do not know ourselves any of the dead or their families. But by the pushcarts Sunday morning and today Rivke heard that two women from Madison Street—in the same house yet—were killed, and another from Monroe.[3] Also, in our building Mr. Weintraub tells us a *lantsman*[4] by his cousin's husband in Brooklyn lost a child. For us (this time) there is no suffering at home, but what person does not feel the pain of others in such a case, and all the more because it did not have to happen as it did.

This is why already mixed in with the grief there are cries of anger. Anger that there was not a decent fire escape. Anger that the doors to exits were blocked by bolts of cloth and old machines or locked altogether. Anger that scraps of material all over the place were just waiting for a single spark.

Already the unions have begun to protest—meetings called, speeches on the corners, petitions to the government. And who can say they are wrong? A person who goes to the job should not be going to her death. The place and the work should be as safe as possible, and since nothing is a hundred per cent, plans for emergencies must be made. This is only common sense. It is also human decency. But common sense seems not to be so common and decency even less, especially if it will cost the bosses a few dollars. The price of the water buckets and the fire escapes they know to the penny. Sprinklers, they will tell you, cost too much. But what is the price of a person's life? The price of the women from Madison Street or the child of Weintraub's cousin's lantsman? Until yesterday it was cheaper by the bosses and politicians to let them die. Tomorrow, with the unions holding the pencil and the angry people the paper, maybe they will figure again.

The hundred and forty are gone. Nothing will bring them back. But if their deaths can make a better life for those who come after, they will be martyrs as much as victims. Good for me to say, who did not know them. But for their families and friends, whether martyrs or victims, they are just as dead. And whatever the unions or bosses or governments do—or what I write here to myself, will bring no comfort in the houses of mourning.

May each of the dead be remembered in the words of Solomon the Wise:

> Strength and dignity are her clothing; and she laugheth at the time to come. . . .
>
> Give her of the fruit of her hands; and let her works praise her in the gates.[5]

AUGUST 24, 1911

I t is almost ten o'clock, and Rivke has been asleep for hours. The pills, they said, would let her rest till the morning. So the children and I and Mrs. Osofsky from next door, who yesterday took her and waited till I could leave the shop and today helped me bring her home, have been able to take a few breaths.

When it happened, who would have thought that it would come to this? *Nu*,[1] so Rivke cut herself in the kitchen. What woman hasn't? Yes, it was a deep cut that bled for half an hour, but with these things you put a little water and tie a rag and that's the end of it.

But in two days the finger was swollen. So she soaked it—in warm water, in hot water, in cold water—in water with a parsley someone told her to use. Maybe this helped and the finger was now only twice the size and not three times. But then it began to throb as if Rivke's heart had moved there from her chest. A thick pus was coming from the wound and the flesh around it had a strange color. So more soaking. But Tuesday, when Rivke could not put her hand to her face because of the smell, we knew that a doctor must see it.

At the clinic, he shook his head. "For yourself, you have come in time," he told Rivke, "but for the finger it is too late." Trying to comfort her as she moaned and wept, I could make out more words: "don't wait," "tomorrow morning," "blood poison." These were said to no one, like at the shop I would talk to the wheel when I put it back on the cart. Then to me he said, "If you want your wife . . ." But I stopped him with a raised hand and said "About this there is not a question."

But with hospitals there is always a question. With an operation even more. Still, without the hospital and operation, we could already see, the two of us, what the answer would be. On the way back home from Essex Street, early though it was, I could feel the heat of the day and wiped a hand across my forehead. But beside me, like a white sheet, Rivke was trembling.

The next morning it was done. Rivke, all in all, was calm. Although when it comes to everyday aches and pains she is an authority on *oy*,[2] in time of a serious sickness she can put all complaining aside. The only thing she said before going in was "Thank God for the ether."

The children, of course, were upset. I tried to make them feel better, telling them that, after the operation, when their mother laid a hand on them it would not hurt so much. This maybe was not such a good idea in the first place, but Asher, who is sometimes a little philosopher, began to reason, "If it hurts less without one finger, then without two . . ." He stopped when he saw my face. "On her other hand," I reminded him, "she will still have five." So much for the wisdom of children and my own foolishness.

Like their mother, the children are asleep now. Mrs. Osofsky came in at supper time with a pot of potato soup and some pieces black bread so we had what to eat. The children made a face at the look and taste of the burnt flour that she had put in the soup.

"Mama never makes it this way," they whined together, but with the bread and butter they managed to get it down.

Most likely I will sleep here in my chair, so if Rivke wakes up and wants something I will be ready to get it. Tomorrow begins changing the bandages. At the hospital, they told us a nurse would come to do this for the first two days and to see how it is healing.[3] After that, we will have to do it ourselves. To this I do not look forward. A stump where a finger was could not be a pretty sight, Rivke will again find her tongue, and the ringing in my ears then will be worse than in my nose now the smell of carbolic from across the room.

JANUARY 30, 1912

The citizen class is not easy. That I am going tired and hungry after work is only the beginning. And it does not help for a grown man to sit in a seat meant for children.

But even with rest, a full stomach, and a good chair the English would be hard. Mrs. Hoffmeyer, our teacher, tells us that the language is a relative of German and Yiddish, but it must be the kind of relative that is the husband of a brother-in-law's cousin from a third marriage. Who knows from it? Believe me, the two Germans and the eight Jews do not have an easier time with it than the Italians, the Poles, the Russians, the Hungarian and the Greek. After "bread" and "butter," we are all the same[1]—joined together by two things—that we want to be citizens and that because of the English we are afraid we will never be.

But one thing I notice is that the younger people do not have so much trouble. Miss Agnello and Mr. Jankowski, maybe eighteen, nineteen years old, speak—to our ears—like the English was *mameloshn*.[2] Maybe they were in a school not so long ago as the rest of us and are used to learning in this way. Maybe when you get to be my age your head turns to stone and nothing can get in or, better, like a shoe at the forge, the brain has already been put to the fire, shaped, cooled, and set. My Yiddish shoe I cannot unmake, but maybe—such a smart smith to leave the holes—I can put English nails.

Little by little, if I remember to keep my eyes in the right direction, I am getting to read more than two words at a time. But to speak is like breaking my tongue. Of course, Mrs. Hoffmeyer insists that we speak only English—for our own good but also hers because, except for a little German and French (not such a useful language by immigrants), she has only English herself. The writing is even harder left to right than the reading, but this I manage to do—like a child, with pressing too hard on the pencil and putting the tongue between the teeth. In the house, the older ones make jokes about Papa doing homework, but they have all helped when I needed, even with the studying for the little tests Mrs. Hoffmeyer gives. About such a thing I am not foolishly proud. Whoever knows should teach.

But since I have been going to the class I have noticed that Rivke's English is better than mine. Not that she will soon give a speech, but, if she has to, with everyday things she can at least manage. There must be a little more English in the streets and stores than by me in the shop. The children, after all, learned some even before they started school. Even without a book and a teacher, the world itself must be a *kheyder*.[3]

Still, English is only the half of it. Learning about the American history and the government is the other. Of course, if I could learn it in Yiddish, it would not be so bad. But I know all about President Washington who was the father of the country and President Lincoln who freed the slaves. (About why there were slaves in the first place we don't talk—a *shande*[4] for the greenhorns most likely.) Also about the Pilgrims, before Washington, I think, Mrs. Hoffmeyer told us, and we learned how many states and their names. (I will not pass the test if I have to write *Mesertshuzits* [*sic*]). A little about Thomas Jefferson and Benjamin Franklin together with Henry Hudson, because we are in New York, she threw in gratis. Not that the class costs to begin with.

I *kvetsh*[5] I suppose because I am a little nervous, but if you asked me the truth, I would say I will pass the citizen test, at least the second time if not the first. But for others I am afraid. Mr. Hymowitz, for one, must learn that the three parts of the government are not the same as the ships of Columbus. Mrs. Pekulin also is a little confused. President Lincoln was not killed in Buffalo, New York by a cowboy named Bill. But I understand such mistakes. Didn't I myself mix up George Washington—first with the English king—his enemy yet—and again with his Irving, the writer?[6] I understand that they want us to know a little something about this country, especially how it is supposed to work, but they are asking us to learn a strange history in a strange tongue.

And yet, this is the struggle that makes from separate students a class. Outside, we go our own way—Jews with Jews and Poles with Poles. Inside, we have to work together with the same thing and for the same thing, like a union, only for learning, and with even more kinds of people. So we don't laugh at a Hymowitz or a Mrs. Pekulin—or we try not to—and we help each other what little we can. Maybe not since the tower of Babel has there been such cooperation. And since we are trying only for our papers and not the heavens, maybe He will allow us, even help us to succeed.

APRIL 17, 1912

Today the newspaper boys were again all over the streets screaming about the ship Titanic that sank in the night two days ago. A terrible accident. Who can imagine a piece of ice so big it could do such damage?

Some say it was fate, others that it was God's will. But for everything there must be a reason, and God does not play with boats in the ocean like a child in a tub water. Someone, maybe more than one, made a mistake. I read about a fog, messages by flashing lights they didn't see—messages from a radio—this I don't understand exactly—they didn't hear. Maybe someone—a sailor—who should have been awake was asleep. Like me that time on guard in the czar's army.[1]

But here, awake or not, messages or not, fog or not—there is something else. A ship that couldn't sink they said and said again ten thousand times—as if the more they said the more true it became. Can a man whose own life is seventy years, eighty maybe,[2] create something that cannot be destroyed? Made in His image though we are, no work of our hands is forever. As Koheles, son of David, says, "I have seen all the works that are done under the sun; and, behold, all is vanity and a striving after wind."[3]

Still, we don't know the whole story yet. We will maybe know more after the reports from eleven bureaus, five committees, and nine offices.

Some say a thousand people died. Some say more. Drowned, all of them, either going under with the ship or freezing first in the water if they jumped off. Hundreds of people—exactly how many we will know maybe better tomorrow—another ship picked up from the life boats,[4] which it seems there were not enough. Some lost a husband; others a wife; parents a child; children parents. Whole families gone—maybe the lucky ones among the dead to leave no one suffering behind.

The dead are of all kinds, but more, probably, from the poor than from the rich.[5] Who would expect different? Sometimes money buys off even death itself. And on such a fine ship, who could complain about steerage or lifeboats that weren't there? Especially when into the bargain, at no extra cost, there is a burial at sea?[6]

But for now I am sorry for the many lives lost and thankful that my own trip across the ocean on the _________,[7] miserable as it was, brought me here in one piece.

MAY 3, 1914

Friday afternoon Goldstein the boss comes to me. "Sol," he says, "I have no money. I can't pay you today.[1] Monday I'll pay you."

I have worked for Goldstein almost three years. He's a man like all men. Not worse, maybe a little better. He has an eye for the women, takes a schnapps more than now and then, but cheating and lying, no, not for something like this.

Still, I say, "No money? Not till Monday?"

"Look, Sol," he says, "whatever you and the rest think, Rothschild I'm not. I make a living. The business gets by. But Wednesday, two payments I was expecting didn't come—for one of them it looks like the goods got lost, and Thursday another customer went bankrupt. I got most of his goods back, but goods isn't cash. Between now and Monday, I'll see my brothers in Passaic and uptown and they'll lend me until I can get things straightened out. A dollar, two dollars maybe I can give you from my own pocket, but the rest not till Monday."

I thought. "Rivke has already made Shabes,[2] and until tomorrow night no one will touch money. If then or Sunday we need a loaf of bread or milk for the children, we can find the few pennies or—if we have to—borrow, just borrow, from the rent money (this we don't pay till next week)—or God forbid, in an emergency, even from the *pushkes*.[3] No one will go hungry or naked for two days.

I looked at Goldstein and shrugged; "Nu, so Monday."

"Monday. Definitely Monday, Sol!" he called as he rushed away.

He should have paid me. On this both the sages and the communists would agree.[4] But like goods isn't cash, should isn't could. If the man doesn't have it, he doesn't have it. Everyone has *tsores*.[5]

I know all about the war between workers and bosses. But there are other wars—not only to live and breathe, but to survive as a *mentsh*[6] with a *neshome*[7] in one piece—not remnants. And in this, the workers and the bosses must be on the same side.

SEPTEMBER 8, 1914

Khavele[1] went to school for the first time and came home with a new name. This is very nice of the school to name our daughter for us, and I didn't even have to announce it in the shul.[2] Maybe the school knows that the New Year is coming in two weeks and our custom is to give the children something for the holiday. But a kerchief, a blouse, a pair of shoes in prosperous times, is not such a fine a thing as a name in English. "From now on," Missus Henley told her, "you will be called Claire." Claire! *Nu!*

Before this I would say our children were lucky. True, they took Reyzl and made her Rose, but at least it means almost the same and the sound is not altogether different.

Asher they let alone. Maybe they couldn't think of anything; besides the name is in their Bible like in our *Toyre*[3]. With Ruven they only changed in the middle a *veyz* to a *beyz*[4]—close. And Esther no problem. Also in the writings, but by them a fine English name. (They should only know it's not only not English, it isn't Hebrew exactly either.[5]) But with Khave, the "kh" sticks like a bone in their throats. If my English was good enough, I would tell them that Khave was the wife of Adam, but who knows what this would be in their language. How do they get to my Solomon from Sholem? Or from Rivke's sister Tsaytl to Therese? And from where, suddenly, do we get our Isadores and Morrises and Sophies?

And last names almost the same. It wasn't enough that they made us take such names in Europe in my grandfather's time—a plain Yosel son of Yakov wasn't good enough. But when we got on the boat for America even those had to change. So from Kagan I became Kahn. It is possible, of course, that the clerk was over-worked or deaf or heard a Jewish name with gentile ears.[6] But if they didn't get us there, they got us on Ellis Island. Like in the next building two brothers, Gold and Blum, each one with a different half of the name they brought over. Maybe somewhere there are two sisters for them, Fein and Berg.[7]

But worse, like by Claire, they sometimes make it English alto-gether—from Rabinowitz to Robbins, from Moskowitz to Moss. For this the *Daytsher*[8] have already given us fine examples. One day I would like to meet on East Broadway Mr. Belmont and Mr. Bloomingdale. To the one I would say, "How are you, Schoenberg?[9] And when he fainted, I'd say to the other, "Quick! Help him, Blumenthal!" And he would also faint.

Kagan to Kahn doesn't really bother me so much. One Jewish name, another Jewish name. Khave to Claire bothers me more. If they can't make Americans altogether from Rivke and me, they will do it with our children. This is also kidnapping— of the spirit—like, I'm afraid, is the English itself.

What can we do? What we have always done in exile—live in two worlds. In their world she is Claire Kahn. But among us she is Khave daughter of Sholem. So was she named before all Israel; so is she known in the mind of God.

OCTOBER 23, 1917

Asher has left high school. His mother and I begged him to stay the couple years and finish. After all, a high school graduate is a somebody, as they measure things in this country, at least someone who could be a somebody. But no, he wants to make money now (much more, he says, than he gets from the little jobs after school), while he learns a business, and one day be his own boss.

And what will he do with his money, after paying something for his board, which is only right that he should do? Buy more hair lacquer? Go to the moving pictures three times a week instead of two? Sit in the ice-cream parlor (at least it's not the billiards parlor) every night of the week with another girl, even if he's not yet sixteen?

One thing I know. He won't buy a book. Not in Hebrew, not in Yiddish, not in English. So in three languages he won't read. Four, I forgot the Latin. This is not a country for scholars. *Toyre*? What for? Talmud? Who needs it? By the *goyim*[1] the same—their Bible they maybe dust off for an hour on Sunday and then goodbye.

No. This is the country for money. How to make money. How to make more money. How to make the most money. How to make money from money. How to make money without money. How not to lose money. The deal. Every schemer a philosopher. The net profit. Every bookkeeper a sage. The clinking of coins; the rustle of bills. Each bank teller a *klezmer*.[2]

But it is done. Tomorrow he goes to Lipsky's on 14th Street. A little stock room, a little counter, a little cash drawer after a while. He'll learn it all.

May he live and be well. And may he remember his people and his God.

OCTOBER 10, 1918

Velvl Weinstock, the husband of Rivke's sister Brayne, died this afternoon. It was not even a week since the fever and cough began. Not such an old man either. Younger than me. But this sickness does not care about age. A *freser*,[1] it devours what it can. An old bobe, a new baby—all the same.

These days, the smallest sneeze, the slightest chill, already they are sending for the undertaker. Everyone knows someone who has not survived, and everyone is afraid. In our building alone we have lost four, on the block maybe twenty, hundreds on the East Side, already thousands in the whole country. It is like the eleventh plague—worse, even, than the war; but no one is spared, and putting blood on the doors this time will not help.[2]

Poor Velvl was a decent man. A worker in the fur business, so almost half the year he didn't have a penny. Except for repairs once in a while he did at home, or got a couple weeks' work in the factory by a sewing machine, or a day or two driving a wagon. In the slack season, two or three afternoons a week and on Shabes he would be in shul. I would tell him that his name should not be Weinstock but Halber because he was a proper Jew only half the year. The joke he took with a smile. "If I could," he would say, "I would change it to Ganz, but since I have to eat . . ."[3]

It was a common story. It is always hard to be a Jew, but in this country it is sometimes harder. Not every Jewish boss, never mind the others, respects our ways. Far from it. Worse still, by some of the Daytsher they have made a Shabes of Sunday. But in this I have been lucky, and sometimes stubborn. So I borrowed two or three days—a week—until I found a place that would give me Shabes off. But more and more are like Velvl— not so lucky—and not so stubborn.

But I do not speak ill of the dead. Velvl Weinstock's head, heart, and hand were Jewish enough. In the months he went to shul he would once in a while sit at the Rabbi's table for a little study, daven with spirit and lead a service now and then, and his hand was always the first to reach into a pocket when the charity box came around. At home the same. He kept a bookcase and read at least a little every week—even in busy season, sang to the babies, went to the union meetings, and on the kitchen shelf was always pushkes—for students, orphans, the sick, the old, the poor.

But he is gone now. And what is Brayne to do with four children, the oldest just past *bar mitsve*,[4] and no money to live on? Move in with us, of course. This Rivke has already decided, and I will not say no. Twelve of us in four rooms will not be easy,[5] but since when is life easy? Brayne herself will have to find work. The older boy, Dov Ber, will get a job after school for a while and go to business altogether when he is fourteen. Our Reyzl already brings home a little money. Of course, we will be crowded, but this will not be forever, and with God's help we won't starve. About only one thing am I worried. Where in such a household does the uncle end and the father begin, if the father begins at all? With the small ones there might not be a problem. Tonight already they let me wipe the eyes and blow the noses. With the bigger ones we'll see.

Velvl's funeral is tomorrow. I have hired old Mr. Sheinkopf to sit with the body overnight and recite from Psalms.[6]

FEBRUARY 28, 1920

Reyzl this morning comes to me and says she wants to get married. This, I think, is itself not such a bad idea. After all, she is twenty-one, twenty-two years old, and if she waits much longer she will be yet an *alte moyd*.[1] But I know already what's to come. Still, I say, "Good. I will talk with the *shadkhen*."[2]

"Pa," she says, "you don't have to talk with anyone. I want to marry Murray Farbstein. You know we've been keeping company."

"Yes, I know," I say, "even if I wish I didn't."

"Pa," she answers, I love him. He loves me. We get along really well and agree on a lot of things—supporting the workers, the Jewish homeland. . . ."[3]

"Do you agree also," I say and feel my face go red, "that he should work on Shabes?"

"We agree," her face also red, "that you do what you have to in order to survive, to live. This is America, not a shtetl near Minsk."

"Out there is America," I shout, pointing to the window. "In here is Israel.[4] My daughter will not marry someone who is not *Shoymer Shabes*."[5]

The red in her face turns to white; her body goes stiff, then she turns away and leaves the room without another word.

This was our first little fight. I do not look forward to the bigger battles still to come.

MAY 3, 1920

It seems that Rivke is pregnant after all. I can hardly write the words. Who would imagine? A woman of her years! And Khave, our youngest, now, I think, past twelve.

Myself, I am happy with the news. Not that I am so old, but it's good to know that I am still able. And six will be a greater blessing than five. True, another mouth to feed won't be so easy. I will have to work more hours, maybe ask the boss for an increase—just a small one but enough. If not, as they say, we can always throw an extra cup of water in the soup. And until they finish school, Khave and Essie can help with the baby in the afternoon.

Rivke is not so happy. And I can understand that she thought she was finished already with the crying and the feeding and the changing—especially in the middle of the night. But also she is ashamed before the neighbors who will know that we still lie together—as if that is not fitting for people of our years. True, we are no longer young, but we aren't ready for the old age home either. And besides, she was always hot-blooded and never shy about making babies in the first place.

But I mention nothing of this to Rivke. I only read to her about the birth of Isaac to a ninety-year-old Sarah, a woman twice her age. Not that Rivke should laugh, like Sarah, at even the thought of bearing a child. But since this is already more than just a thought, Rivke at least could smile. What is truly not fitting and a shame for the neighbors is to mourn over miracles—even the smallest.

With God's help, all will be well.

AUGUST 30, 1922

Esther and Khave have been fighting again, again over clothes. A blouse this time. Whose it was and who took it without asking still isn't clear. I wish that we could afford to dress each of them altogether separately. But they are only maybe a year apart and about the same size. So why can't they share—at least some things? In Russia they would have been lucky to have even one change [of clothes]. But here, it seems, the more people have the more they want. And what they want are goods, things, money—of course.

They are good girls, both of them already working for a year or two. What little they make they bring to their mother and she gives back to them carfare and a little extra—for an ice-cream maybe or a glass of soda water—who knows what. It's not much, really. They are not "spoiled," as they say here, and certainly not ignored. Believe me, we watch over them, Rivke and I.

But we are here in New York, not Minsk, and soon it will be Rosh Hashanah. If I can put in some more hours and save a penny here and a nickel there, maybe Rivke can buy for each of them something nice—a blouse—a skirt, if there's enough—for the holiday. Reyzl too, naturally—we wouldn't want another world war—though these days she buys a little for herself. The boys don't care so much. A new collar. A necktie maybe. As for Rivke and me, as long as the children are content, we'll be happy with an extra patch or a couple stitches to fix the holes.

JANUARY 14, 1923

Reyzl once again troubles me. It is not a question of going on the stage this time. She gave up that foolishness and spared us that shande some time ago. No, this time she wants to give up her marriage to Mr. Krumbein's son.

We have already signed the agreement, so just the ceremony is left. And to put the wedding aside now would shame us.[1] Also, at more than twenty-five,[2] Reyzl is no longer a child.

Young Krumbein is Shoymer Shabes. He is not a poor man, or won't be when he takes over his father's store. He is strong, healthy, even handsome. So what is her complaint? She doesn't love him.

This I understand. I loved--I love my Rivke. And I never meant to marry Reyzl to someone she did not love. But why did she not speak sooner? Before the agreement was signed? When I first mentioned that Mr. Krumbein and I were talking?

Still, the love I think she means is an American love, the kind they show on posters outside the theaters (and in the moving pictures too, the newspaper tells me) or in the signs for tooth powder and soap. I don't deny such a feeling, altogether. Our sages themselves discuss it, and we have it also in the Song of Songs. But this is only one book out of thirty-nine.

Passion? There can be love without it. I have seen marriages prosper even when the bride and groom were altogether strangers. My brother Zalmen and his Gitl saw each other for the first time a week before the ceremony. And from a little seedling of respect has grown a love. It must be now more than thirty years with eight children, and, if I remember his last letter, five grandchildren. Yes, I know the rose of Sharon and the lily of the valley, but for how long do they blossom? And how do they bloom at all except for a healthy plant?

Still, I do not know what to do about Reyzl.

AUGUST 12, 1923

I am calmer now, thankful that Shabes is not only a day of rest but also of peace—even if the one just ended did not begin so peacefully.

Erev Shabes,[1] after the meal and *Zemires*,[2] Essie disappeared. I didn't miss her at first. Friday night she meets her girlfriends, takes walks with them through the neighborhood in nice weather—even not so nice weather. Or they stroll along East Broadway or Delancey Street looking in the shop windows. Sometimes it's with the boys, which I am not too happy about. But no matter what, she's home at ten thirty, eleven o'clock at the latest.

Not last night. At half past eleven I went downstairs to see if she was on the steps out front. But no, just some neighbors who had not seen her. I went in the next block to her friend Molly. Not there either. Also not by Shirley around the corner or Zelda two streets over. When I got back home, it was closer to twelve and I was beginning to worry. Mrs. Glicksberg was on the stoop, guarding the entrance like a watchdog. Earlier she was not there. "I'm looking for my Esther," I said. "Did you see her?" "No," she answered, "but I heard music from the fifth floor, by the *Taleyner*,[3] and young people were coming and going all night. Try there."

I gave a "thank you," but the words came from my mouth like ice. My Essie listening to music on Shabes? By the Taleyner? Impossible. But when I reached our third floor, I could just hear—now that I was listening for it—the sound of a gramophone coming from upstairs. Impossible, but why not just make sure.

When I caught my breath, I knocked at 5D, loud enough to hear over the jazzmusic [*sic*]. The door opened with such a sound and such a sight of dancing—men with women, boys with girls—you could go deaf from one and blind from the other. Essie was in somebody's arms. She screamed as I came toward her. "Pa!" I slapped her once across the face and she was silent. The crowd parted like the Red Sea as I grabbed her arm and led her out.

If we were still in Russia she would be maybe already spoken for and surely not out working. But here, she is away from her mother and me most of the time. And if the tenement is no village, the shop is surely not. And there she has been eight or ten hours a day since she was fourteen. Tempted by strange people, strange ideas, strange behavior. In America the *yeytser hore*[4] prospers too.

I am angry at Essie and myself, ashamed of both of us. You could count on one hand, two at most, the number of times I have hit the six of them. It goes against my belief and my nature. And in this case the spirit of Shabes as well. But she too knows right from wrong, our ways from the ways of others.

Essie has not spoken to me since. I don't know when she will. And I am afraid this is not the end of it.

JUNE 29, 1925

When I finish a hem by ladies' dresses, it will come not more than four inches above the ankle, once in while maybe six, if the pattern maker went a little crazy or the cutter got a little drunk and left the material short. But by Essie and Khave (and all their friends and the other young women I see in the street or on the streetcar) it seems the hem goes ten inches, twelve, whatever they need, from the ankle to above the knee. I am not happy with such shamelessness, but all my talking, my complaining, my shouting doesn't help, and they are too big to lay a hand on. But this would also do no good, and in laying a hand I am not interested anyway. They are not exactly independent, but not exactly children either, the two of them going to business every day a few years now.

And why are they (and all the others) dressing like this? The fashion. And what is the fashion? Whatever they are showing in the newspaper advertisements, on the covers of the magazines, on the posters for the moving pictures. "This is what you should wear" all of them say, so this is what they wear. Never mind the fashion could change every Monday and Thursday.[1] And, of course, never mind what an operator by sewing machines will say. Who is he, after all, but a poor observant Jew, who is also your father? Listen better to the sign painter and the actress Frieda Baron.[2]

I suppose it could be worse. It is only the legs and the painted knees[3] they show without shame. The hats, like a helmet from the Kaiser's army, covers as well as a *shaytl*.[4] Not that there is so much hair left to cover. If I see only the back of the head, I can hardly tell Essie and Khave from Asher and Ruven. The bosoms too are like by the boys. How, I don't know. Maybe the cut—I have not examined the garments, and in my shop we make only for older women. Maybe something else I don't need to know—something only for the women themselves. So, in the end, the fashion this week is to look like a skinny tree with two branches hanging down. But on those branches not a shred of bark. Naked altogether. And to put silk stockings you might as well put clear glass.

Rivke, of course, does none of this and feels the same. But even her skirts are higher than they used to be. When she got off the boat, they were at the top of her shoes; now you can see the ankle. And ankles among the Elbaum women, thick as they themselves are stubborn, are not the best feature. Not that I have studied ladies' ankles like a page of *Gemore*,[5] but with gathered skirts here, a kick from beneath them there, even a shy and modest man would see enough. When I was a young man, I could look away, but now if you look away from one you will see two others, as visible, even by bobes, as the forbidden tree in Eden.

With Rivke's hemline Khave and Essie have no problem except it should be higher. What bothers them is the slip hanging (as they say) nine yards underneath. Maybe this is not so neat like a pink [*sic*] edge, but because it covers more I don't complain. The two of them kvetsh the same about my long drawers that show from the pants legs when I sit down. Such craziness. Two daughters to be so upset by their parents' underwear. Maybe just to make them happy we should go without altogether. But I am afraid to write such a thing. Today is Monday. By Thursday, to go without might be the new fashion.

APRIL 23, 1926

With Rivke sick off and on and with Reyzl now married and out of the house, the cooking and cleaning fall to the other two girls. (What sewing there is, I take care of.) But Esther seems to do more of it than Khave. Maybe it's that she's so fussy. Khave cleans, but with Essie it's a war against dirt. And if she missed a spot, what would be so terrible? And haven't we—I certainly, lived in more *shmuts*[1] than we have on Keap Street?[2] But no, it must be war! Out come the buckets, the cloths, the brushes, the mops, the powders, the brown floor soap, all used with such an energy that I wouldn't wish an attack like this on my worst enemy—if I had an enemy.

And fast too. This war is not the Great War with the dirt in one trench and the cleaners in another for four years. No, for the dirt it is like airplane bombs and mustard gas all at once. In one hour an armistice. Still, it is not the cleaning to end all cleanings, and Essie is soon at it again.[3]

She is the same with the clothes too—from scrubbing to starching to pressing—everything perfect. A wrinkle Essie hates as much as a stain. This her brothers Asher and Ruven saw already and asked her to do their shirts and collars. But after a week or two, she told them that she would not be their servant. They could either pay her or do the work themselves. Now, at eight cents a shirt and two cents a collar, she has maybe an extra eighty cents a week, more than carfare to her job. The boys took advantage, but everybody should do for the family. Sometimes Essie is not so generous. She is also not a fool.

OCTOBER 14, 1926

Asher will soon be married and, thanks to the One on high, without all the trouble we had with Reyzl. The bride will be Leye Blank, a plain, quiet, *heymishe*[1] woman, but one who already in her young life has had plenty tsores. The same sickness that took Velvl Weinstock took also her parents, both. So she was left together with an older sister, girls maybe 12 and 14, orphans. But like by us with Brayne and her children, someone, a mother's cousin, I think, took them in.

The family, Asher says, was from Romania. This he knew already, but was reminded the other night when he went to Leye's cousin for supper and ate eggplant.[2] From this food I never heard. For me an egg does not grow from a bush but from under a chicken. Asher tells me it is a vegetable with a purple skin that Romanians (Jews or not) roast, or fry, or bake. By us, vegetables, except for carrots, are mostly brown or white—a potato, a *posternak*,[3] maybe a little green like a celery. And these we boil, unless for *latkes*[4] on *Khanike*[5].

So for the *forshpays*,[6] he says, there was a mashed-up eggplant that was roasted, together with some pieces onion. To look at, it almost turned his stomach, but the taste he enjoyed. With the meat they put slices fried eggplant. Who could complain about fried? Whether there was an eggplant cake to go with the tea, Asher didn't mention.

Nu, if we were from Romania, we would eat eggplant too. I suppose that wherever our people have been we have found what to eat, and if it was tasty and kosher and we could afford, we ate. Maybe I would like an eggplant. After all, the Romanian pastrami is *geshmak*.[7] And maybe after she and Asher are married, Leye will invite Rivke and me for supper (if I can drag her out of the house) and cook some eggplant for me to try.

FEBRUARY 27, 1928

This afternoon I had another argument with Rivke. Or she had one with me. I brought home the wrong milk. One brand, another brand, what difference can it make? But, no, it must be Sheffield's. Still, I don't raise my voice. She's a sickly woman, after all—though not very old. Better to cross the street to the grocery.

Later, with the milk now in the ice box, I sang to her as I used to:

> *Ikh vel geyn in ale gasn,*
> *Ikh vel shrayen "Vesh tsu vashn,"*
> *Abi mit dir, Abi mit dir, tsuzamen zayn.*[1]

As I sang it for the second time, I took her in my arms to dance. By now she was not angry, so she let. Maybe she also remembered the walks in the village[2] after supper. I hummed the melody a third time then kissed her on the lips.

But in less than a second there was a small gasp from the doorway. Little Avrom stood there, his eyes and his mouth wide open. So that already was the end.

"Go," she said, pushing me away, "bother someone else with your foolishness."

She smoothed an apron that had no wrinkles, then turned her back on both the child and me and found something to do at the stove. A pot rattled. "You should burn," she shouted, "as you have burnt every potato!"

I shrugged and smiled as I looked at Avrom. Young as he was, he nodded and smiled back.

AUGUST 5, 1928

This time Brayne has gone too far with her joking. Rivke and I do not have to be shamed before the neighbors, and the smiles and winks from some members of the morning minyen I could also do without.

The weather this week has been unbearable. A person can hardly sleep even with all the windows open. Some go up on the roof. Others in the apartment houses try the fire escape. But Brayne, with a mind of her own, dragged a mattress out in front of the house in the space between the bushes. This I didn't know at the time, and if I knew it, who is to say I could have stopped her? To give her credit, she says she slept very well.

But in the morning, between the birds and the sun, she was up by 6:30, sitting on a mattress in the front yard, in her nightgown. (I am happy it was not hotter still.) A few minutes later, Mr. Tischler, the *shames*,[1] passed by on his way to open the shul. He is a quiet man, a scholar. And even if he was something else, who would not have been astonished to see such a sight as Brayne? He stopped. He stared. The blood went from his face. He could not make a sound.

And Brayne? She could not help taking advantage of the poor man. With a smile on her face she calls out, *"Reb Yid,"*[2] taps the mattress, and shakes her head for him to come. Tischler runs off to the shul in terror. And Brayne, laughing, I am sure, drags the mattress back inside. A little while later, I leave, knowing nothing of what has happened.

But at the shul I learn almost everything. Not that Tischler tells stories, but this he had to tell somebody, and somebody told someone else, so when I got there everyone, including Rabbi Magerman, had heard about the loose woman in the garden by Kahn. Nu!

What the coarser ones said I will not repeat. The best I could do was explain that it was my sister-in-law (who else could it be?) on a visit from Baltimore, and that sometimes she was not altogether in her right mind—a lie, I admit, but not so far from the truth. I am sure all our prayers this morning were ruined because whatever words we said the picture of Brayne managed to get in the way.

Later, at home, I lost my temper. And Rivke, by her silence, seemed to agree that I had a good reason. But Brayne herself would not give an inch. "If it is hot tonight like last night," she said, "I will sleep outside again. My rest is more important than the opinion of a timid shames, your rabbi, or even an entire *beys din*.[3] But if it makes you happy, Sholem, I won't say a word to the people in the street. In fact, I will put a sign to explain: "A hot woman lies here."[4]

What to do with such a person I don't know. But at the evening minyen, even though it is the wrong season, I included the prayer for rain.[5]

JULY 11, 1929

Again we are at Lowenstein's in Spring Valley.[1] Not that we can afford every summer, but every few years we go for a week. This year only Avrom is with us the whole time. Essie and Khave came up with us before Shabes but went back to the city Sunday afternoon to go to work on Monday. And the others are altogether on their own. So with mostly just three of us, the trip was easy. Especially because Lowenstein's is now a hotel, no more a *kokhaleyn*.[2]

But when we came before the war and even one time after, we had to shlep not only the whole family, but pots and pans and dishes—everything two sets—like making *Pesakh*[3] a hundred miles away. Then there were towels and pillows and sheets for the three or four beds we were sharing. Altogether, going to America was easier. But Rivke insisted the children needed fresh air, and I didn't mind a week away from *shvitsing*[4] at the sewing machine or from the apartment without air at all.

They have no more bungalows. Now everyone stays in rooms in one long building. The toilets are inside, but outside still is the shower house with cold water only. The dining room is another long building but with screens for half the walls. Not to have to cook or buy what to eat is for Rivke a pleasure. And for me it is also a change to have her sitting at the table and eating almost like a mentsh instead of always running from the stove to the table with a pot. Here the waiters bring what you want, as much as you want, as many times as you want. I am eating more than enough but not like Mr. Helfand at our table who always has two waiters (sometimes more) running for him at once.

For Helfand and some other fresers, eating is all they do. But I have brought my *Khumesh*,[5] so I can study the portion for the week. The radio I brought up, but a Jewish program half the time I can't find and the other half not clearly. A Yiddish paper I can get if someone goes to "town"; whether they mean the little village or some other place, I don't know. Every day before breakfast and after supper there is a small minyen in the back dining room. On Shabes they use the entertainment hall for a shul.

These things are not too different from home. But also I take a little sun in one of the big wooden chairs on the lawn, or go for a walk in the woods and every once in a while pull a berry from a bush. Sometimes I go along the road past the farms to look at the cows and horses and maybe talk for a minute with a farmer. I use my bad English because his Yiddish is still worse. Once, I helped one of them put his team to a wagon. Another time, I showed a different farmer's son how better to hold the horse's leg when he was putting a shoe. When I get back to Lowenstein's, maybe someone will greet me with *"Vos makht a yid,"*[6] or I him, and we'll talk for an hour. Cards I don't play, and for ball I'm too old even if I wanted. In the hot afternoons I will go to the lake and get in the water to the waist. This Avrom likes too, and Rivke just her feet. By us we have no swimmers except Krumbein, which is why Reyzl says when she's angry about money, "You didn't come over steerage; you swam to save the fare."

With jumping and running, Avrom has a good time, like the others when they were small. By the table tennis and the handball on the wooden wall he doesn't even have to play. If in the afternoon it gets too hot, he takes a book under a tree for a half hour. This week it is Robin Hood with his men who, Avrom tells me, take from the rich and give to the poor. But this is not the same as politics. Avrom also says that they have bows and arrows in the woods like Rabbi Shimon bar Yokhai and his students,[7] but I read myself a couple pages (it is a child's book after all), so I know that in Sherman's [*sic*] forest they are not studying Toyre. After supper there is more running, this time after the fireflies, and maybe looking at the entertainment if it is a juggler or a magic trickster. And then the child is in bed sleeping like a dead one.

Rivke and I do not stay up too late either. To the *klezmorim*[8] we will listen and tap a foot, but neither one of us likes the joke tellers. Half their stories are filth and the other half dirt. Why they have such people at a kosher hotel I don't know. But I notice that for them Helfand, our friend from the meals, always takes a seat in the front. Still, for all of them Rivke has just one word—"*Fe!*"[9] And on this we agree.

In two days we must leave. I wish we could stay longer, not so much for the boy, who can run and jump in Brooklyn, even without the grass, but for Rivke. She is just beginning to enjoy. Not a sharp word from her or a hard look since Monday. And once or twice she even laughed. Next week, I'm afraid, the looks and sounds will be more familiar. Lord of the world, from what tree have we eaten to be driven from this Eden?

SEPTEMBER 2, 1929

Today is a holiday for the workers, so I was at home. But for Fishkin the commission merchant it was not a day off. Like clockwork, he showed up on the first Monday of the month with his record and receipt books to collect his dollar or two. Of course, I am almost never home when he comes, and so we talked a little about how we were, how was business (not too bad, *Got tsu danken*[1]), what people who know each other only a little talk about. Then it was time for him to deal with his customer, Rivke.

"We have here, Missus," he says as he opens the bigger book and looks, "a balance of seven dollars with forty cents. So, how much you are paying today?"

"Paying?" Rivke begins. "I should pay nothing. Better you and your boss, the Nissenbaum brothers, should pay me for taking the rotten goods."

I could see already that for Rivke this was a formal negotiation. Usually, she calls the brothers "the little men" since two of them are not taller than I am and two are shorter still. Never mind one is almost six feet. But today it was "Nissenbaum."

"And what now is the matter?" Fishkin sighed.

"The matter is that not six months there are already holes in the dish towels. The matter is that I bought white sheets, not yellow. The matter is that already by my husband's shirts the cuffs are growing little beards."

"Missus," Fishkin answered patiently. "If you stab with a knife and fork the towel is not to blame. If you put a bleach with a blue to the soap, the sheets will be like new. And if all day I pushed material through a sewing machine, I would rub out my cuffs too. Nothing lasts forever. Not me. Not you. Not a piece cotton."

Rivke, of course, was not satisfied.

"Mr. Fishkin, I am off the boat now twenty-five years. I am not green anymore—except for the color that ran from one towel, I forgot to mention. Also, I have been doing business with you for years. Do I ever complain?"

Fishkin rolled his eyes toward the ceiling. Rivke saw.

"And if I did, was I wrong?"

Fishkin pulled his watch from a pocket. He had other stops.

"All right," he said, "all right. I will make you an adjustment—but only for the cuffs. Twenty cents."

Rivke did not answer.

"Twenty-five," Fishkin offered again.

Still not.

"Thirty-five cents. Leave or take."

"All right. But today you get from me just half a dollar."

Fishkin was not going to argue. He put out one hand for the money, and changed his records with the other.

"That's $7.40. Thirty-five cents adjustment makes $7.05. Half a dollar you are paying," he looked up as Rivke dropped a quarter and five nickels into his palm. "So that makes a new balance—$6.55."

He sat back in the kitchen chair without closing the book.

"So it is coming next month to holiday," he said to both of us. "You are all right for the holiday, Missus? Something you need?"

"Strength," Rivke answered. She was not buying, yet.

"Tablecloths we got. Just came in. Nice. Beautiful. One a white on white $2.75 for your size and one white with the needlework in the middle $2.25."

He showed the samples.

"On Eastern Parkway[2] you're not," Rivke said. "You have a plain white?"

"1.75."

Rivke stared.

"All right, for you $1.50. Something else?" Fishkin asked as he wrote the tablecloth down.[3] "For the boy, maybe?"

"Always something with a growing child," Rivke sighed. "Yes, a white shirt size 12 so he'll have yet another year. The cuffs on the old one are almost to the elbows. And three pairs socks. A blue, a black, a brown. The seconds. But good ones."

So Fishkin wrote.

"Three socks. Blue, brown, black. Seconds. At fifteen cents is forty-five. One boy's shirt, $1.00—the cheapest. All together with the cloth is $2.95. Add to $6.55 is $9.50 exact."

He looked up and stood. "I will bring so you will have every-thing in time for *yontif*."[4]

"Not so fast, Mr. Fishkin," Rivke said. "The money and the order you remember, but the receipt you forgot."

Fishkin, shook his head, a little embarrassed, and made out a receipt.

"So, goodbye Missus," he said as he handed it to Rivke. "And to you Mister, if I don't see you, a good sweet year."

After he left, I thought how even after the "adjustment" and paying cash we owed more than when he came in. Maybe it is not such a bad thing to be a commission merchant. You get paid for collecting money on goods sold in the store and even more for what you sell yourself. Walking from house to house in the winter is not such a bargain, but the rest of the year makes a good exercise. And a person is not locked in the four walls of a factory or even an office or chained like me to a machine. Of course, if like Rivke every customer takes your *neshomeh*[5]. . . . But what job doesn't have its tsores? What life?

MAY 4, 1930

All day Essie has been in the bedroom crying her eyes out. She doesn't say why, and Rivke and I don't ask. But it must be she was out with him last night and put an end to it.

To the children, their mother and I are still greenhorns. It is true, of course, that we don't know everything about America and its ways even after so many years, and some things we will never know, and other things we wouldn't want. But we are not like we just arrived, green from top to bottom, like every day for us was the Irish yontif. After so many years you learn what is the picture they call a "heart" and what it means to have the letters from the names inside with an arrow through everything. So last winter, the middle of February I think, when I saw Essie drawing such hearts with V. R. and E. K., I asked who was V. R.

First she turned white; then she turned red. "Nobody. . .somebody at work," she said finally.

"And does Mr. V. R. have a full name, or maybe his family couldn't afford?"

A few seconds she said nothing. And behind the eyes you could see the brain working like a machine.

"It's Victor . . . Victor Rosenzweig."

"And what does he do at work?"

"A bookkeeper."

"That's not so bad. Tell me, Essie, he also makes such pictures?"

Again she turned red.

"I . . . I don't know, Papa."

And that was that. But two weeks after, we saw from the window she got into a fancy car in front of the house. And when I asked later who it was, she *fomferd*[1] but said in the end it was the boy from work she had mentioned before.

"Rosenzweig?" I asked.

"Yes, yes," she said, as if I had reminded her of the name. "Rosenzweig. . . Vi . . . Victor Rosenzweig.

I said nothing more, but I knew such a car no bookkeeper could afford. Maybe, maybe something was not so kosher. Rivke thought so too: "What kind of boy is it that won't come into the house for two minutes?" For this I had no answer, and Essie only excuses. Later on, Rivke also saw him with Essie by the street lamp a couple times when he brought her home. "A Victor, maybe," she had said, "but like a Rosenzweig he doesn't look."

Then two weeks ago, I picked up an envelope that had fallen under the long table in the front room. On it was Essie's writing. Again and again she had written "Mrs. Vittorio Renna" or "Mrs. Vito Renna." So at supper I asked her who was Mrs. Renna, and she almost choked on her soup. After the coughing, and banging on the back, and a glass water, I asked again.

"The new forelady at work."

"So you can't remember? You have to write it twenty times?"

Silence.

"She is V. R. too, like Rosenzweig," I went on.

"Rosenzweig? Oh, yes," she tried to laugh, looking at her sister Khave for help, "like Rosenzweig. V. R. What are the chances?"

I could not control myself. "I believe that now there is not such a person as Mrs. Vittorio or Vito Renna. And I know that such a person there will never be!"

By now I was at the top of my voice and had struck the table with my fist. But somehow the blow reminded me of the time years ago when I had struck Essie for breaking Shabes—also by a Taleyner. This I would not do again. In a second, my anger turned to ice and my voice almost a whisper.

"I will not argue with you Essie. I will not give you reasons. If you don't know them backwards and forwards by now, you are not such a smart young woman that both of us think you are."

She was staring at me, a tear down each cheek, fear and grief in her eyes but also, I am ashamed to write, hate. But my voice grew colder still.

"I have said Kadish, Essie. For my parents, for a brother, for the bobe whose name you carry,[2] for the sister in Europe you never knew. The first few times for each of them the words stuck in my throat. It will stick maybe more if I have to say them for you, my second child dead. But if I have to, I will *take*[3] say them."

We left the table in silence, and I said nothing more to Essie after that. But Rivke, at every chance, made herself heard long and loud enough for our daughter to run from the room or the apartment with her hands over her ears. Whether my quiet or Rivke's screaming would do any good we couldn't tell. But a strange visit gave us a little hope. Thursday afternoon the boy's mother knocked on the door to talk to Rivke, asking her to help keep Essie away from her son. Her family didn't want any more than we did.

Afterwards, Rivke was as amazed as she was pleased.

"Such a person," she said, "I have never had in my house in my life. Once we understood each other—with Avrom's help—and were happy we agreed, she stayed ten minutes for a glass tea I put in a cup for her."

"Regular Yankees," I said, "with not a hundred English words between you." But I was glad that the true Mrs. Renna was a woman of sense.

When Essie came in last night, Rivke was still up. It was clear to her that the child had been crying, but before she could say a word, Essie had slammed the bedroom door.

And there she stays. And it is good for her, such tears. A *mikve*[4] for the soul.

MAY 7, 1930

Now that peace has returned for a while to the Kahn household, there is still one thing that bothers me. Khave. From the look Essie gave her across the table the other day she must have known. But in all these months she never said a word. The way the two of them are always fighting, you would think she would say something the minute she knew. I will not discuss with Khave—let the whole thing be over.

But I have two thoughts about her silence, and I like one less than the other. First, that in this land the idea of a "romance," as they call it, is so important that it makes lions lie down with lambs, dogs with cats, even landlords with tenants. Even worse, in a country that goes by struggle and competition, we have here the children united against the parents. Was my father my enemy? My mother? No more than they were my friends. What were they? My creators, my teachers, my guides, my examples of *yidishkayt*[1] and mentshlikhkayt. Children here, I suppose we are fortunate, do not ignore a father and mother altogether. But parents as teachers? Not after twelve years old. Guides? We are so old fashioned. And since yidishkayt and mentshlikhkayt you find less every day, for what kind of world are we giving examples?

JUNE 29, 1930

ot two weeks ago, when I wrote how Ruven became a rabbi,[1] my eyes were as full as my heart. Somehow, I wiped the tears, so the Waterman's did not become a pale smear. But today, with another kind of tears, I am afraid the ink will be thin. Ruven left this morning to lead a shul in Indiana. Whoever thought of such a place, let alone imagined it had Jews?

Because he is now a rabbi, Rivke and I, of course, are filled with pride. But this is not just simple *kveling*.[2] It is more than that—a reality that once was a dream. Ruven's, naturally, and ours—especially after that unpleasant business about the birth paper and getting him into City College.[3] And if such a thing is possible, maybe it means a little more to me than to Rivke. She has always had rabbis in her family, something she reminds me of every Monday and Thursday, as if my relatives were all peasants. I should hear less of that now that there is a Rabbi Kahn as well.

But no matter how much his mother and I may boast and swell to bursting, it is Ruven who has studied and learned and gained honor, not the least by his own hard work. A special child—even at the ceremony, you could hear the sweetness of his voice among the others[4]—the last of them born in Europe, the only one born without me there. A gentle boy, who would run from the house when his mother took the live fish from the tub.[5] Of all of them, he is closest to the ways of his elders.

And now he has gone to lead the Jews—in a wilderness—worse yet than Baltimore.[6] If we were not with him at the train this morning, I would think he went maybe in an old wagon with a cloth cover. Indiana—about this place I remember from the citizen class two things: the first, Abraham Lincoln was born there; the second, he didn't stay.[7]

But to complain about the place does not make me (or Rivke) feel any better. It would be the same no matter where, and it is not even the distance—unless, may He spare us, California—but the going itself. Yes, if he lived next door, or a couple blocks away, even in New York[8] or the Bronx, it would not be so bad. But, like his older brother and sister, who live near us, he would still be gone.

What father and mother do not rejoice in the growth of their children—the first step, the first word, going to kheyder, a bar mitsve, marriage? And which of them does not weep, at least a little, at the same time? Time passes. And all of us are on one clock. Or maybe we are joined fast to them as if by a rubber band. Fat and thick with the small ones, it stretches thinner and thinner through the years. With God's help, it will never break, but sometimes it seems as fine as a spider's thread that will not survive a well-used broom or sweep of sudden wind.

But enough. May Ruven, wherever he goes, be blessed with all things good.

So I (and so would Rivke) say. Still, I remember once my little Avrom showed me, wasting half a good lemon, how to write with the juice. But how to write with plain water I never learned, or even with salt water that is burning the eyes this minute.

FEBRUARY 4, 1931

Reyzl's baby was born dead. There will be no *bris*.[1] No name. Only a burial.

In the house all is quiet. Even the tears. Krumbein, like always, comes and goes in silence. But this is the silence of suffering not of rage. Little Arnie[2] plays in the corner, sitting still for once more than two minutes. Once in a while, he looks up with fear and questions in his eyes.

Since the doctor left, Essie and Khave have sat by their sister's bed. Leye made supper. Max, Zelig, and Asher will stop in a while after work. We will read together from Psalms. But for Reyzl there is no comfort. A nine-month budding without fruit. And without a life at all, not even a memory to ease the pain.

Only Rivke brings relief. She sends Avrom to play with Arnie and Mindl in the parlor, brushes Reyzl's hair from her forehead, and takes her by the hand. "I understand," she tells her. "I understand only too well." Reyzl looks into her mother's eyes, then bursts into loud sobs against her bosom. The poison of grief comes out like a boil opened in the soul.

I wipe a hand across my own eyes. Since this morning, I have pushed the old memory aside but can no longer. In Europe, our first—Rivke's and mine—our Gitele,[3] dead before a year. We had as little comfort then, maybe less, with no other child already in the house. But with so many others losing theirs we weren't so alone in our suffering. Here in America, with the needles, with the medicine, it happens, but not so often. Still, how can you measure pain—or compare yours with someone else's? A child that lived ten months with one that never took a breath?

There is nothing for the living to do but mourn and go on. And to trust in God. Our sufferings are not Job's, and even he kept his faith. He would not take his foolish wife's advice to curse God and die. Still, Reyzl now and I then could understand such a temptation.

MAY 10, 1933

Whether what happened today will mean something we will have to see. But even if not, at least we are trying to make a change or to call for help from those who can make changes. To do nothing—even for fear we will make it worse for our brothers in Germany—will surely end with nothing for them and for ourselves. This the Congressman La Guardia[1] said himself. And this is why it was right for the Jewish Congress[2] to have the march.

People were there by the thousands—from all the squares—Madison, Union (where I was myself), Rutgers[3]—most of us waiting for a couple hours to march to the Battery Park. Fassbinder gave everyone half a day (that by him was at two o'clock) and was himself going to walk, but not, of course, with the unions. By other Jewish bosses and workers the same.

But it was not just the Jewish workers and bosses. Children from the schools were there, old soldiers,[4] goyim more than a few—I was surprised—even their priests.[5] The leader, they tell me, was a general, I think a brother to the mayor,[6] who himself stood outside City Hall as we went past. Some of the speakers also were not Jewish, but I could not hear all of them because they began the talking before everyone got to the park or we would still be there. And even if I could hear, I could understand in such English maybe two sentences together and otherwise every fourth or fifth word. But there is language also in the sound of a voice, an arm raised in the air, a fist banging a table. And from the Jews you could still hear some mameloshn.

But to go with the sounds there were such sights—uniforms, hundreds of flags—American, of course, and Zionist—together with signs that said what all of us were feeling. Except one, that when I saw it first turned my stomach and then made the blood rush to my face: "We want Hitler!" Azoy![7] But before I could take even half a step to tear it down I saw underneath "Society of Undertakers." So who could argue, and who could not laugh?

One thing I learned today is that maybe we are not altogether alone. Even the books the Nazis are busy burning[8] are not only Jewish books. So if the others will not help because it is right, maybe they will see that if it's the Jews today it will be themselves tomorrow.

What matters now, of course, are human lives, Jewish lives. To this you cannot compare a book, even the holiest. Still, of the little I have in this world, to lose my books would pain me most. And whoever would destroy such things must be coarse and ignorant, an enemy of the spirit as well as the flesh, evil beyond redemption.

And this I'm afraid they are. Large as our protest was, the Nazis will not be overcome by men making speeches or carrying flags and signs. Nations, not citizens will have to stop them, and if worse comes to worst, by beating the ploughshares back into swords[9] and putting these into the hands of other marching men.

But for now we have at least spoken loudly with one voice, just as at the end they played *Hatikvah*[10] together with the Star

[Spangled][11] Banner. And this stirred the heart so, that I felt I must write, even though it is nearly twelve o'clock, and in the morning Fassbinder will not hear excuses for being late.

JUNE 19, 1933

This evening Essie was *farputsing*[1] and her sister Khave teasing more than usual. So the signs were clear.

"Another young man?" I asked.

I got a look for an answer.

"So, who is he?"

"A friend."

"Thank you," I said. "This I already know because for an enemy you don't put powder. This friend has a name?"

"Max," I thought she said. Who could tell with her making the lipstick?

"Max?"

"Yes, Max. Max Rothstein."

"Max Rothstein," I repeated. "Yes, yes, that is definitely a name."

Then from the drop by drop all of a sudden came a waterfall.

"You'll like him, Papa. He's a nice guy. A salesman. Piece goods. And last week when it was so hot and I was on the picket line he bought me an ice cream cone. He came up just like that and offered. Naturally, he asked where I lived. So I told him the neighborhood. He asked where in Brownsville. You know, you have to be careful, so I gave him an address on Riverdale. But it turns out he's also from the neighborhood and knew the house. So he caught me in a lie, and then I was too embarrassed not to tell the truth. So we made a date, and he'll be here in a minute. You'll like him. Not that much to look at except for his curly hair and cute moustache. But he's funny and smart. You'll like him, Papa. He reads a lot."

While Essie took a breath, I asked, "His books, they open from the left or from the right?"

For this I got an "Oh, Papa," which was at least better than another look.

But then came the doorbell and a knock, and soon Max Rothstein walked into the apartment. As for nothing to look at, Essie was right. Some of Rivke's cooking would not have hurt besides. From cute moustaches I don't know. But about the reading also she was right. A book was sticking from a pocket. That and the eyeglasses made him look like a scholar. "Funny," I couldn't tell from the little he said. But he spoke in Yiddish and was respectful enough. So a *grober yung*[2] at least he's not.

Rivke was not happy that he refused her tea and cake. "A thin one," she said, after they had left. By her this is not a compliment.

I was left thinking about how they met. An American match altogether, settled between an ice cream cone and a lie.

JULY 25, 1933

Twice now in two years I have lost a grandchild. Asher and Leye's son, two days old and gone. Like before, the women have gathered around the mother. This time Reyzl feeds Asher and the girls. Rivke sits by the bed, but Leye, after all, is not her child, and she is only the mother-in-law. Leye herself has no one but a sister, orphans, the two of them, at a young age.

Asher, I can see, is suffering. Not from just losing the baby but from losing a son. Who knows if he will ever have one? Of course, he loves his girls—Ellen the sweet one, Phyllis the fire—from the kiss on the cheek to the doll carriage to the *patsh* in *tokhes*.[1] It's not the name that he worries—Kahn/Shmahn, what does it matter? Or someone to leave the money or the business. When we were in the desert yet the law was that the daughters could inherit if there was no son.[2] But where is his kadish?

Still, even for this problem there is an answer.[3] And the Talmud only says it is the duty of a husband and wife to replace themselves. This already Asher and Leye have done. And even if some of the sages understand this to mean with another man and woman,[4] I wouldn't worry. For every family with two daughters there seems to be a family with two sons—like right across from us by the Kesslers. But why even go across the street? I am one of twelve brothers, Rivke one of eleven with nine sisters.

I will say almost nothing about this to Asher. Now is not the time. Now is the time for him to cry himself out together with Leye, to hold on to what he has and let go what he doesn't. Between the partner and the workers he can be home a few days with his wife.

Tonight, before the girls went to bed, he sat across from Leye with one on each knee and told them a story. He didn't know what he was saying; they didn't know; I surely not. What the children knew was that their father's arms were around them, and what he knew was that their faces were pressed to his chest. Then I knew that with God's help they would be all right.

JANUARY 22, 1935

Nu, done. Over. Tomorrow I won't have to go to the job except to tell them and pick up the couple dollars pay for yesterday till two o'clock. After this they won't see me in the shop either by Fassbinder or anyone else. Since this afternoon, since the visit with Dr. Sussman, I am retired.

Retired. Who is Sholem Kahn to retire? A millionaire he's not. An a*llrightnik*[1] also not. No, the Sholem Kahns of this world work till they drop dead. My problem, I think, is not so much the arteries or the heart but that I have lived too long.

And what kind of living will it now be? When I asked Sussman if it was better for the heart to be working or to worry how to eat, he gave for an answer half a smile and a shrug, as if to say "who knows." I can almost be thankful that I have been a poor man all my life. From next to nothing to a little less it is not so hard as to go to such a little from something much more. Not that we will starve altogether or be put out in the street, Rivke and I. The government with an old age pension[2] will see to that. (This, at least, is better than by the czar.) And the children—though what parent wants to go to them—will help if they must.

But, Sussman or no Sussman, I have been thinking of how to make a little money, as they say, on the side. Already I have had pupils—two or three—to teach for bar mitsve. More I can get and maybe with some to do more than the blessings and the readings. Maybe—if there are still some Jews in America who don't want such teaching, like everything else, by the "streamline" and the "short cut." For most of them these days, a year is enough to become a Jew, and for their children even this is too much. Go tell them that with luck it takes a lifetime.

But it is not just for the little money that I think about teaching or even to bring some yidishkayt to the pupils. Or even just to take up a few hours of an empty week. It is more to—how can I say it—to be someone. Not that I am no one. But in this country—so maybe I am more an American than I often think—to be someone means to do something. As if there is a comma after the name followed by a job. Henry Sussman, doctor; Mendl Fassbinder, businessman. Until this afternoon, I was Sholem Kahn, cloak and suit operator.[3] Now I am just Sholem Kahn, altogether naked. If I were Sholem Kahn, *melamed*,[4] I would have at least a leaf to cover my shame.

But maybe, since I read so much in Ecclesiastes, this too is vanity. And this, like other luxuries, I can't afford. What I must do now is keep Rivke calm. I have convinced her already that the process server is not coming in the morning to put us out. What remains is to have her believe that we will have what to eat. After all, without food in the ice box and the pots there would be no more Rivke Kahn, *baleboste*.[5] Once this is done, I must prepare both of us for a greater terror still, that she will have me at home from morning till night every day. Already I can hear her blessings on Sussman for creating such a yontif without end.

NOVEMBER 10, 1935

For the second time in three months the house is being turned upside down because of a wedding. In the summer Khave married Zelig Wexler. Saturday night, after Shabes, Essie will marry Max Rothstein. The two of them, as they say, have been "keeping company" for over a year. They were going to wait until the spring, but the thought that Khave would have a husband for so long and she not was too much for Essie to take. Bad enough that Khave was first. (Such a competition we have in the Kahn house someone would think we lived on Wall Street instead of Herzl.) So in a few days, after Shabes, we will marry off our last daughter (if not the youngest), and everyone will put Rivke and me on chairs with crowns on our heads like a king and queen and dance in a circle around us.[1] Good. I wish Essie and Max what I wished Khave and Zelig—a long, healthy, happy life together and *nakhes*[2] from the children.

So two new son-in-laws we will now have. And they are night and day. Zelig is a quiet man, dark, and strong from the lifting he does forty hours a week in the plant. A *yeshive bokher*[3] he was and goes to shul whenever he can, but he is far from a scholar. The family, of course, we met. *Frume yidn,*[4] and his father you would swear has his picture on the Rosh Hashanah cards the children like to send.

Max is almost a hundred percent the opposite. Skinny, pale, a salesman by piece goods. He is never without a book or an opinion, which he is not embarrassed to tell you. Mostly he loves the socialists better than the communists and both of them better than the shul. You wouldn't know this from his parents, who are as frum as Zelig's. The father is, like me,[5] a sewing machine operator but is out of work as much as in, and, when he is out, will sometimes play a little pinochle and take a schnapps or two. The mother is a sick woman like Rivke, if not more, but Max maybe gets his reading from her. He tells me she is always sending the children to the library to get books in Yiddish. Not politics like him but romances and plays—a King Lehrman[6]—something—who knows what. Whether Max's books or hers are more foolish I can't tell.

But while Max's ideas are not what I hoped for, other things about him bothered me more. And bothered Essie too. So much that they asked Ruven to help them. The trouble was that when Max was not on the street corner making speeches, he was in the poolroom. And also in the poolroom were the gangsters. Not exactly that he was one himself. But even if you go to clean out a stable you will need yourself to take a bath after. What we know is once in a while he carried a little money for the gamblers, and one time—such a *mitsve*[7]—he hid for one of them a gun. Twice, by accident, he met even Meyer Lansky[8]—who the Jews and the world can do without. And there was a story—what it was I will not even tell to myself—that if it was the truth, would have put an end to the "keeping company" for good. As it was, it almost ended anyhow.

What saved it was, first, that Max told Ruven everything and, taking Ruven's advice, told Essie the same. He agreed also to give up all his friends. His job he made an excuse for not being *shoymer*

Shabes,[9] but promised to keep kosher outside of the house as well as in. (Such a negotiation from Essie would put even Lewis and Dubinsky[10] to shame.) Naturally, Essie would not just take his word, so the "engagement" went on longer than it would have so she could see. If not for this, she would have been married maybe before Khave.

Now, I should not make Max the angel of death altogether. First, that he loves Essie very much is not a question. Also, he is very good to Rivke. Just tonight he went special to the drugstore on Saratoga to get her a bottle pills. And the BC powders he buys for her every month. That he eats whatever she puts in front of him pleases her, even if he does not gain an ounce. With me he is respectful. And it is not so much he hates the shul. He hates the difference between what the shul is, he says, and what it should be.

"So staying away will make it better?" I ask.

"It will make me better," he answers.

But this is a discussion, without anger. Anger he saves for talking with Asher. What Max wants, it turns out, is justice. With this who can argue? And maybe it was for this idea (besides Essie) that he has given up the Lanskys of the world—big and small—who are anything but just.

One other thing to mention. Max gets along with Khave the same as Essie does. Not that this is a reason to marry. But at least he will be ready for some of the Kahn family quarrels.

MARCH 24, 1936

This morning when they were going to work (God be thanked, the two of them have jobs in these times), Essie and Max saw an old man sitting by the elevated. His hair was in front of his face with the hat pulled down over his eyes, and he was shaking a metal cup with pennies and maybe a couple nickels that people put in on their way to the train.

A beggar. Not such a rare thing these days. Even the people who sell apples in the street—shoelaces—who knows what else—are not so different from the ones who beg. Do you give the little money because you want the apple or the laces, that could be cheaper in the fruit store or by the shoemaker, or because it is a poor person you take pity on? Maybe someone who not so long ago was making a living, even a nice living. So with a little selling and a little buying, everyone pretends that it's business and no one feels so bad. But the beggar does not need to pretend. He is already past shame. And maybe whoever gives believes it is a mitsve altogether, with no goods involved, and feels better for the two of them.

So this morning Max dropped a few cents in the beggar's cup and with Essie started up the steps. Near the top they turned around (who knows why) and saw the beggar staring after them full in the face. When he saw their mouths drop open, he took the box he was sitting on and limped away. If there was any question, the limp answered. "Eisenberg!" the two of them called out together. But Eisenberg was already around the corner and out of sight.

The question is, why would Eisenberg, Reyzl's landlord and the owner of other properties besides, go out to beg? Some of the tenants could be behind in the rent, but I can't believe all—or even most. It could be his bank went out and he lost all the cash. But this did not happen so much to the big banks, and the bank yontif for the East New York Savings on Pitkin Avenue was maybe a week.[1] According to the neighbors, Eisenberg does not go to the bank anyway but saves instead by the shoebox and mattress— not to bear false witness against him. But it is true that Mrs. Eisenberg wears a muskrat coat not two years old. She could not wait to show it off, Rivke says, the Rosh Hashanah before last, even if it was eighty degrees.

So it seems Eisenberg sits near the elevated (this was not the first time Max and Essie saw him) not because he needs but because he wants. And if this is so (I leave it to the Judge on high), he has broken the commandment about greed. He is not the first, and he will not be the last. But his foolishness seems greater and sadder in these days because it was greed that brought us to the misery of the last six years in the first place and maybe also stopped President Hoover from doing some of the things President Roosevelt is doing now to help. And what is worse, the money Eisenberg collects each week could go to people who need it. So instead of feeding the hungry and clothing the naked, and protecting the widow and orphan, the man helps them starve and freeze and suffer.

For a minute I stopped to put a pill under the tongue. I do not often get so angry. In this house and in the rest of the country it is not like by Eisenberg. With God's help, most of the people still out of work will get jobs. But Sholem Kahn never. It is already more than a year that Dr. Sussman made me stop because of the heart. And as little as my pay was, the pension is less. So especially now what Eisenberg is doing aggravates me more than an all-day kvetsh of Rivke's.[2]

But it is not for myself, who has a very little, that I am mostly angry. It is for those who have nothing or next to nothing. And even if the story gets out and the neighbors put Eisenberg to shame, what will stop him from sitting by the Utica station or Pennsylvania? There, they won't know him from Adam (as Essie says) and, not knowing, will take pity. This, of course, in one way he needs. But not the money.

APRIL 21, 1937

It is almost three weeks after Pesakh with nice weather, so Rivke in the middle of the afternoon decides she wants to go "shopping," as my daughters call it, for a new housedress. This is altogether a surprise. Unless for a doctor, a funeral, or an affair Rivke hardly ever leaves the block. Maybe once in two years Khave and Essie will drag her to buy a new dress, maybe a second—as they say, with kicks and screams.

"Who needs it?" she tells them.

They answer, "We can't stand looking at you in the same *shmates*[1] every day."

After a month or two, Rivke gives in, and the three of them go find a brown shmate to replace the blue, and this is fine until it is time to change the brown for a green or a pink for a purple. About shoes every three or four years she does not complain until after with her corns and her bunions. But a coat is altogether impossible. She will not give up the old seal until it is more holes than fur—that I am afraid will soon be.

And this I can understand. Why should a person buy who doesn't need? But today, the housedress I could also understand. With the patches, and the seams I sewed seven times, and the colors washed out, and the cloth so thin you could look through, it was almost time. So we went—after, of course, Rivke closed all the windows in case it should rain, pulled the shades if it should not, and made sure the water was not running and that the gas was off together with the electric. So in half an hour we were finally on our way.

Myself, I would have walked. But for Rivke, I thought, the few blocks to the streetcar were far enough. For five cents each we would be, as Reyzl says, "sports." On Belmont Avenue with the stalls and the pushcarts together with the stores it was such a noise that I knew tonight would be at least four aspirins for Rivke. But past one "*gevalt*"[2] she didn't say a word. In the first block she stopped at Levine's to look and feel the goods and in the next by Finkel and Graubart and in the third by Wolkowitz. All with the squeezing and pushing and bumping, the shouts of the peddlers and women, the smells of the fruits and vegetables, some good some rotten—until, of course, she went back to Levine and bought what she saw an hour before. But outside with the package she was angry and wanted to go back to Wolkowitz, "that *ganif*,"[3] and have him tell her how he could charge $3.98 for something she paid $3.25. "Maybe better," I said, "we'll take a stroll on Pitkin." So, when she agreed, that was the second surprise of the day.

Years ago, when we lived on Saratoga, we used to walk on Pitkin all the time. Now I'm there not more than twice a year and Rivke not five times since we moved. Still, everything seemed the same. Busy, but wider than Belmont and with fancier stores and no stalls or pushcarts. The men were still in front of the bank talking politics. Other men were talking more politics—also a little gambling, I'm afraid—by the cafeteria. There were the shoe stores, Beck's, others, some with glass cases on the sidewalk or standing between the big windows to show more goods. The Ripley was on one side, the Howard on the other for the men's clothes. And just where it had always been the Woolworth five cents and ten. Here there were no signs in the window—Jews should not apply—I looked—but I thought one must still be there on the face of the manager. By the Adam Hats window we stopped for a minute. Oy, the prices since three years ago when I bought the one I was wearing! And "oy" again for the prices that would be the Rosh Hashanah after next when I might need a new one!

But with the walking and looking in windows, by now it was getting late. One by one the lights on the storefronts, "neon" they call them, began to go on—Ripley, Jack Lewis, others. By the Loew's theater the lights were already burning, but now you could really see them—off and on, off and on, with running the colors and patterns all around the sign. Such a thing Rivke and I did not see every day.

But what amusement is without a price? We would not get home in time for me to go to shul, and so I would have to daven alone in the house.[4] Supper also would be late. Of this, the smell from the doorway of the delicatessen reminded me. But not only the delicatessen, the knish and the sweet potato carts too, that I forgot to mention.

Between the thought of supper and the smells, by now the mouth was watering. The delicatessen was out of the question. First, who could afford to eat in restaurants? And second, I knew anyway we would have dairy for supper.[5] So it was between the other two. Twice Rivke and I walked from one cart to the other, never mind for the traffic light and the sounding horns. The carts looked the same, a silver color with a coal fire burning inside, and the man at the one and the woman at the other, dark and red themselves from sitting so close to the heat and still bundled in their winter coats and hats. Which one to burn the hands on—the sweet potato in an orange wrapper or the knish in a wax paper? What decided was Rivke getting back to being herself and telling me that I was not Ahashueres[6] choosing a queen and also the kosher sign on the knish cart.

But now another question—what kind of knish—kashe or potato? Comes another *nudzh*[7] from Rivke: "Sooner *Meshiekh*[8] will come than you make up your mind." All right, so potato. Rivke does not want one herself but will take from me a crumb that on our way back to the streetcar becomes almost half.

Except for missing shul, this was not a bad day altogether. With carfare both ways and the knish just a quarter. And for Rivke tonight it has been only two aspirins till now; but the two basins hot water for the feet I didn't figure.

JULY 12, 1937

Sunday, Rivke and I came back from Spring Valley, where we had not been for maybe ten years.[1] Thanks to the children, we had a good time, even if two of Rivke's sisters were there, and a good rest too. Also, Rivke was not so nervous about leaving Avrom by himself at home. He would eat by his three sisters and Leye, and all he had to do was lock the door when he went in and out. And then go to work.

The job in his brother Asher's ice cream parlor was why he stayed home. He started in June after school was finished and was going to work the whole summer so he could have a couple cents in his pocket. He worked for Asher before— a day here, two days there—shlepping from the freezer to the counter, from the cellar to the back room, washing the floor and wiping the tables. But now he was behind the counter, making the cones and the sodas with ice cream and working at the register. When we left for the country, everything was fine.

When we got back, there was no more job. Asher had fired him. And not only did he fire him, he fired him on the night Leye invited Avrom for supper and in the middle of the meal. Azoy! And why? There was a whole *megile*[2] of reasons. Avrom was too slow; he sometimes gave the wrong change; the ice cream cones he made too big; and instead of putting the syrup first in the malted, he put the milk. I am just happy he didn't also hit a rock with his stick.[3]

How fast Asher expected him to be in two weeks I don't know. A person without experience does not go so fast as someone with. This I know from the piecework. Every time a green one came to the job, it took a good while to catch up with the others, even if the person had worked on other kinds garments.

With the cones and the change, I can see it cost Asher money, but you must take time to teach a beginner. Avrom was making the cones he would want himself to eat. So you tell him he must think not like a customer but like the shopkeeper. After all, a profit must be made. The wrong change you could tell him to take his time, to be careful, but Asher wants him to go fast.

But exact and fast by a beginner who can find? I remember that when Asher was just starting his lessons I asked him once to say the *alef-beyz*.[4] This he did in maybe eight seconds. Of course, four letters he left out, and five others were in the wrong place, but I did not fire him from being a pupil.

The syrup and the milk is Asher's craziness that he gets from his mother. By Rivke the taste of the soup changes if the carrot goes in before the onion. Does the water or the chicken know the difference? But vacation or no vacation, all in all, I am not happy with my eldest son.

Still, Asher has taught Avrom two lessons. The first is that the dollar in this country means more than the blood. The second is that it should not.

AUGUST 11, 1937

Every day there are more reports of how the Jews in Germany are suffering. And not just in the communist papers or on WEVD.[1] My *Morning Journal* also has stories—for years now. So many, how can you not believe?[2] The government, the president must know. But will they do something? Can they do something? Why would they care?

And even some of us, mostly the Daytsher allrightniks, don't seem so worried. And some of us, among the frume yidn, even say that the Nazi evil is God's punishment.[3] The other day on Pitkin Avenue my son-in-law Max had to shout down an old man preaching this nonsense on a street corner. God's punishment! What, for the innocent as well as the guilty? For the little children who don't know their right hand from their left? Punishment? By God who spared even Nineveh?[4]

But everyone looks for a reason, for an explanation. Is it the victory of evil, after all? This I cannot believe. Maybe it is time to read Job—again. Maybe better to keep asking painful questions than trying to find simple answers.

MARCH 17, 1938

Tonight is *Purim*,[1] a time of celebration. A time we must be so drunk that we can't tell Haman's name from Mordecai's.[2] But to me this is a day of shame. Asher was arrested this morning and sits in jail. From what my son-in-laws tell me, it's not so serious that he will stay in prison. He will only have to pay a fine. I suppose I should be thankful he is not a thief or a murderer. Still, besides whatever law, he has broken the commandment to honor his father and mother.

Max and Zelig say that in the ice cream shop he put some machines for gambling. And such machines no one is allowed to have. Or not have without a license. Something. And why? To make a little more money, naturally. I didn't know his business was so bad. I didn't see Leye and the girls thin with hunger. I didn't see them without clothes. I didn't see Asher sell the car he bought two months ago. I didn't notice he couldn't take the family to the mountains last summer. I didn't realize we need to make an appeal for him in the shul: "I beg you, give what you can to help a man who makes more than a nice living."

But I forget. This is the land where whatever you have is never enough. The land where Israelites have no patience for Moses on the mountain. Better to have Aaron and the calf.

Max (who understands such things better than I would like) went with Zelig to get Asher from the jail. Leye, of course, knows. Also Khave and Essie. But not Rivke. And Reyzl we shouldn't tell because if Krumbein finds out, Asher and everyone else won't hear the end of it. But how to keep it from her I can't imagine. Maybe she won't tell her husband.

But there is one from whom we can keep nothing. And fine or no fine, it is before Him that my son must atone.

Meanwhile, I feel as if the whole world knows. Maybe I could put on a mask and costume to hide my shame. A *purimshpil*[3] all my own. Already from such excitement, disappointment, and anger, my head is turning like a *grager*.[4]

JULY 7, 1938

❧

This afternoon before *Minkhe*[1] I was standing outside the shul for a while and watched Avrom with Arnie and some other boys playing—what else—ball. Avrom, soon eighteen, is, *take*, a little old for games. But by Arnie and his friends he is a teacher, and it wasn't so long ago he was a child like them himself. Besides, he had put in a day's work already, saving for the books for college in the fall, so I suppose a little amusement wasn't such a terrible thing. And in the long days, there is plenty light after supper to see what you are playing.

I am not myself interested in their games, but since they were banging a ball with a broomstick, it seemed to me that in America they are always finding something new to do with something old— like a wheel from a cart becomes a wheel from a car or from a bird's wing the wing of an airplane. A broomstick, after all, is for holding a broom, not for banging a ball. But not only this, when the ball went down the sewer by the corner, Arnie found somewhere a wire from the milk bottles, twisted it around the end of the stick to make a loop, and the broomstick with the wire became now a fishing pole. Five times, six times it went down, and finally up came the ball in the loop. Somewhere, I know, there is a broom sitting without a handle and a bottle milk leaking from the cap.

And this is not the end of it. When they don't have a ball and a broomstick, they find a can and make a game from kicking it and running. A can, of course, is to hold something. All right, so the peaches have been eaten or the tomato juice drunk up, but the can could still hold some pencils, maybe some nails and screws—and last for years. But by the boys it holds nothing—only the dents from their shoes—and in half an hour is not even good enough for them to play with.

So, no ball, no can—what then? The rubber heels, they took maybe from a pair of shoes still good. With this they throw and try to make it drop on the cracks in the sidewalk and then do some other foolishness, I don't know what, on the same cracks. Or if they have a ball and not the stick, they will put pennies and with the ball try to hit them. President Lincoln must again be a target for the *banditn*?[2]

The girls are not so bad but not altogether so much better. How many of them are jumping with the clothesline while their mothers do not have where to hang the wash?

But soon—I was happy—it was time for me to go daven. By now the boys were playing a game where one of them is called the pillow.[3] With their running and jumping like wild beasts, a mattress I did not want to become.

OCTOBER 30, 1938

Friday night was livelier than usual. Asher came with Leye. Reyzl was there (without Krumbein) and Esther and Khave with Max and Zelig. Also the children, Reyzl's Marcy and the two boys, Arnie and Nokhem. Together with the three of us there were thirteen in the small kitchen. It was a cold night and Shenkman's heat goes off at nine o'clock. So we didn't mind crowding together. The one burner going on the stove helped a little,[1] and the tea going round helped more. Since Rivke had a good week, there were *rogelakh*[2] to go with the tea though the three or four sugar cubes with each glass were sweet enough for me. Before everyone came, the Shabes candles had burned themselves out and left only the light bulb, not bigger than a 40 I think. But with the talk and the singing there was no gloom.

Asher and Max, of course, were arguing as usual. For Asher, business was business and religion was religion, For Max, if you cheated your customers and whoever you owed, or ruined the competition with unfair prices, going to shul, no matter how often, was worthless. The truth is neither one of them goes often, if anything Max less than Asher. Still, Max has the point. Religion is not just the prayers, or listening to the Toyre reading or the rabbi's speech. It is also what a person does. *Frumkayt*[3] from mentshlikhkayt you should not separate.

So I say, "Business and religion are like sides of a slice of bread we call living. Are they different sides? Yes, but of the same slice, from the same ingredients. And if one side gets moldy, you can be sure the other will too."

Asher, who would rather argue with Max than with his father, makes a joke. "And which side of the slice do you butter?"

"The side that will fall facing up," Max answers.

"Not with your *mazl*,"[4] Essie joins in.

She is not smiling. Max is out of work now six weeks, and just yesterday two jobs he thought he had fell through.

"It takes more than mazl," he says.

But before things get too serious, Rivke pours out some more tea and the rogelakh get passed once again.

Reyzl hums a tune. Her sister Khave asks if she knows the words. At once she breaks into Hatikvah. The others join her. Maybe we should have let her go on the stage after all, she is that good. And the others, Essie and Asher at least, are a near match. As is Ruven who isn't here. I don't know where this musical talent comes from. Not from me. And as for Rivke, she can kvetsh but not sing. Arnie, too, has it, but with him I know it comes from his mother and Krumbein. Still, everyone is singing, the Yosele Rosenblatts[5] with the so-sos. The children are amused as their uncle Avrom, not much more than a large child himself, keeps time on their heads with a teaspoon. And there is good feeling and joy in everyone's eyes.

NOVEMBER 12, 1938

The attacks on Jews in Germany (also Austria and Czechoslovakia)[1] that began Wednesday night were more terrible than any that had happened there before, and I am afraid that worse is still to come.

Before this, there were laws—Jews couldn't do this or that, signs telling Germans not to buy from Jewish businesses.[2] Sometimes a beating, even a murder, but these were here or there, not throughout the whole country at the same time.

But now, in two days, hundreds of shuls and kheyders, thousands of homes and businesses have been destroyed, and dozens of Jewish lives taken. They say that thousands of Jews were arrested and will be sent to special camps--not for vacations, I think.[3] I can't imagine, refuse to imagine, for now at least, what dreadful pogroms might lie ahead.

For now, at least, I can't bear to think about those who have died, especially by fire in the burning shuls. For now, I think only about the Toyre scrolls that burnt with them and of Rabbi Khananya ben Teradyon, who the Romans put to death by fire while wrapped in a scroll from which he had been teaching. Although, like himself, the scroll was burning, he told his students that the letters were flying free.

If the letters survive, the Toyre survives. If the Toyre survives, we survive. This is something to hold onto, at least for now.[4]

MARCH 6, 1940

I don't know how Max worked today. Reyzl and Essie both tell me he was up all night again with Arnie. What it was this time I don't know either. But almost never is it anything someone could give a name. The boy gets upset it seems for no reason. And when there is a reason—his baseballers lost a game, the cat had trouble with her kittens, another Nazi speech or victory—he acts just the same. He walks—almost runs—up and down the room, talks like water pouring from a broken pipe, waves his arms like by the exercises in the school yard. *Shpilkes*[1] he has enough for ten. Sometimes he cries, or sweats, or shakes without a stop.

No one knows what to do with him. Reyzl sometimes tries to hold him in her arms, but he is no longer a small child. The doctor thinks maybe he will grow out of it—or maybe not. His father long ago decided he was crazy. If not for Max the last few years, Krumbein would have been right. What Max does exactly it is hard to say. Most of the time, he just stays with him, listens, once in a while gives a couple words advice—quietly. And when Arnie is calmer, they walk for hours through the streets, talking. Or they play a little cards with Arnie's friends, or go once in a while to the moving pictures.

It is not as if Max is the boy's father. This Arnie never had and never will. (What kind of man is it that puts a lock on the ice box his children shouldn't "steal" the food?) No, Max is more like an older brother, like my Ruven with Avrom or me with Eliezer[2]—about the same years apart. Someone more like himself than a father—even a good one—can be, and someone to follow a little bit. With Arnie, I am afraid he is following Max to the socialist meetings, but this is better than the other madhouse.

With all the *meshugas*,[3] Arnie is not a dummy. A head he has for what he wants. Numbers he is good with. When he used to come study, Rivke would always ask him to check the figuring by Sherman on the paper bag. This Arnie would do without a pencil, with his eyes alone. And when he found a mistake, Rivke would go herself to Sherman to get the few cents and give him good, because she knew I would do one but not the other. And enough times it happened that Sherman used to send his regards to her grandson the adding machine.

But to teach him, good head and all, was not exactly a pleasure. Between rocking in the chair, humming the songs, tapping with the feet, and banging with the pencils like a drum, I was surprised he learned as much as he did. The stories he liked—Cain with Abel or the spies in the land of Canaan—and paid attention. In the laws and the prayers he was not interested. But because between his father and his mother he could sing and wanted, learning for the bar mitsve was not so bad.

Like the other Jewish boys in America, he would rather play than study and from everything he made a game—even the Toyre. He would sit in shul with his brother Norman or one of Helzner's boys, whoever was there, and take turns opening the Khumesh. If they opened to the beginning of a chapter, they would give the letters their worth as numbers[4] and keep a sum. Whoever got a hundred "points" or whoever had the most by the time the Toyre reading was finished was the winner. From this maybe comes amusement but not learning, and not the wisdom even a child can reach.

I would not know this if one afternoon during a lesson he didn't show me. He wanted, I suppose, that I should tell him how clever he was. This I could not do altogether. "Such a use for the Toyre I never heard of," I said, "but even by the accountants' shul[5] they would pay attention to the words at least as much as to the numbers."

So, after last night we expect there will be peace with Arnie—for a while. Max tonight will get some sleep. I don't know how long he can go on this way with his nephew. After all, he has his own child at home to think about now, even if it is such a little one. May the Holy One give him strength to be to his own children what he has been to Arnie—only as a father and not an older brother—and Essie the patience to let him do what he can for Arnie still.

JUNE 27, 1940

Today in the house was pushke Thursday. All the collectors from the charities showed up the same day. Two of them even the same time. So it was an entertainment for Rivke and me to talk with people we see maybe twice a year. Not exactly that it's a visit, but it's not exactly business either.

In the house we now keep four boxes: one for the orphans, another for old rabbis and scholars, a third for a yeshive, and also for a hospital. Altogether, we go from the just born to the close to dying. Every Friday before Shabes, like everyone else, we put in each a few cents, sometimes before holidays, sometimes because we notice them when two cents are rubbing together in a pocket. So we put the pennies in the box, they shouldn't start a fire. At least twice a year, sometimes more, someone comes to empty a box, count and take the money, and give a receipt. Though little it may be, they are after all not counting by Rothschild, they never say a word. Once in a while maybe they give a look. But to this Rivke and I say nothing. After all, the orphans and the others will get the money, ugly face or no.[1]

But about this my son-in-law Max thinks different. The collectors, he says, take half for themselves. So it is not for the orphans and students they make the face. And what if he is right? Someone has to collect, and should he do it for nothing, a poor man himself? The old and the sick at least get something, much more than half, I think. By Max the dark is never black enough. Max himself, of course, gives to charity. But when he gives, Mr. Socialist, he writes a check. And where, Max, I could ask him, do they get the money for the bookkeeper that opens his envelope? The collectors are also bookkeepers, only with a kitchen for the office and a table for the desk. Still, Essie keeps a box or two anyhow.

So this morning at 9:30 comes the hospital. An old man, tall, skinny, with long fingers. So pale, you would think he's a patient himself. It's a "how are you this morning," a word about the weather, and a refused glass of tea. Nu, so straight to the box. He separates the pennies from the silver then the nickels from the dimes and the dimes from the two quarters. The quarters Rivke and I are surprised to see. Each of us points to the other and asks with a shrug and a raised eyebrow which of us put them in. Meanwhile, the collector has put the nickels into threes and is doing the same with the dimes. When he is finished, he takes a paper and piece of pencil from a pocket, counts the stacks, multiplies by three, and again by the worth of each kind of coin. He adds everything together, including the two quarters. Two dollars and sixty cents. Rivke and I nod at each other as if to say "not bad." But the collector is already with the pennies that he puts out by five. Again with the arithmetic. A total of eighty-four cents. So altogether with the silver it makes $3.44.

He pulls out a little receipt book and starts to write. Then stops.

"Mister, Missus," he says, "this is a nice amount. From the hospital a heartfelt thanks. Still, another sixteen would make it twenty times khay[2] cents."

Almost without thinking, I reach into a pocket and Rivke gets her purse. I find a nickel, she the eleven cents. The collector already hands us the receipt for $3.60. With another thank you and a wish for our good health he goes.

Two hours later there is a knock on the door. Who is it? The yeshive! Rivke and I are astonished. Only once before, maybe eleven—twelve years ago, we had two such visitors in one day.

This one is a much younger man, short with a small beard. To look at him he is not starving. Tea he also refuses. But some crackers[3] with the chocolate pieces he takes after checking to make sure they're kosher.

And then to work.

He spills the pushke onto the table. Rivke and I wait for him to separate the coins. But no! He has a way of his own. He takes from his pocket a paper bag, and whatever he takes from the pile he puts in and counts—forty-eight, forty-nine, fifty, sixty, sixty-one, sixty-six, sixty-seven, seventy-two, a dollar twenty-two. . . ." Both Rivke and I are stunned by the half dollar.

He goes on like a factory. Finger, coin, bag, number. Finger, coin, bag, number. With the figures he is faster than Sherman by the grocery, so who knows how many mistakes. But soon he is finished. "Two dollars ninety-two cents," he announces. Do we know? We take his word for it and nod.

Right away he makes out the receipt. He is not interested in how many times khay. But Rivke, maybe out of pity he doesn't know any better, maybe because she likes exact, finds eight more pennies in her purse and gives them to him.

"Three dollars, just," she says.

"But I made the receipt," he says. He, too, likes exact.

"Don't worry yourself," I tell him. "The One above keeps all records."

He smiles, thanks Rivke, and puts all the coins from the bag into a heavy leather pouch inside the little suitcase he carries. So with a good day, a good year, and another couple crackers, he goes.

By now Rivke and I are exhausted and a little upset because we have things to do. She with the pots and I with the books and papers. For an hour Rivke cooks while I read. After, there is a little lunch with black bread, a piece farmer cheese, and coffee—Postum[4] for her, and then back to our work. By the middle of the afternoon, everything seems normal again. Rivke is even muttering quiet curses to her frying pan, the oil, and the peanuts it came from. Then another knock.

It is the orphans' home. The two of us can hardly believe it. The collector, rosy faced like a child himself for all his years, stands shyly, also like a child, in the doorway. In our astonishment, we have not asked him in.

"Come in," I say, finally. "You are not the first one to come for the boxes today."

"Not the second either," Rivke adds as he sits down.

This one, it turns out, will have some tea. Rivke takes a new bag (nothing is too good for company) and pours from the kettle into the glass. This she puts next to him with a box sugar cubes he should help himself. The collector just puts a cube in his teeth and raises the tea to his nose before sipping when there comes another knock at the door.

"May my enemies have such knocking in their heads as we've had knocking on the door today," Rivke says.

Still, we open it.

And there stands the old age home. Not only do we not believe, but the two men are also standing with their mouths open. But soon, when both are at the table, sitting on opposite sides, they are looking at each other like two roosters in the same yard. The newcomer, more gray and bony than the hospital this morning, will also have tea. After all, he seems to say, if the other one has it why should I go without?

After a few sips, they reach slowly for the boxes. But the old age home stops.

"Missus," he says to Rivke, "maybe you have something to put on the table we shouldn't mix the coins."

"Yes, Missus," says the other, looking across the table all the while, "we wouldn't want the money to go to the wrong place."

Rivke finds a rolling pin and places it between them not too softly.

After another sip of tea, the collectors reach again for the boxes. Slowly. This is a dance of the hands. And it is into the hands that each pours the coins before placing them on the table. They try to make no noise, as if someone could tell the total from the sound of the jingling.

These two work in piles of ten for the pennies. First the old age home puts one. The orphans matches it then puts another. This the old age matches and puts a second. Till the pennies are finished and the orphans smiles. Each of them has fourteen stacks, but the last one for the old age is short a couple cents and the orphans has one extra. They move to the nickels and do the same by fives. But no one smiles at the end. Both with six stacks that look full. By now they have lined them up in rows on either side of the rolling pin.

It is time for the dimes, also by fives. One stack. A match. Two stacks. Another. The seconds pass. And the old age almost laughs as he puts a pile nearly full with only two dimes for an answer. But his happiness disappears as the orphans takes from under the rolling pin a quarter. But before he can show even a sign of pleasure, Rivke has already put another nickel for the sages. "So, both the same," she says. The three of us men are amazed at her addition. To tell the truth, I couldn't tell that one pile of nickels was short.

But what pleases Rivke, does not so much please the collectors. They make out their receipts without a word and mumble a thanks and goodbye like two *goylems*[5] as they leave separately.

With such excitement, Rivke has swallowed two aspirins (if not more), wrapped her head in a *bobishke*[6], and taken to her bed. Myself, I couldn't study, so I just read the newspaper and listened to the radio. Our four boxes are empty, and if our little donations helped even one person (though I think more), I am content. Still, tomorrow is Friday, and the boxes we will start to fill again.

FEBRUARY 12, 1941

My daughters have all inherited their mother's tongue along with her knack for giving names. And each one, it seems, has gotten more than just a share. This morning I was in Khave's house ten minutes to bring figs and dates for the holiday[1] And in the ten minutes she cursed poor Zelig ten times. I'm sure under his breath he was cursing President Lincoln for having a birthday (also today) to keep him home from work.

Most of the time she was satisfied to call him "peasant." This she mixed in with a "teamster"[2] and once or twice "block of wood." Not exactly compliments. Did he leave his cigar in the soup plate? Did he not move fast enough from her carpet sweeper? Who knows why? Maybe nothing was a reason, maybe everything.

In the middle of this, Khave's shouting woke little Yoyne.[3] Naturally, Zelig got blamed.

"Even the baby suffers with you home today!" she told him. "The way you woke him, you should be wakened by worms in your grave."

Speaking for once, Zelig said, "I'll never die." But he forgot that he was dealing with Khave *bas*[4] Rivke.

"Oh, excuse me, Mr. Goylem," she answered. "Then go be a lump of clay."

Zelig has not yet learned (as I have altogether) that the best thing is to say nothing.

When Khave went in to Yoyne, I started to go. But before I left I saw Zelig was putting the date pits on the coffee table. I pointed to them and toward Khave. He understood and picked them up. But it seemed to me that one of them he pushed between the cushions of the couch.

At Essie's I didn't stay even ten minutes. Max was out getting the paper, so their house was certainly peaceful.

"Why he needs another paper, I don't know," Essie said. "He already has a pile of them behind the club chair."

I could see already it might not be so peaceful when Max got back. But even if I didn't hear anything today, I know what Essie's tongue can do. By her, each curse is an arrow, and she is maybe better with the bow than the students of Rabbi Shimon bar Yokhai.[5] For practice, she'll maybe throw in "May an evil spirit take you" or "a husband like you my worst enemies should have," but these are almost blessings. If Max's clothes fall from their hangers, she wishes the same his fingers from his hands. If the clothes do not fall, but he hangs them the wrong way, then she wishes he would walk with his head turned backwards. For what crimes I don't know, she would have him spit blood or vomit green gall.

But Max is different from Zelig and me. He has a temper and answers not only with a voice. He also bangs on tables, slams doors, throws whatever he puts a hand on, and tears from the walls the fixtures. But Essie is always ready: "May you bang on the gates of paradise and never be let in"; "This Yom Kippur may the Book of Life slam shut without your name"; "The next time you throw, may it be a fit"; "The way you ripped out that towel rack, wild beasts should only tear out pieces of your flesh."

So I do not wait for Max to return but leave my little present. At least over this there will be no arguing. Max likes this kind of fruit, and if anything tastes sweet, Essie will eat it.

At Reyzl's it is different. Except Krumbein growls at the children, it is always a funeral parlor. At least by Khave and Essie it is lively, and you can hear a person laugh. When I come, the children are out—in the schoolyard, by friends, so it is just Reyzl and Krumbein silent in their dark rooms. He is by the window reading with the paper in his face so not to use electric.

When he sees me, he lifts up the paper like a Toyre and says, "Every day the news is the same. Half the world are bastards; and those that are not are fools."

A fine blessing and a way to greet a father-in-law.

Reyzl offers him the dates and figs.

"Too sweet," he says.

"Naturally," she answers, "what isn't too sweet for you?"

He lowers the paper altogether. "You're not too sweet for me."

He smiles enough to show one gold tooth, then goes back to reading.

Reyzl says to me, "A man who takes no tea with his lemon."

No one raised a voice. But it was worse than with the others. By Khave and Essie, there is a harmless explosion, mostly noise, over with and back to normal. But here normal is frost, creeping forever like slow poison. Again I had a reason to regret the marriage, not that I needed another.

After this, I walked home a little faster than usual. Rivke was having a good day when I left, and I knew she would have been at the figs and dates, no matter how she would deny it. When

Pharaoh got up in the middle of the night it was to relieve himself in secret. How would it look for a god, after all, to be so human? When she gets up, it is to eat. How would it look, after all, if Rivke Kahn?

When I walked in the door, Rivke greeted me: "You're out so long, I thought you died already in the street."

"Maybe next time," I said.

But I was right. She had been at the fruit. A piece of date skin was stuck to her lip. I took it off and put it in my mouth.

"Still sweet," I said.

She poked me in the chest, saying, "Go already—go study."

But she could not keep from smiling.

DECEMBER 2, 1941

For months, for years better, the newspaper and the radio have told us about the gangster Lepke. Finally, he has been found guilty of murder and will be put to death.[1] If even half the stories are true—maybe even if only one—he is an evil man. Sometimes we hear that he supports his mother and that his wife and son—a stepson, I think—he treats well. Nu, very nice. Hitler also, I suppose, has put a child on his knee and (however hard to believe) sang it a song. But those he makes suffer do not feel less pain because of this, and such a singing does not make his crimes less evil. As for Lepke, to the murders we must add stealing, beatings, burnings, bombings.

For such a man all of humanity must blush, but, since he is a Jew, he is especially a *shande far yidn*.[2] And he is not alone. Where do we get them all—a Buchalter, a Lansky, a Rothstein[3] (not, *Borukh Hashem*[4], related to Max)? In Europe we had our Jewish thieves, yes, a *bulvan*[4] here and there who might beat someone, once in half a lifetime a murderer. But first, there were not so many, and if they were talked about at all it was in whispers, not like here with screaming to millions in the paper every week or in the news on the radio. When we spoke above a whisper in the old country the names on our lips were *Rambam*, the Vilna *Gaon*, this *magid* or that[5]—not criminals but sages.

But in this time and place it is the Lepkes that are the heroes, or, if not heroes exactly, the ones respected (and feared) for their power. Respect also for the prize fighters[6]—in an ugliness and inhumanity allowed by the law—and in a different way for all kinds [of] entertainers. Because it is not just guns and fists but money that is power in this world.

Still, I ask again, where do we get such men as Lepke? From the tenements, Max says. From the lice, the filth, the crowding, the poverty. Maybe this is so. And poor in America is worse than poor in Europe. There, no one had anything. Here, some do, and those who don't see it and want. But this does not explain altogether. If a starving man steals a loaf of bread, you can understand. Even if he hurts someone to get it—I don't say kill. But when he is satisfied, should he go steal again? Or make a habit of hunger and theft? And then maybe of theft without the hunger? No, it is not just the tenements. The yeytser hore must be at work too. Otherwise, every immigrant and his child would be a criminal. And that is not the case. Even in Lepke's own family not. Brothers and a sister he has—one a teacher, another a dentist, a third—I can hardly believe myself—a rabbi! Never mind Max makes from this two criminals by the Buchalters. They are, except for Lepke, respectable people.

But respectable people are maybe too many for the newspapers to make headlines. Who would read "Berel Shmerel Works Hard and Makes a Living" or "Yente Dvendl, Regular Baleboste, Keeps a Fine Kosher Home"? This would be their own story or their neighbors'. Altogether not too interesting. Soup without salt. But must the paper give us Lepkes for a seasoning? Too much of such salt will kill the soul and even one grain stings in the wound of our embarrassment.

And as for Max, who keeps coming to mind here, it is a good thing he has stayed out of the poolroom on Pitkin and the candy store on Saratoga. Let him find his newspapers elsewhere and not find himself in them.

AUGUST 23, 1942

We buried my brother Yisroel a week ago this morning.[1] One might have cursed the sun for a liar on such a day.

We all went to the funeral parlor. We all cried with his children, his Miriam dead now for years. Our two families had been very close on the East Side and the cousins see each other still.

The rabbi spoke the truth. Yisroel was an ordinary man, frum, a good husband and father, and—like all of us—a better grandfather. His children and grandchildren loved him. (What was there not to love?). He was not an old man, a little more than the seventy allowed us,[2] and his life had been filled with the usual sorrows and the usual joys.

At the cemetery, waiting for the rabbi to begin, I thought how of the five of us who came to America only three are left—Borukh, Eliezer, and myself. Khaim was lost in the epidemic after the first war, maybe two weeks after Brayne's Velvl,[3] leaving Rivke's sister Tsaytl also a young widow. And my other brothers? Those we left in Minsk? The eldest, Menakhem Mendl, Zalmen, and Naftali, are long in their graves. But from the four others no letter in almost a year.[4] I'm afraid that they have fallen into the madman's hands and are lost—along with all those other brothers and sisters whose names I never knew.

In this age of evil and death, when I light the *yortsayt* candle,[5] sit shive, and say Kadish, it is not for Yisroel alone.

MAY 17, 1943

Avrom left this morning for the war. He would not let us take him to New York. Not his mother and me. Not his sister Essie. Not his brother-in-law Max. Alone.

He kissed us goodbye. At the kitchen window, we saw him wave once, smiling—I don't know how—then turn and walk toward the elevated. He swung his one small bag as he went. With our eyes, we followed him across the street and down the block past Malkin the butcher. At the corner, by Persky the tailor, he disappeared.

All the while Rivke held my arm, crying softly, trembling.

"You gave him the apple cake?" I managed hoarsely.

She nodded.

"A *sider*[1] also I put in his bag. What more could he want—a piece apple cake and a prayer."

We fell into each other's arms. As my shirt grew damp with her tears, her hair with mine, I recited the *Sh'ma*.[2]

AUGUST 22, 1943

Ruven spent the past Shabes, the first weekend of his vacation, with his mother and me. Golda and the boys, Dovid at least, he tells us are fine. Nathan, Golda still takes from doctor to doctor, but there seems to be nothing they can do. The polio took both legs and part of an arm. Thank God it spared his life.

By now, Ruven is back with his family on their way to the mountains for a week. But while he was here, Rivke and I were happy to have him. Especially with Avrom gone to the army, Ruven made the house livelier than it has been since his brother left. And on Friday night when the others came, as they do each week, it was a pleasure to hear him join in the singing as he used to.

But I don't know how happy Ruven was himself. He was glad to see all of us, of course, but otherwise he seemed quiet—as if there was something that troubled him. Nathan alone is enough to cause sorrow and worry. And more and more the boy fills Golda's fears as his brother fills her hopes. One can understand this; children are the center of their mothers' lives. But in all this filling, where is there place for Ruven?

Still, I think it was something more. He is now with his third shul, and has not yet found one where he can stay. It is never the members. They listen to his speeches; they can talk to him. He visits the hospital when they are sick, their houses when they sit shive. With the board, with the president, it's another thing altogether. What exactly, I don't know. But in America how are you a rabbi without a congregation? A yeshive is possible. A kheder somewhere. Maybe, with the war, the army. But then, what happens after?

So Ruven left me thinking about such things. But while he was here, I must admit I was kveling. He came with me to shul, naturally, and I could hear the whispers "Reb Sholem's son, the rabbi." But when someone spoke to me it wasn't the usual "Reb Sholem" but "Mr. Kahn."[1] Of course, they honored Ruven, asking him Friday afternoon to daven Minkhe[2]—*Mayriv*[3] they must have thought was asking too much—and called him to the Toyre Shabes morning. His fine Hebrew and good voice impressed everyone there. And when Rabbi Magerman gave his speech, he introduced Ruven to the congregation as Rabbi Ruven Kahn, son of Mr. Sholem Kahn.

Even if no one had said anything, they could tell he was not just a plain man. Every hair of his short beard was trimmed and in place. The creases in the pants of the dark blue suit were like razors, and his shirt so white and starched I could believe Essie was still washing and ironing for him. If anyone had yet a doubt, the gray hat—a homburg they call it, brushed just so, could have told them. Just to look at him was enough to set the women in the gallery upstairs chattering, even before they knew who he was.

At home, we made *Kidesh*[4] over the wine from the grapes he brought last fall.

Rivke, of course, tried to fatten him up, serving him soup with so many noodles they couldn't swim, both thighs and legs from the chicken, plenty of her carrot *tsimes*,[5] and half a shtrudel with his tea. Such a meal he doesn't get from Golda, and at the hotel in the mountains not so good.

Not that he needed; I could see no bones beneath his flesh. But with all the singing, and the honors, the food, and the kveling, it was his spirit in the end that seemed thin and hungry, yet, so weak at times, it didn't have the strength to eat.

So Ruven's visit was the sweet with the bitter, the sun with clouds, a flood with a drought. For paradise you must go to *Gan Eydn*.[6] For misery one hundred percent, to *Gehinem*.[7] In this world there is only so-so—whatever is in between.

NOVEMBER 3, 1943

Avrom is home on leave and we are all overjoyed to see him. But he has changed a good deal. In a few months, of course, no one would expect him to become altogether a man, but he is not such a boy now either. He has lived a little, not only in the army, but away from home—so in two different worlds. Even Max, who tries to know everything, asks him—as if Avrom is a *meyvin*[1]—if what the socialist books and magazines say about Southerners hating black people and Jews is right. Rivke and his sisters try to treat Avrom like a baby still, but he enjoys it less than he used to.

Except when they are feeding him. Maybe fifteen pounds he lost since he went to the army. From the letters we already knew he was eating just enough to live. *Treyf*[2] we knew the food would be before he went in, and we were not surprised to learn that it was bad treyf. The meat absolutely he would not touch. And with all the training, someone wouldn't put on an ounce from the canned vegetables and the eggs maybe made from a powder. Fortunately, this army, like the czar's, has great respect for potatoes or he would be a skeleton altogether. It is a good thing also that he got now and then meals away from the camp at some Jewish homes. And, a couple times Asher or Zelig sent him a salami, but how much of this can a person eat?

But now, his mother and sisters take turns stuffing him. Rivke feeds him *flanken*[3] with beans; Reyzl, herring she pickled herself; Khave, *kashe varnishkes*[4] by the bowl; Essie, armlets [*sic*], whether with the vegetables and tomato [sauce][5] or lox (she was lucky to find) with onions, of course, and real eggs.[6] The plate chopped liver Leye sent over did not go to waste either.

The men too have not been shy. Asher shlepped him off one afternoon to his shop long enough for a slice pie with two scoops ice cream and a malted (two more scoops) to wash it down. And a couple nights after supper Max took him for an egg cream[7] in the candy store. So Avrom will go back to the army with a little meat on his bones. And I also will add a couple pounds because not even a half-starved soldier can eat everything the women put in front of him.

But we are afraid that when Avrom goes back they will send him overseas. This we have already seen with other families on the street—Schreiber, Aaronson, Feldstein and more. But Avrom knows even better than us. And maybe this is why he is sometimes so quiet. And maybe why at other times he plays so hard with his little nephews, Ari and Yoyne, tossing them in the air (never mind their mothers are screaming), rolling with them on the floor, and letting them ride on his back or shoulders. In these moments he is like a child himself. After they send him over, this he will never be again.

OCTOBER 2, 1944

Wherever I go in the neighborhood, I see the same dog. A small one with long, pale fur that lives around the corner from Esther. From what I can see, he is not taking a walk just to enjoy the fine weather. And not exactly for his health either. Though I suppose to deny himself (if an animal could do such a thing) would be unhealthy.

However it is, he seems to be making a new nation of dogs all of his own (not that the lady dogs don't cooperate). If like paper, and rubber, and scrap iron, dogs were needed for the war, this one would get a medal from the president.

There are some men who behave the same way. They will lie with any woman who will let them and pay no more attention to the results than any beast. They are men of the flesh, of the senses but not of sense. What, after all, is the difference between us and the beasts but to be able to think, to be able to control our sinful passions—in the name of sacred law and for the sake of peace among us?

I have known just a few such men, but they always made me uneasy. As if they were goylems controlled by a power not their own—maybe of a better clay but also a more slippery. These made me shudder.

But at the dog, such a little bandit, I smile, admiring his energy and respecting the urge (itself God given). I might even think about giving his furry tokhes a patsh of approval. For he is living out his dogginess, and a dog should live like a dog.

And a man should not.

APRIL 12 1945

President Roosevelt is dead.

When the news came, I was teaching Ari at the little table by the kitchen window. His mother was listening to the radio in the front room while she waited for him. We rushed in when she screamed. Essie was in the Morris chair already in tears. Between sobs, she told us what happened, then buried her face in her hands and cried on for twenty minutes or more. (How Rivke and the baby slept through it all, I don't know.)

Ari was frightened. I think he had never seen Essie cry, at least not for so long and so hard. The lesson, of course, was over. Instead, I tried to explain about the president and death and how his mother felt. He knew who the president was and what death was—from his dog five or six months ago, if nothing else. He is a bright child, sometimes even wise beyond his years—but with a child's wisdom. He did not know what his mother felt. It was for the president, yes, but for herself as well, for all of us, for all our lives.

The death is not altogether a surprise. Such a sick man, especially the last few years. So there is not shock so much as sorrow. He was a friend of poor people, after all, and there are many who remember, even if now, Got tsu danken, they make a living. And if he brought us into the war—what else could he have done—he was, with God's help, bringing us out of it. So even by the Jews you could find his picture on the wall—Reyzl has one—even if he could have done more—something—to save our people in Europe from the madness.

The streets have been still since the news came. As if after the first loud lamentation the world at once turned dumb as stone.

AUGUST 15, 1945

At last it is over. Two big bombs, terrible bombs the newspaper said, and finished. Now maybe Avrom can come home, and Schreiber's son and Feldstein's and Ginsberg's and Max's brother. All of them. And all the other brothers and sons. Only the secret horrors remain to be told. Maybe it was not like in Europe, but the Japanese had their camps too.

In New York they were dancing in the streets. Here in the neighborhood there was everywhere a "block party." Not too fancy. Frankfurters, soda water, pretzels—like what they call a picnic. But everyone laughing and having a good time. Almost everyone.

Max was hanging the paper ribbons—red, white, and blue like the flag—from one side of the street to the other. The other side was the shul, so he tied the paper to the big iron gate. Karpowitz, the president of the shul, comes out to yell at him he'll maybe do damage. Max says something he shouldn't say to an old man (or to anyone else) and keeps tying. Karpowitz keeps yelling till he's red in the face but finally goes back with a warning that Max will pay for any damage and he knows where Max lives.

I have never heard of paper harming iron. As an old blacksmith, I know that sometimes even iron won't harm iron. So how to explain Karpowitz? He suffers from *makher*'s[1] disease. A little money and a little power sometimes damage—*take*—the eyes, the head, the heart. Karpowitz is a wholesaler from groceries. Because he has some properties and more money than the other members, he becomes the president. By him he's King David in Jerusalem—only without the psalms. And the worst thing would be if someone else took away his little city and his throne. So he barks like a peasant's dog if someone even comes close—maybe even at the peasant.

But is Karpowitz a learned man, a wise man? He does not know more than the rabbi or our shames, who unlike most has spent years in study, or maybe even me who knows very little. What he knows is business, and here that is the source of all honor. For a scholar they might have some respect, but not for a poor scholar. Such a person must be a fool.

My son-in-law, the socialist, knows this. Still, his problem is not with the money but who has it and who hasn't. He himself has nothing but his wages. What he wants is to take from a Karpowitz and give not only to himself but to all his brothers and sisters, whether he met them in his life or not. Max, after all, is a generous man. But then we might have everyone a makher, and to me this is not an improvement. One or two, at least, you can keep an eye on.

So the argument was more than about the ribbons that hung across the street almost the whole party. (Finally, the boys on the block tore them down.) No, it was the old argument between the rich and the poor. The prophets and sages knew all about it—without the help of Mr. Marx.

The party for the neighbors was very nice. That the war is finally over is wonderful. But no one should be surprised that even after fifteen years of war and depression the Karpowitzes and the Maxes are still tearing each other apart. Who can expect to settle in four years what hasn't been settled in four thousand and that might never be settled at all?

AUGUST 16, 1945

I have just read over what I wrote yesterday about the sons coming home. Aaronson's boy will not come home. He is home more than a year. More than two months ago already was the yortsayt. I am ashamed that in my own joy I forgot another father's, another mother's misery.

The two of them, Aaronson and his missus, walk around like the bullet that took their Mickey also took them. Their talking is "hello" and "goodbye." With a joke or a *kibits*[1] you get maybe a smile, a laugh not. For them, even with other children, with grandchildren, the world has grown gray, like a mist, without color, almost without light. Worse it must be for them than when Rivke and I lost the baby. Mickey, a young man already, was a whole person—with such a voice, with such a walk, with memories, ideas, things he did, things he wanted to do—but who can compare suffering?

The flag with the star the Aaronsons did not hang in the window. I think this, with the letter from the War Department, with the medals and ribbons, they must have put in a box, in an envelope, or with a rubber band somewhere in a drawer. One day they will give to the nephews and nieces, maybe with a picture, and say "This was your Uncle Mickey who died in the war." Children of his own there are not and will not be.

By the politicians, the newspapers even, you hear that such a death was a "sacrifice" together with "honor" and "glory." Without Mickey and the other Mickeys by the tens of thousands America would have lost the war, and the Jews surely would have been destroyed. Who can say no? But to the parents of all the Mickeys, such a "sacrifice" with "honor" and "glory"—who can say no—is still a hole in the heart.

APRIL 14, 1946

Tomorrow is Erev Pesakh[1] and the house is altogether ready. The dishes have been changed.[2] Rivke is doing her cooking even now, and I have grated the horseradish—so strong this year that four times I wished it taken by cholera as I rubbed my eyes. This afternoon I brought the wine up from the cellar in gallon bottles, and I have just gathered the *khomets*[3] to burn early tomorrow morning. Then I will go to Mr. Mermelstein to buy the *kharoyses*[4]—why we don't make it ourselves I don't know—and done.

Then tomorrow night and the next the *Seders*.[5] Like always, the whole family in the neighborhood is there (except the first night Max takes Allan to his family—traveling yet on yontif). Like always I will wear my white *yarmulke*[6] and *kitl*.[7] And one by one all the men and the boys past bar mitsve will say the Kidesh—myself, Krumbein, Asher, Zelig, Max (the second night only of course), Reyzl's Arnie and Norman and their brother-in-law, Marcy's Joe. Asher tells me that maybe his Elke, almost engaged, will bring her Neil (also a name—but it could be for Nisn). Our Kidesh will take twenty minutes at least, but by then with the repeating, each in a different voice, we will all be in the yontif spirit.

Like always we will have for the fruits of the ground, not lettuce or parsley in salt water but sliced radishes, green onions, and cucumbers. Yoyne will ask the four questions, translating from Hebrew to Yiddish word by word and phrase by phrase, as I have taught him; then we will read the answers. All the while, of course, the little thieves—Jerry by himself the first night, Jerry and Allan the second—will try to steal the *afikoymen*.[8] Essie's Michael is too small to help.

But in the middle (like always) there will be dinner. And this can become a little crazy. For each of the women cooks for her family at home and brings the meal in pots to be heated or on plates to be served. So there are five kinds of gefilte fish, sweet or peppery, dark or light depending on how much carp—none in Essie's almost white. Only Max eats the fish jelly, so the first night the women mix all of it in a bowl to save for him. It sits like Elijah's cup.[9] Naturally, there are five different chicken soups, some pale some dark, some fat some lean, some with more vegetables than soup others with just a piece celery or carrot. *Matse*[10] balls the same—big ones, small ones; ones that float, ones that sink; some that fall apart when you look at them; some cannon balls left over from the war. But the meat dishes are altogether different. One person will have pot roast, another chicken, a third turkey—which I don't mind, since I will always be offered a couple slices—who knows what else.

But another thing that confuses is that Zelig eats backwards, meat before soup. Allan, if Essie let him, would do this too, only starting with cake and cookies.

The truth is these nights no one goes hungry, and I have said nothing about everything else from *kugl*[10] to compote. Let us hope that this year we will not have to get an ambulance again for Krumbein. Thank God, what we thought last year was a heart attack was only indigestion.

After the tea, I must buy back the afikoymen—from Jerry the first night, from Jerry and Allan the second. Last year, thanks to Max, who is a troublemaker in such things, the boys asked for a dollar—for each of them! My offer was some pennies or a patsh. But in half a minute we settled, and after yontif I gave a quarter each.

But this year, even if I have written "like always" twenty times, is different from other years, just as the night of Pesakh is different from all other nights. It is the first Pesakh after the war; Avrom, we hope, will soon be home; some of our people in Europe—a few, a few—have escaped the slaughter, together with those in America and elsewhere, and the voices calling for a Jewish land in Palestine are growing louder every day. For such a Pesakh a quarter will not do. I will give a dollar each night—to be shared— even for Allan the first night he won't be there.

APRIL 18, 1946

From beginning to end, the Seders this year were all that I had hoped. Everyone was there, at least the second night, and it really felt like yontif. Krumbein managed not to stuff himself, so we did not need the ambulance again; Elke brought her Neil (not for Nisn but Nokhem, like Reyzl's Norman) to meet the family—a nice boy, it seems, except he has not read a Hebrew word since his bar mitsve—if he had one; Ari (the second night) and Yoyne were excited about the dollar I would give them for the afikoymen. Max, for once, had nothing to say about the amount.

From the blessing after meals to the last song you could hear our voices like a chorus of twenty or more over the whole neighborhood—if not for all the other voices coming from other apartments. But we were happy just to hear ourselves. Asher, Reyzl, and Essie led the way as usual, together with Krumbein, who can sing when he is not growling like a mad dog, and also the grandsons Arnie and Allan (on the second night).[1] Even little Michael, not two years old, chirped a note here and there.

Between the singing and the four cups of wine, that even Krumbein said was good this year, we were all hot and red in the face when we were through, even with the windows open. And in this happy mood, over the noise of pots, and coats, and children being gathered, we wished each other a *zisn Pesakh*[2] and a good year.

And if this morning's mail is a sign, a good year it will be. Avrom writes that with the war now over he might be home by summer.[3] Rivke has spent half the day thanking God and weeping for joy. The other half she spent making and unmaking his bed, which she will do a hundred times again before he returns. As I polished Elijah's cup before putting it away till next year, I said some blessings and wiped the eyes myself. But more than a hundred times, I imagined rising from my chair to open the door for my son.[4]

JULY 23, 1946

The best thing is to sit and study by the window. But it is not the only thing. To sit all day long would be a pain, not a pleasure. And if I have always been a student, I have never been a scholar. The Almighty, after all, gave us other parts besides a head, and we should use them.

My hands tell the story. From the broken knuckle to the dark, rough skin. A man who has worked with his hands. Not just with the needle and machine sitting in one place all day long. But in the blacksmith shop or by the pushcart and wagon repair. Even today fixing a chair or a table. The one good thing about the farm in Connecticut years ago was I was out in the fields, in the barn, in the shed—with a hoe, a shovel, an axe, a hammer—bending, banging, lifting. The farm failed but not the health.

These days I don't do so much with the hands besides the little fixing. The arms, the eyes, the fingers are not what they used to be. But if the hands are out, I use the feet and legs. And this is what has kept me long past the seventy years of the psalm.[1] Almost every day I am all over the neighborhood. To teach my students. To go one of the journeys Rivke sends me on. And not just to Sherman on the corner. For some things—like pot cheese—I need to pack a valise it's so far.

Twenty years ago Rivke tasted pot cheese she liked by Auerbach. So that's where I have to get it. Never mind it's the same company like by Sherman and almost all the others. (And never mind that only Rivke can taste the difference. Also never mind it could be from the same milk from the same cow.) So every other week I walk back and forth the eight blocks to Sackman Street. But it does me good to walk. Auerbach (may he rest in peace), who only sat by the cash drawer, is dead maybe twelve years. So now I shlep to Winokur, the new owner.

And it's the same with the green store—Dvorkin's special apples (seven blocks back and forth)—and the butcher—Krieger's pullets (ten blocks) always fatter than Malkin's.

But the laundry (two blocks) at least I can do nearby. And so I don't need the used baby stroller that Khave and Essie want to give me. But like my daughters, the neighbors take pity on me for my age. If one sees me, it's always the same.

"Reb Sholem, where are you going with that bundle on your back?"

I say, "To America. And you'll please excuse me—I can't talk. The boat sails in ten minutes."

Besides all these regular trips, twice a year (at Pesakh and Rosh Hashanah) I visit Shubin, the old barber near Sutter. He trims my few hairs, evens out the beard, and cuts the hair from the ears that Essie has threatened to make braids. Do I have to go this far? (Maybe I am more like Rivke than I believe.) No. But the place around the corner—between the communist papers, the pinochle players, and the fancy music on the radio—is not for me. By Shubin it's WEVD on the radio, if anything, and a little talk about the holidays or what's happening with Palestine. Besides, on

Shubin's price list he still has cupping. Only twice in America have I seen this done. So a visit here is an adventure. Maybe, maybe I will see it again. But the truth is I doubt this. Because cupping, of course, helps a living person as much as it helps a dead one.[2]

In spite of my travels, I sometimes don't feel so well. What person doesn't? But calling a doctor is for Rivke, not for me. Instead, I walk an hour to the clinic at Kings County. Most of the time it's take an aspirin, soak the finger, put a compress. Sometimes, if I tell them how I have come and how far, they ask how sick could I be if I walked an hour to get there. I tell them, "Wait, I still have another hour to walk home."

OCTOBER 2, 1946

At the start of the New Year, with Yom Kippur just days ahead, Rivke gets more nervous by the hour. It is true that our fate for the coming year is written on Rosh Hashanah and sealed on the Day of Atonement. But only prayer, repentance, and good deeds can change what is written—not announcing your husband's ten thousand faults—like a *shoyfer*[1] blast for the whole neighborhood to hear—or greeting every small misfortune—a spill, a dropped spoon—with curses fit only for a Haman or Hitler or for the Evil One himself. But this is always her way. She thinks if she survives these ten days she'll live out the year to come.

She believes this, but how can she know? Who can know when the end is near? Moses knew at Mt. Nebo. King David knew he would die on Shabes, even if he tried to avoid his fate by studying Toyre all day long.[2] But ordinary people don't know, and you can make yourself crazy if you think you do. And anyone around you, a husband, for example, as well. The Angel of Death comes when it pleases. But while we live we must follow the Toyre and the teachings and so live well.

Of course, these *yontoyvim*[3] are solemn days—I am in shul from early morning till dark—but, Rivke's nerves apart, the holidays have their pleasures. And I mean besides the apples and honey, the kugl, the tsimes, the *tayglekh*.[4] Every Jew in the neighborhood is in shul, everyone all dressed up—even the children outside, playing with the hazelnuts like marbles. (They should be careful not to rip the knees out of the pants or their mothers will give them good, yontif or no.) And the entire family buys tickets for the shul together—Asher, Max, Krumbein with his Arnie and Norman and son-in-law Joe. Asher's brother-in-law Yitskhok is also there with his Henry along with their neighbor Mr. Rosen and his son Bernie who I taught for bar mitsve. Ari and Yoyne, too young to need a ticket, come in and out, and Zelig, who davens at his father's shul, comes for an hour or so just to be with us. We take up a row or more.

Now, my father taught me long ago that with so many we should not all sit together because, if they compared, people with small families or none might be upset. (Never mind that to have a pride in numbers is a foolishness itself.)

During the year I would follow this teaching, maybe sitting with Asher or with him and the boys, Ari and Yoyne. But if Arnie and Norman also came, I sat apart from the grandchildren or took just one if I needed to teach him something. On Rosh Hashanah and Yom Kippur I make an exception. Why, I don't know, but it feels right and good to have all of them with me.

Is it possible that I am sinning and tempting fate? Maybe I, not Rivke, need to be nervous. I do pray, I do give to charity, I do repent—but maybe not for everything. He alone is perfect.

FEBRUARY 1, 1947

This morning, Essie, Max and half the tenants in their building went to court. Again they were dragging in Orloff, the landlord. Nine or ten years they are living there, so five or six times they took him to the judge. It was the same thing as always—the middle of the winter and no heat. It was for this that Rivke and I moved down the block—not that Plotkin, our landlord now,[1] is such a bargain. But at least we get enough heat not to freeze to death.

By Orloff, Rivke was turning blue half the time from November to March. And he always had an answer for every complaint. "I'm not cold; the bricks keep me warm. You're cold? Put on a sweater." And if not an answer, an excuse: "The coal man forgot to come this week." Or, "The boiler broke. Two days they will fix it, maybe three." Last year he made an "improvement." He changed the building from coal to oil. When? In January, of course, so he could save a couple days heat. With painting and fixing the plumbing he is also so generous.

Today, the judge, who knows him already, gave him a fine fifty dollars and said that if they bring him again Orloff will sit in jail. Naturally, Max, Essie, and their neighbors are satisfied, and maybe for the rest of the winter there will be no problems. It seems Orloff was afraid about the jail because when Allan came for his lesson this afternoon, straight from the house, his face was red and he was shvitsing like it was summertime. Orloff must have pushed the *shmitshik*[2] up to ninety degrees already.

Rivke gave Allan a glass seltzer and wiped a wet rag over his face and neck. While she gave and wiped, she had some suggestions for Orloff—that he should boil like a bagel, that he should cook slowly like a *tsholent*[3] for a day and a half then burn to the bottom of the pot—who knows what else. When Rivke murmurs it is like the children of Israel against *Moyshe Rabeynu*.[4]

But Orloff's sins are three. First, he does not give full measure. The thirty or thirty-five dollars a month is not just for the four walls. Second, he helps make well people sick, especially the children, and makes sick people suffer, especially the old. And last, I am ashamed to say, he gives my son-in-law Max another reason to attack the rabbis, the shuls, and what he calls the snuff-smellers that go there. The truth is that in other ways Orloff is a pious man. But Max would say, what good is his davening and keeping Shabes if he is unjust and the cause of misery?" I could say that if he didn't daven and keep Shabes it would be worse. But Max, if not exactly right, is not altogether wrong either.

The trouble is that Orloff, like other landlords, like other businessmen, even my own Asher, has two gods. One is Our Father, Our King; the other is money, the father of nothing but a king of another sort. And Orloff and the rest try to keep them separate, an Israel and a Judah. But does the same person go to shul on Shabes and to a church on Sunday? Impossible. I remember years ago in the citizen class I read an English *khokhme*,[5] "No man can serve two masters." We also have such a saying: "I am the Lord thy God; thou shalt have no other gods before me." And this means not only Baal but also golden calves and green papers.

MARCH 2, 1947

A cold Sunday, gray, with sometimes still a little rain. Too cold and damp to be outside. So Esther and Khave sit in the front room with their mother. Each rocks a small child on her lap. Rivke's cousin Big Reyzl (so called not to confuse her with our own smaller one) is visiting. She comes maybe twice a year, so the women have a lot to talk about. Even though the little ones are asleep, all of them are almost shouting so that Rivke can hear. She won't use the hearing aid, even after all the fittings and refittings, especially when there is a guest in the house. I have read the first part of Ecclesiastes to her, but it does no good.

Because they must speak so loud themselves, they don't mind the noise Allan and Jerry are making in the kitchen. Sitting on the floor, the boys have pulled the shoemaker's last from the closet together with a hammer and pretend to fix each other's shoes. I have taken away the leather knife, but their mothers are afraid that they will hit themselves or each other with the hammer. Now and then they stop talking with cousin Reyzl to call for the children to be careful. "We are!" they call back, and to prove it, they bang the last until the house seems to echo with the metal sound.

In the kitchen with the boys, I work at the little bench that I have taken from under the sink. It's one I made myself a few years ago. After I stopped working with horses and pushcarts, once in a while I would do something with my hands. Sewing at the machine doesn't count because there the hands only push the material or lift or lower the needle. So I made the bench. Sometimes, if I find pieces of wood, I change a knife handle or two. The blades you can always sharpen, but the handle and bolts wear out.

The work now is to roll a cigarette. Not that I am a smoker. In shul Erev Shabes, if I'm offered a pinch of snuff, I'll clear my nose. But maybe once in a year and a Wednesday[1] I'll treat myself to "a smoke," as the younger people call it. The papers must be more than two years old; the tobacco I'm not sure. But it stays a long time in the back of the icebox where Rivke won't see it. I tap the little tobacco can over the two papers in front of me. Allan and Jerry look up at the sound. They stare, asking with their eyes.

"I am making cigarettes," I tell them. Both their fathers smoke but buy ready made by the package.

The children watch carefully. I pack the tobacco, not too tight, not too full, lick the edge of the paper, press, and tap all four ends against the bench. The children are not so sure about the job I've done.

"When you make your own cigarette," I tell them, "it will be flat, not like by by the machines. Machines make the ones your fathers smoke."

With the leather knife that I have taken from the children, I cut one cigarette in half and put one half and the whole one in my vest pocket. The remaining half I light. Holding it between two fingers and a thumb, I breathe out and cough a little. Allan and Jerry scatter the blue smoke with waving hands.

I take two more puffs. Just as I am relaxing, Big Reyzl calls out, "What's burning?" On Rivke's side the ears might not be so good, but there's nothing wrong with the noses.

"The enemies of God," I reply. "Also a cigarette."

"Pa, the doctor told you not to," Esther and Khave shout together.

"Nu, since you for once agree on something, I'll put it out soon," I tell them. Not such a big favor for the size of the cigarette.

The boys go back to fixing shoes once again. I puff once more, slowly, and after a while again. When I can feel the heat as the tobacco burns down toward my fingers, I run the water and crush the stub in the sink.

"Nu," I say, rising from the bench, "It's time to daven Minkhe." Jerry hits the last dead center as if—like at the *Mizrakhi*[2] meetings—with the great noise he is bringing the business to a close. But this one sound wakens the little ones. They are probably hungry and wet and so begin to cry.

"Didn't I say to play quietly!" Khave shouts, and Essie, louder still, adds, "Now put those things away!"

"All right, we're doing it," the boys yell back. The last and hammer clash and clang.

"What kind of tumult is this?" Big Reyzl wonders aloud, adding to it herself. And Rivke, who has heard something at last, begins to moan about her head.

I take my hat and coat and leave this peaceful afternoon behind me.

MARCH 6, 1947

Avrom might be home, but he is not settled even if he will soon be a married man. I write "a man" because he is not a boy any longer. The years and what he has been through have brought a change. He is more nervous now than before the war, talks a mile a minute, and cannot sit still. When he walks up and down, speaking and waving his arms, he reminds me of Arnie—not such a healthy thing. Then all of a sudden he becomes quiet for an hour, the eyes almost empty. But on his face you can see the twitch of a cheek, an eyebrow, and you know that he is remembering.

What exactly he remembers I don't know. He will not talk about it except to say it was terrible and to mention one or two things he saw, but he will only mention, not discuss. This I understand a little. I almost never talk about when I was in the army. It was itself not such a pleasant thing, and by the Russians I was as good as the enemy. Not all. Once I fell asleep on guard duty, for which they could shoot me, and a Russian, for a joke, took away my rifle, which for losing they could kill me a second time. But when I woke up, he only laughed and gave it back.

But with Avrom there is not even smiling. He tells about men on the supply trains killing for a can of beans, women—even children—giving themselves for the same (never mind some of them said "Heil Hitler" and waved to the Nazi soldiers), and, of course, the camp—the camp. A day after Dachau was freed,[1] Avrom arrived there with his company. About this he never tells a story, only three words— "skeletons," "sickness," "stink"—again and again. From the newspaper and the radio, I know the story only too well. But this Avrom understands with his own eyes, his own flesh. Without a reporter. Without even a brain to understand the report. Straight to the neshome. Sometimes he has awakened screaming in the night.

Max thinks he is suffering from the "shell shock" and that maybe in time he will recover. If not, Max says he should go to the veteran's hospital for help. But maybe it is his Ruth that will be Avrom's real help, especially after the wedding. She is a calm woman who says everything in the same quiet voice. Naturally, of this Rivke and my daughters are suspicious. But for their son and brother, especially now, such a woman is maybe the best thing.

MAY 12, 1947

Rivke tells me there's a new peddler, not with a pushcart or even a horse and wagon, but with a truck. And not only does he sell fruit and vegetables of all kinds but also fish. Because he has "everything," she calls him Wanamaker—after the department store.

For Rivke, giving people names is a sport—not like Adam by the animals. Sometimes the names are not so clever. The woman up the block who has dark skin and hair is to her "the black land-lady." But other times she really gets them just so—maybe, after all, exactly like Adam with the animals. Our landlord Plotkin's daughter, a tall, thin girl with a long face and neck, is by Rivke "the stork." A homely woman in the apartment house on the corner is "the beauty." The young man with the high voice across the street she calls "the flute." Our block also has "the dancer," "the broomstick" and "the latke," for the man who seems to walk on his toes, the skinny boy across the alley, and one of the twin sisters with round faces, flat noses, and tiny mouths and eyes. The other, not surprising, is "the frying pan." Of course, any one of the mischievous boys who bang the garbage cans, swing from the branches of trees while screaming like wild beasts, or throw a ball too close to the window may be called "the angel of death."

But Rivke does not spare her own either. "Mr. Consumption" is a cousin who will drink from a cup only at the handle because nobody else does—never mind it has been washed a dozen times. Another one, "the flood," always weeps at her own sad stories. Closer to home, our grandson, Reyzl's Arnie, is "the frog" since every five seconds he must speak or jump from one place to the next—sometimes both. And her youngest sister, with rouge and lipstick and jewelry, always dressed for a fancy ball—and now with a third husband, is, truly, "the American."

What Rivke calls me is another matter. But something like "Wanamaker" would be a pleasant change. As for the peddler and his truck, I'm glad forty years ago I stopped fixing pushcarts and wagons. There are more machines on the street every day, especially now after the war. Maybe there is nothing new under the sun, but everything seems to change. It would not surprise me if one day there was not a pushcart or wagon left in the whole neighborhood. Maybe also the machines will stop the boys playing ball in the street in front of the shul. But maybe not. Children here can find as many ways to play (and not study) as Rivke can find names.

JULY 16, 1947

Ruven came today for a couple hours and brought not just himself but news. He has left his shul and will not look for another. Instead, he will become a rabbi in a hospital for crippled children. A "chaplain" they call it, like in the army, only with tsores not exactly the same. Some of the children cannot walk or use the arms or hands; some with broken backs can move only the head; some can move but with such a shaking it is almost as if they can't; one or two are in iron lungs. And with these children he will have a kheyder, make bar mitsves, daven at least Shabes and yontif, and give what help and hope he can. For most of them, it is the body, not the mind, that is broken. But the spirit is always a question, and for this Ruven more than the doctors should have good answers. And not for the children alone, but for the parents too.

Experience himself he has plenty. It has been almost five years since his own little Nathan was paralyzed. And as Golda has given herself over to the care of the boy, so Ruven will give himself to others. And, maybe it is not too much to say, in the child's honor.

Of course, there is a price. The hospital is more than two hours from the Bronx, so Ruven will not be home more than a day or two each week. And to be a husband and a father from such a distance is not so easy. But this is better than to have his heart eaten out by a board of directors from the shul. In Europe a rich man respected the rabbi and his judgment—even if he didn't agree or accept. But here, outside the oldest neighborhoods, everything is a corporation—the Almighty and Company, A. Gantsermakher, Pres.; A. Kleynermakher, Vice-Pres.[1]—and the rabbi, like the janitor or *Shabes goy*,[2] is an "employee." Nu, as Rivke would say, what can you do?

Ruven has a good head and a good heart. He is more than ready to begin his new work. May he be content and prosper.

AUGUST 6, 1947

Once (sometimes twice) every summer, thanks to Asher and his machine, Rivke and I make a short visit to the ocean. Today was this year's visit. Asher took half a day from his ice-cream shop (he has enough help, so he can leave even in the busy season) and at two o'clock drove us to the water. Slowly, because if he goes faster than a team of horses Rivke starts to grow fearful and shouts at him not to drive as if he is being chased by an evil spirit. This happens at least once every trip, so I am convinced that Asher terrifies his mother on purpose. As long as he doesn't do it too often or too long, I don't take it seriously. It is almost a joke between the two of them, just another part of the journey—a little ceremony that all of us would maybe miss if it didn't happen.

Because today Asher was not at all in a hurry, he did not drive on the main streets. Instead, he took back ways past the little houses of the Taleyner. In every other front yard we could see the big yellow flowers with the black centers. And in the backyard vegetables—cucumbers, the purple eggplant (that by our family only Leye knows how to cook), and plenty tomatoes (what do they know that Borukh and I did not a hundred years ago in Connecticut?). And this is besides the farms, five or six they have left, with not only these things but cabbages, carrots, even watermelons. The watermelons we knew already because three or four times every summer one of the farmers sends his son with a wagon and little brown and white horse to sell.

But all of this was pleasant to look at, and very different from our neighborhood. (By us we have rows of brick apartments with buildings separated on one side just by a narrow alley and in the front maybe a bush without flowers or a tree by the gutter.) And the people, plain people working hard with their hands, this I could understand too. Once, we passed a stable, and I smiled to see the sparks fly from a hammered shoe.

But one thing was not so pleasant. At the end of a road, the one where Asher decided to make his mother yell at him today, was a wooden house. It was not much bigger than a chicken coop and was falling apart. A man with dark skin was chopping wood beside it, and I could see (and smell) wood smoke coming from a metal chimney. A woman (just as dark) on a rotting bench in front of the one window I could see cutting up potatoes. Three small children played in the dirt next to her but hardly made a sound. (By now Asher had come almost to a stop.) You could hear only the axe and the insects. And you could see from the torn clothes and shoes (on the few feet that had them) that they have even less than us. Max tells me that these people must be some of the last Indians—all of them poor—that remain in the neighborhood or in the city altogether. If this is true, then even more than any disappointed greenhorn they have the right to curse Columbus.[1]

But when we reached the water, such troubles, for a while at least, were forgotten. Asher took two folding chairs from the car and led us along the little boardwalk. We sat, Rivke and I, next to each other, like a king and queen—she especially, under the umbrella that Asher had tied to her chair—and stared out at the sea. In the distance, to one side, of course, were the beaches and summer bungalows. But in all other directions there was just the ocean itself, rolling toward us then back without end, a sign of His might and of eternity.

A breeze came in from the ocean, but it was still hot. So Asher brought us ginger ale from the cart with the treyfe "hot dogs." This was in bottles, Hoffman's, so it was all right.[2] With the heat and the smell of salt in the air, the soda was *take* geshmak.

While we drank, I looked over by the pier. Some men and boys were fishing. Taleyner mostly and a few blacks, with one or two Jews. The older ones were teaching the younger, how to put the bait, how to throw the string, how to roll it in. Not Talmud exactly, but this is also learning. As for the Jews, most of us know fishing only by fat Zalmen in the fish store with a net in the live tank. But Mindl's Joe goes with his father since their days in the country, and Essie has a neighbor who sometimes brings a child or two. Still, taking the life of even a fish must be done with care and a clear mind. There is a reason that not every Jew is his own *shoykhet*[3] and that every shoykhet is trained and approved.

Even with the breeze and the ginger ale, more than an hour in the air and sun were enough for Rivke, and so by four o'clock we were on our way back. Asher would be home in time for an early supper, so he and Leye could go to the moving pictures. The theater, he said, now had "air conditioning" so it was just like an ice box inside. Nu, if people want to feel like a farmer cheese, who will say no? Rivke and I had our little meal as well, and I had yet an hour or two by the window to read before it got dark. While I was eating, I thought about the eggplants in the gardens this afternoon and about whether Leye had cooked some for Asher tonight. It is years since I had any and I would like to taste it again. It may be another American *maykhl,*[4] maybe even as good as sweet potatoes or French toast.

But enough about stomachs. With the trip, the sun, and our lungs filled with the fresh air, heat or no heat, Rivke and I are sure to sleep well tonight.

MAY 14, 1948

It has come at last. Six months already we knew it would happen, but today it is changed from becoming to being.[1] Independence. After two thousand years Israel is again a nation as well as a people. The dream of Herzl, of all of us, of millions down the ages come to pass. We have not forgotten you, Jerusalem, and our right arms remain strong.[2]

And this strength we will need for Israel to survive. Maybe one moment to shout or weep our joy before the Arabs are upon us with all their power.[3] If this must be the Shabes of blood, may it also be the Shabes of victory.

But the children of Ishmael are not our only enemy. Even among ourselves, some, a remnant of our remnant, have argued against us. When Meshiekh comes, they say, He will restore us all to *Eretz Yisroel*.[4] And since he has not come, we must not go. To this argument Max shows his two hands and says, "Here is your Meshiekh." What would you expect from him? Still, there is a point. If, as we say in the *Ani Ma'amin*,[5] we will wait for Him no matter how long he delays, that does not mean we must sit like stones.

There has been enough of exile, of being scattered among the nations of the world. Now we are ourselves a nation. Yet this is a blessing not without its fears. Will we be a Jewish nation or a nation of Jews, which should be the same but might not? Who knows if this is not a scattering of another kind? But if such thoughts are not an old man's foolishness, they are at least for another time.

For now, I fear the Arab numbers and the Arab guns. We must put our hopes in the "two hands" of the Israeli army (I cannot believe I have written these last two words) but our trust in the Almighty to set a table for us though we are surrounded by enemies.[6]

MAY 30, 1948

Today Rivke and I celebrated our fiftieth wedding anniversary. Are we married fifty years? Who knows? It must be more because Reyzl, I think, is already past fifty, and before her was the baby Gitl, may she rest in peace. But the family decided to have a party. So for them it is fifty, even if not exactly. I could mention again that Rivke and I were married in winter, the Tuesday before *Shabes Shire*,[1] and today is Sunday in a different part of the year altogether. But let them enjoy.

It was a very happy, lively afternoon. The whole family, even the grandchildren, were there, except for Golda and Nathan. I have seen the child no more than three times since the polio. Golda keeps him mostly in the house, and if they go out, it is not to such a gathering as this. So all we could do today was for Rivke to send a healthy piece of the anniversary cake home by Ruven. Otherwise, all of us were at the banquet hall, in our best clothes—they even dragged me to buy a new suit and Rivke a new dress—with an accordion player who sang, and white cloths on all the tables with baskets of flowers. And in the middle of each basket was from gold cardboard the number 50. With the dancing and singing and drinking and eating, everyone had a good time.

When we started the meal, I made the blessing over the bread. Where they found an oven to bake a *khale*[2] three feet long I don't know. When I stood it on the table it was taller than me—but maybe that's not such a wonder. As for the meal, there were dishes Rivke stopped making years ago or makes maybe once in a while, like the boiled white fish for an appetizer—delicious with the carrots—and a meat borscht, very tasty, for the soup. But also a roast beef which she never made in her life and inside so pink I thought it was raw or had not been koshered.[3] But when I asked the *Mashgiekh*[4] he assured me. So I had a second portion. Of the *kishke*[5] too, that was almost as good as Reyzl's, who learned from her mother well. From the string beans I tasted one or two but ate the pieces of almonds they sprinkled in. For a nosh between courses—and maybe the best—there were on the tables pots of *shmalts*[6] and *gribenes*.[7] This I smeared thickly on the pieces of khale and the little rolls.

Before dessert and tea, the children gave presents to Rivke and me. The eldest, Reyzl and Asher, performed the ceremony. Their mother they gave a gold butterfly pin with a little ruby in the middle of each wing. This she will wear to all the weddings and bar mitsves to come. Rivke loves butterflies. When we would go to Prospect Park, she was not so crazy about the monkeys. Such tricks, she would say, she could always see at home by Avrom and his friends. She liked better across the street in the gardens to watch the butterflies go from one flower to another. A gentle heart after all.

For me there was a bookmark, also gold, with my name in Hebrew engraved. Maybe I will use it. But if not, I will keep it in the bookcase to remind me of this day.

At the end of the ceremony we drank a *l'khaim*,[8] the third, at least, for the afternoon. Then we sat down to the false ice cream—how they make it *parev*[9] I'll never know—followed by tea served with the big cake that Rivke and I cut together. For the thousandth time the flashbulbs blinded us, and Asher's little moving picture camera wheezed like an old man with bad lungs.

I had been cheerful all the while, but when Ruven led us in the blessings after meals, with all our voices rising, and (almost) all of us together, I could not hold back the tears. Rivke too. But she had recovered enough from the butterfly to tell me, "They should have given us golden umbrellas; it's raining all over our face."

Still, this was a gathering of the Kahn family, so of course perfect you wouldn't expect. Trouble there was even before the party. The children—they are, after all, not made of money—did not invite the cousins. The cousins—also without a Rothschild among them—understood. But my brother Borukh's Dina decided to be insulted for her children and stayed home. I don't know how after eighty years a mouse suddenly becomes a lion. So Borukh, who can hardly walk even with the cane, came with our brother Eliezer and his Sorke. But by the time everything was over, Eliezer also could hardly move. Past sixty-five—youngest brother or not—it is better not to dance the *kazatske*.[10] So for the last two hours Eliezer sat with a bag ice Zelig ran to get him.

Meanwhile, half the dinner, Max, my son-in-law the humorist, kept nudzhing the waiter to bring him calves' foot jelly. This he had by his mother when he was a child but not in twenty years otherwise. Finally, the waiter, another comedian, brought from the kitchen a soup bone and a wooden hammer. "Here," he said, "make it yourself." To keep joking, Max tried. So he broke the plate, and now has to pay damages and a cleaning bill for Reyzl's dress where the bone landed—and I am sure Krumbein will collect. Then later, luckily after the tables had been mostly cleared, Asher's Phyllis, another jokester, together with Ari and Yoyne, tied the ends of the cloth from table to table together and made little Michael run through the knots. Before they caught him there was one lap with cold tea and two with frosting from the cake. More cleaning bills, and since Asher and Max will have to share, we should maybe call in the United Nations. But today even these things added to the amusement.

We have been home for hours now. A basket of flowers with the gold 50 sits next to the little radio, and Rivke is still wearing her pin. I have decided, after all, to use the bookmark here.

JULY 14, 1948

It is harder to be a teacher in America than in the old country, whether in a kheyder or not. Over there, the pupils were taught and had to learn "what." Here, it's "what" but also "why." Not that "why" was unheard of; not that everything was absolute this or that. The Talmud itself tells us to study with one other at least, not only to correct each other but to discuss, and the rabbis themselves don't always agree. As is often said, where you have two Jews you have three opinions. But in America the "why" seems almost to come before the "what," a thing that is impossible.

Today Allan again was asking why. "Why did God harden the heart of Pharaoh?" "Why did he do it ten times?" "Why, if Moses was the leader, did Aaron do the talking?" And when I answered this last one, it was "Why did God choose for a leader someone who could not speak so well?" And Allan's "whys" began almost from the day I started with him—"Why do they write Hebrew backwards?" That one at least I could answer: "People were writing Hebrew long before English, so it is the English that must be backwards." But, of course, it didn't stop. There was "Why did God like Abel's sacrifice better?" and "Why did Sarah chase Hagar away?" and "Why did Jacob have two wives?" Once in a while, just for a change, there was a "how." "If Jacob wasn't married to Bilha and Zilpa,[1] how could they have children?" Nu!

These questions I answered from what was taught me—as a child I also asked "why" once in a while—or made up an answer, or sometimes gave an answer that was a way not to answer, whether to say something was God's will or that he would learn when he became a bar mitsve. Such questions, hard as they are for me, I don't mind. First, from an answer to questions you can learn something yourself. Second, asking questions shows you have a good head. And this Allan has, young as he is.

But sometimes there are questions I don't like so much. "If in the beginning there was nothing, from what did God create something?" "If God is the Almighty, why did he allow the Jews to be slaves and to have their sons die?" Such questions do not come from the head of a child maybe nine years old, not even a genius, which Allan is not. They come, I think, from the head of a socialist father who asks his son such questions and maybe even tells him to ask such questions by his *zeyde*[2].

I don't want Allan to be torn between Max, on the one side, and Essie and myself on the other. He will end up altogether an *apikoyres*[3], knowing nothing and doubting everything. The workers of the world are important, but better to unite first with your own people. We were already in chains for thousands of years before Mr. Marx and his friend Engels noticed them by others.

SEPTEMBER 12, 1948

Today Essie is not so happy with Max. This is not altogether something new, but the reason is another story. While they were sitting on our stoop after supper, I saw from the window a young man came by with a paper. Would they put their name. The others, the neighbors, shake their heads.

But Max takes it to read, and Essie, without reading, says "Don't you dare."

Max gives her a look because if it's on a page he is the king, not like in the house. "It's only a petition for Marcantonio to save the five-cent fare,"[1] he says, and reaches right away for his own pen that he is never without.

"I don't care if it's to save Meshiekh," she says. "If you sign, they'll put your name on a list."

"You think it's not already on a list? They don't bother with me because I'm not big enough or in a job big enough to get them headlines. Can you see 'Name 86 Red Piece-Goods Salesmen; Max Rothstein Number 82'"?

So right away he signed.

"I'll visit you in jail," Essie says.

"Bring me some *mamelige*,"[2] Max answers.

"You'll take whatever you get and like it," Essie laughs.

The neighbors laugh; Max laughs; I smile. The times, after all, are not so funny. When the government starts with the lists it is not a joke. Hitler had a list with millions; the czar with his secret police had thousands; by Stalin we don't know yet how many. And now the lists have started here. With the one hand we shake a fist at the enemy; with the other we put down names, just like them.

On the television, "the *meshugener*, "[3] as Rivke calls him, raises one hand to stop the clapping and with the other, at the same time, waves it should keep going. This is funny—on the television. In life, such a thing can drive a person crazy. And a country too.

NOVEMBER 2, 1948

Today was election day, so like every election day for over thirty years I went to vote. This from the night school I learned is important. In Russia, nobody could vote for the czar, and plenty Russians would not have voted for him if they could. It wasn't for nothing they threw him out.

Of course, they can't vote for the new czar either—the one without a crown. But this is the point. Unless God chooses a Moses, the people should be able to pick their own. Not that they don't make mistakes—I remember that Harding with his thieves and Hoover who could do nothing. And even when they find a man like Roosevelt, it's not a hundred percent—or even ninety. But in this country, you can fix the mistakes every four years—or two years by the Congress. And even if you have a good, you can always find a better. Also, on this day, at the voting place at least, all are the same. Rabinowitz or Rockefeller, one vote.

So in the afternoon I took my citizen paper from the top drawer in the wardrobe, wiped off the glass and the frame, and walked two blocks to the school. Allan and Jerry I took with me, they should see what the voting was about and that their zeyde thinks it is important. Allan understands something already. By Max, his father, politics is on the mind and lips every day, not every few years like me. So Allan helps explain to Jerry. Thanks to Max, he knows a lot about Mr. Wallace.[1]

But I didn't need to know about Mr. Wallace, and Mr. Dewey I knew only too well. All I had to know was where to find Truman's name on the ballot. And almost every Jew (not counting a few millionaires and Wallstreeters and Maxes—who should only see who I put him with) today felt the same. Where he is with the workers, what he is doing with prices and places to live, how much taxes he is spending to build Europe (even Germany) again—doesn't matter this time.[2] Because without Harry Truman there would be no state of Israel. And that's the end of it. Enough.

Whether he will win we have to wait and see. On the radio and in the paper they say no. People want a change. The unions are angry. Some are upset he's doing for the black people. If he wins, then wonderful. If not, we will have to suffer most likely with Dewey. But this in New York we are used to. And soon we will get a chance to throw him out.[3]

Meanwhile, the citizen paper I put back in the top drawer.

DECEMBER 19, 1948

Reyzl's Marcy had a baby girl this afternoon. She is my first great-grandchild. This makes me an *alte zeyde*[1] and officially an old man—in case there was a question. Of course, I am happy for Marcy and Joe, for Reyzl, for the baby who is healthy and screams her lungs out, and even for Rivke and me. In our prayers we often say from generation to generation. Nu, I can say now from generation to generation to generation to generation. So the years pass.

Tonight I sat at the window watching the snow that is still falling this minute. Across the street, Max walked by with Allan on the way to visit Marcy and the baby in the hospital. My children's generation and my grandchildren's going to meet the newest one. And then I couldn't see them, and there was just myself in the darkness, looking at the whiteness piling thicker and thicker over the empty street.

MARCH 14, 1949

This afternoon we had guests for lunch. Yontif or a *simkhe*[1] aside, we don't eat in each other's houses. But today was a special occasion— tsholent. Maybe twice a year Rivke gathers the strength to make it—mostly to see that it doesn't burn while it cooks all Friday on the stove and sits on the asbestos all night till after shul on Shabes.[2] She makes a good one too—plenty of meat and potatoes, not too many beans, enough salt and pepper, with onions just so and the fat mixed through and through. Too good not to eat right from the pot. Except today we had Khave— who would also eat from the pot if her mother let—and her family. Why Khave? Because she enjoys it more than the others and can't or won't make it herself.

Not that any of my daughters cooks or bakes like Rivke—or the way Rivke used to. Reyzl you can count on for rogelakh and shtrudel once in a while, but Essie and Khave don't bake at all. Essie can cook—a tasty stuffed cabbage, a tomato soup. When she makes she sends some with Ari. And on Pesakh a ginger candy with honey and nuts, so good that Yoyne finds excuses to visit his aunt four times a day all week. But also there's the flounder [filets], the vegetable [cutlets], the salmon krikets [*sic*][3]—things one can hardly pronounce and that Rivke never made or ever heard of. Not such a loss—if they weren't fried, they would have no taste altogether.

But for fried you can't do better than potatoes. Why they are called French I don't know. But Reyzl and Essie both claim to make the best. I can't tell a difference except by one the pieces are flat and by the other they are wrinkled. Maybe the wrinkled are better if they hold more oil.

But Khave, our guest, has disappeared in all this kitchen talk. To tell the truth, I don't know that she cooks at all. Maybe it's no wonder that she and Zelig and the children enjoyed so. But she must feed them something! The children look healthy enough and she and Zelig are not losing weight. Maybe it's a family mystery backwards. Just as no one never sees Rivke eat, no one never catches Khave at the stove. Yet she and her family somehow survive.

Our old landlord used to say that what kept him alive was black bread and herring. But I would add to his menu a tsholent once in a while. For this is not only a way to survive but a test for the *kishkes*[4].

MAY 30, 1949

Almost three hours ago, Rivke's sisters left to go back to Baltimore. With the four of them in the house—six with Rivke and Hinde, who lives in the neighborhood— two days were plenty. My head will soon stop spinning and I will be able to think again. One or two, maybe twice a year, is one thing; all of them together is something else. But they are gone now, with Arnie and his brother Norman together with Allan and Jerry going with them to shlep valises to the subway, and from the subway to the Pennsylvania Station. How much the smaller ones can shlep I don't know.

Baltimore. Also a place for a Jew! Brayne we know went there after years in New York. The others, if you believe them, got there by accident. For one of them a storm blew the ship. Another bought the wrong ticket. The third landed in Boston and on the train to New York fell asleep. Each one another story.

But yesterday for the first time in many years the six sisters were together. Rivke, naturally, was so happy you would think Meshiekh had come. For two days before she lived in the kitchen, and what she couldn't make she sent me to buy. From two poor people the bakery, the grocery, and the delicatessen did a nice business. To tell the truth, except for the tumult and the headache,

I was also happy to see them together. There might not be many more times, and with those we know and those we fear are dead, half our families are already gone. But this was not *Tishe Bov*,[1] so there will be no Lamentations.[2]

If someone didn't know they were sisters, you couldn't guess. These two might look alike, those two, the last two not like each other or the rest. And the same for their character. Rokhl, a little younger than Rivke, is white altogether, and with the curls in her hair she looks like the President George Washington. But a refined woman who collects money for the Mt. Sinai hospital[3] and the home for the aged. Hinde, from the neighborhood, and Tsaytl look almost the same, and both are sweet like a citron. The two of them have hair they never had when they were young. Hinde says it is a wig. Tsaytl says nothing. On both it is the color of spoiled liver. And from neither one a pleasant word, especially for me. They are jealous that Rivke's husband is still alive. And Tsaytl worse than Hinde because her Khaim, may he rest in peace, was my brother.

Brayne, who my Essie is almost the image of, I know and like the best. Didn't she live with us for two years after Velvl, may he rest in peace, died and left her with four little ones? She has had the hardest life of all, but is always helpful and good-natured. Today and yesterday she washed almost every dish while the others hardly lifted a finger. Brayne is a clever woman, with a quick tongue, and a joke, not always decent, never far from her lips. (No wonder she gets along so well with Max.) But foul mouth or not, Brayne is an honest, lively woman—if, like the others, not so frum. But this is what happens in Baltimore, even worse than here.

The baby, Freydl, twenty years younger than Rivke, is like none of the others. From her red hair, "rinsed," she tells her sisters, to the jewelry on the neck, the wrists, and fingers, to the powder and lipstick and rouge, she is altogether farputst. Khave or Essie would look like this for a wedding, but with Freydl it's every day. This, I'm afraid, and know from my granddaughters, is the new Jewish woman in America. So maybe it is a good thing that I will not be here much longer.

Different from the other sisters, Freydl is not at this moment a widow. She has buried two husbands, but is now married to a third. Freydl speaks a good English and goes to business every day in a department store. Also, she reads the paper and knows something about the world. I remember on her last visit, almost a year and a half now, we talked what could happen with Palestine if King Abdullah made peace or not. Definitely a smart one, but whatever else one can say, the Elbaum women, Rivke included, are no dummies.

———

Arnie and Norman just came to tell us that all of them got on the train. (And that their cousins fell asleep on the subway on the way back.) Rivke is now content, at least as much as she will be until she gets a postcard from Baltimore saying that they arrived and are safe. Any minute she'll be yelling at me to put away the "Seyfer Toyre,"[4] as she calls my writing book. In two short words sin together with scorn. Aggravating but clever. An Elbaum through and through.

JULY 5, 1949

Long ago I learned that the streets in America were not filled with gold. But later I found out that they are filled with amusements—and not just what the children make for themselves. There are also the men with the little horses that take children half a block and back or put them to take a picture. One man comes with dogs that do tricks, and for this the little ones give a penny or two.

But since the war, we have on the block a regular Coney Island from the trucks with rides. One of them has wooden horses that go in a circle and at the same time up and down. Another is a big swing with two sides and three benches each—a high, a low, a middle. This the truck man pushes, like in the park, and like in the park, the children scream "higher" and the mothers "not so high." A third one there is, electric like the horses, with little cars that go around and around, so fast on the turns you can get dizzy watching. Of course, with the twisting and turning, with up and down, the children (even if they are screaming for more) sometimes get sick to their stomach. This should not be a surprise, because twenty minutes before most of them had (also from a truck) an ice cream that is now shaking in their kishkes like a malted. The rides maybe we should make *fleyshik*[1] and not have them until an hour after dairy.[2]

Still and all, amusement here is a serious business, and I have said nothing of the moving pictures or the radio or the baseball—in America they pay good money to see grown men play a game for children. But what I want to know (in a foolish moment) is what do these amusement people do for a change, a vacation—go a week to the shop?

OCTOBER 31, 1949

O ur Khave is a nervous woman. And sometimes people take advantage. Today it was Allan and even her own Jerry.

Tonight is the *goyishe*[1] yontif Halloween.[2] But my Jewish grandsons, no matter if I tell them that on this night in Europe all of us would hide to not be beaten or killed, think it is only a purimshpil with a witch and a ghost instead of Queen Esther and Mordecai. If there was here a pogrom, which, blessed be His name. there is not, they would understand. How to tell them when all they see is the masks and candy is a problem I have not yet solved. But besides the masks and candy, there is other foolishness: an orange melon with a face and a light inside, flying mice from rubber, black cats (that, of course, don't eat such mice), spiders also rubber, and I don't know what else.

It is the spiders that were the problem today. Allan had one, so with Jerry he got Khave turned in such a way that he could put it on the shoulder she couldn't see. Then they told her it was there, and when she turned her head and saw, she went screaming through the rooms. When she changed from white to red, she gave Jerry a good smack on the tokhes and yelled at Allan she would tell his mother to do the same. From their faces, I could see that both of them thought their joke was worth the smack and maybe more than one. I said nothing, but when they see me tomorrow for their lessons we will talk about respect and cruelty.

This is not the first time such a thing has happened. If it's not a spider, it's a mouse. And if the mouse is not on the shoulder, it's on the table, or on a full plate. Sometimes, the boys have a mouse they wind like a clock to run in front of Khave or over her feet.

All this would have stopped if Essie and Max would tell Allan "no" louder than a whisper. But Essie tells him with a big smile on her face (she forgets she can't go near a cat because somebody once threw one on her), and Max not only doesn't tell him "no" but buys the toys! Essie and Khave live only by the armistice and Max, who gets along even less, sometimes forgets there is one.

In the teasing, once—twice maybe—there is a joke. But more than that there is anger and meanness. And with a jokester like Max, where the one ends and the other begins it is hard to tell. Sometimes he does or says or brings something—a *tsatske*[3] from a store—that is funny. Once, I remember, he had a Pharaoh in a coffin—a good place—that when you took him out you couldn't put it back without the secret. This was an amusement. But even with himself, Max will laugh and tell you through the laughter that he is really angry. Such a meshugas he has, which I don't like; more important, I think it is not such a good example for Allan. Still, I know that a zeyde is not a father. So when I talk to Allan tomorrow I will say nothing about Max.

I am happy the Halloween will be gone for another year. Maybe by then the grandsons, a little older, will be a little wiser. But it will be hard for Allan, especially, not to go from door to door to beg for candy. Better he should stay home and eat from Essie's candy dish. It is always full and what's inside is tastier than the three-cornered pieces—orange with yellow with white—Allan gave me this afternoon. They weren't too bad, but a cube sugar has more flavor.

DECEMBER 10, 1949

With Shabes over, I started to clean the candlesticks and found two dimes underneath them. So this time Rivke has lost her "*shtup*[1] the grandchildren" game, and they have won.

Really, there are two games, and in one of them everybody wins. In the first, she shtups them with sweets, and, like little *khazeyrim*,[2] they do not refuse. On Friday night after shul, Ari and Yoyne come home with me for Kidesh. (Their own fathers, I'm ashamed to say, are not back from work to do this, especially in the short days.) After Kidesh, Rivke gives them a piece shtrudel (if she's had the strength to make it) or, more often these days, apple cake. If she had a bad week, maybe the crackers with little pieces chocolate in them—the ones she makes me get by Isaacson because Sherman doesn't have. But for the children it doesn't matter. Whatever she gives them they eat in two seconds then stand there and beg for more with their eyes. This time she gives them in a piece wax paper to take home for after supper. Good. Finished. Unless she catches Ari reaching for even more.

Saturday night, when they come back for *Havdole*[3] after Shabes, they play again. Maybe Michael is with us, if I have taken him to shul for an hour, and little Merle, if Khave has spent the afternoon with her mother. So there could be more mouths to feed. But no matter how many, Rivke always has enough—except for Ari not even too much is enough.

But then comes the second "shtuping," this time in coins. Nickels for the little ones, dimes for the bigger ones—sometimes a quarter. But their mothers do not let the children take money because they feel we can't afford to give away from the little we have. So the children refuse, or if Rivke forces it into their hands, try to give it back. And if Rivke won't take it, they hide it where either their bobe or I will find it later. But one night a week Rivke is sharp-eyed. Cataracts or not, half the time she sees what they are doing and sends them out the door with what she gave them. Tonight her eyes were not sharp enough for Ari and Yoyne. And so tonight they won the game. And I found the dimes.

My daughters should let the children keep the money. Giving to the grandchildren, no matter how little, is one of their mother's few pleasures. And we don't need them to tell us we are poor. This we already know well. And how much is it, really? Not even a rye bread and a bottle milk—and, thanks to the One above, we are not starving.

If I can, I keep Rivke happy and never tell her when I find what the children hide. But I also have a game. The hidden coins, like the dimes tonight, do not go into my pocket. Instead, they go into the box for the orphans. So one way or another, the children get the money after all.

FEBRUARY 14, 1950

This afternoon, between Ari's lesson and Yoyne's, we went down to the cellar to taste the wine. It was the second time since Ruven brought the grapes in October.

The boys were excited—the cellar by itself is an adventure for them, with the old coal bin and everyone's storage—trunks, valises, a rusty bicycle, drapes that won't go upstairs again unless for the trash, summer rugs that maybe will, and, in the tall Horowitz-Margareten[1] cartons, the Pesakh dishes. If a mouse or two scurries by, all the better.

I never know whether the light is working down there. Plotkin does not care to spend money on a new bulb, so I bring a candle. This time I need it. The flame flickers as I lead the way down. Ari follows me with a bag of sugar, just in case, and Yoyne with a cup.

No mice this time, just two roaches that run from even our small light. The barrel is in the far corner, so the boys get to see the whole cellar, as much as they can by the light of one candle. But on their way, Yoyne spins the bicycle wheel, and Ari has me stop so he can look at some picture cards of baseballers.

"Not much here," he calls to Yoyne. "Everyone has vilmans [*sic*] and the medzhik o [*sic*]."[2]

Who knows what it means?

"Not much there, but something here," I say, going on. At the barrel, I drip some wax and make a place for the candle. Then Yoyne hands me the cup, and I let a little of the wine flow into it. I take a sip and pass it to the boys.

"Just a taste," I warn them.

Yoyne swallows a mouthful, then quickly passes the cup to Ari, who, of course, swallows two.

"That you call a taste?" I protest.

The rascals grin.

"Nu?" I ask.

"Sour," they say together.

When I taste and agree, Ari hands me the sugar. I pour in a good amount. Then a little more. I roll the barrel slowly where it rests. It's not even ten gallons, after all, but enough for the whole family for a year. Done, I open the tap again. We all repeat the tasting.

"Nu?"

"Better," the boys say.

"It should be sweet, but not too sweet," I tell them.

Yoyne asks if it will be ready for Pesakh.

"It will be ready even if it isn't ready," I tell him. "A lot can happen in almost two months."

As we go, Yoyne finishes what's left in the cup. Ari rolls up the sugar bag—almost empty.

In the apartment once again, I begin Yoyne's lesson. Ten minutes later, his head drops to the page. Ari, who was waiting for him, is asleep in a chair at the kitchen table.

Rivke has been fussing around us making supper; she grows aware of the silence, deaf as she's getting.

"Sholem," she scolds, "how much have you let them drink!"

"A drop, two drops," I tell her.

"A drop, two drops," she throws back. "Why not an entire ocean? Maybe now you're a tavern keeper?"

I suffer the attack. At least there's some justice in it this time.

One by one I rouse the boys enough to walk them to Rivke's bed. In half an hour they are awake and almost back to normal. As they leave, Rivke who has kept to the attack all the while, gives them two cookies each to save for after supper.

"Ari, Yoyne," I call after them, "Next time we go down remind me to take water."

"Okay, Zeyde," they yawn and close the outer door behind them.

"They should remind you?" Rivke is not finished (and tomorrow I will hear from my daughters who have inherited their mother's tongue). "Why, have you lost your own senses?"

"All things are possible," I tell her.

There will be a tsimes for a day or so, but, God willing, by Pesakh we'll all be laughing about the whole thing.

MAY 7, 1950

Yesterday Reyzl brought over the child from the orphans' home.[1] She is not exactly an orphan. A father she has, but who knows where? And a mother who cannot take care of her. So, an abandoned child, and this is maybe worse than having parents who are dead. Reyzl calls her Diana (the same as Avrom's girl) and tells me the Hebrew is Dveyre.[2] But when I called her by that name she did not know who I was talking to. So the child is not only without a mother and father but maybe without a name in Israel.

Dveyre is a pretty girl, eleven or twelve years old, with dark eyes and blond curls. Except for the hair, she looks almost like Krumbein. And, whatever his faults, Krumbein is a good-looking man. Of course, she was shy with her new aunts and cousins, but after a while she talked with Ari and Yoyne and played one of their games. Once or twice she kvetsht or nudzhed, Reyzl made her behave. So, it seems, a child like any other. But who knows what to expect between the parents, the home, and the other families she has lived with already. One thing, for certain, is that in Reyzl's hands she will not lack care or attention. As for Krumbein, he is no more a mentsh than before, but he had to agree to take the child in, even if there was no expense. Besides, he was always better with Mindl than with his sons.

What Reyzl has done does not surprise me altogether. Her two oldest are married and gone, the third out of high school and working. Soon he will go. And what then, to be alone with Krumbein forever? But still more, Reyzl was always a giver. Even with animals. Cats she kept, kittens. After the cats, birds. When she was small, I couldn't walk down the street with her without her patting every horse and shtuping them a piece carrot or half an apple she found. Also more than a few sugar cubes were sometimes missing from the bowl on the kitchen table. And more than once, Rivke gave her good for feeding the mice. With people the same. Making a soup for the old woman next door; pinching the nephews and nieces till the cheeks were red; finding members for the Mizrakhi women. So she will give to the child—maybe double—to make up for what Krumbein will not.

Of course, a mother's love might not solve any more problems than a mother's curses. With whatever Reyzl gave her Arnie, he still has troubles. But who knows how much more and worse they would have been without her? So for this new child, Reyzl will not only help but maybe fix a little what damage has already been done.

Naturally, taking the child in is for Reyzl a great mitsve. Maybe a greater mitsve than bearing a child herself. With her own, she simply had a child; with Dveyre she chose special to have this one. It is the story of Ruth and Naomi turned upside down. Ruth chose to be Naomi's daughter, and with choosing the mother also chose the Jews and God. Here, my Reyzl has chosen her daughter. And if with God's help she saves this one life, it will be as if she has saved the world.[3]

MAY 24, 1950

⌒

I have been thinking—maybe not such a new idea— that Brownsville is itself a shtetl. There are others, of course—Taleyner mostly, some Polish, a Russian here or there, black people on a couple streets, and, Ari tells me, even an Arab boy in his class. Still, it is mostly our own who live here.

And more than that, we have not only brothers and sisters in the big *mishpokhe*[1] to which we all belong, but also many generations in the small ones.[2] So, Rivke and I have four of our six children no more than two blocks away together with their children, and by Mindl and Arnie, who are already married with their own apartments, children of those children.

But this is not even half the story. My son-in-laws and daughter-in-law also have other family on their sides. Leye's sister with her husband and two children—not so little anymore because their Henry, like my Avrom, was in the war—live right across the street from us—the daughter's name I forget. This means that Asher's Ellen and Phyllis have grown up with aunts and uncles and cousins on both sides. True, Krumbein has no one in the neighborhood, which I'm sure does not bother him, but Max has a cousin and her family a block away and other cousins just past Brownsville in East Flatbush.[3] It is Zelig, though, who has the most. A brother he has with his family, a sister with hers, and his own mother and father together with their three or four (a pity) unmarried daughters. Yoyne and Merle see both their bobes and zeydes together with their eight or nine aunts, five uncles, plus whatever cousins all the time.

And not only this, but the families on one side, like by Leye's sister, know the family on the other. Even sometimes by the children. Zelig's nephew (his brother's son) is also, like the Arab boy, in Ari's class. And almost every Shabes Ari walks with Yoyne to visit the other grandparents and the single aunts.

In all this we are not alone. In Essie's building, for an example, is a woman with children. Her mother lives two houses one way, her sister with her children half a block in another. The sister's husband has a brother with a family on our block. So we have again cousins on both sides for the sister's children. Yoyne and Ari, of course, know all these people (not that it matters if I am talking about families), and the boy who lives on our street is also in Ari's class, that seems *take* to be getting crowded.

Who knows how long this closeness will last. After all, how many people can one shtetl hold? By us already Asher's Ellen and her husband are in Borough Park. And it's not like the old days in Brownsville when sometimes there were more apartments than people who wanted to rent. But for now, except for an Ellen or two, we are here and will stay.[4]

OCTOBER 26, 1950

Today Allan asked another question I could not give a good answer. We were reading in Bereyshis[1] about the children of Adam and Khave, how they took wives and what the generations were. In the middle, Allan stops.

"Zeyde," he says, "if Adam and Eve were the first people, and they had only three sons—Abel, Cain, and Seth, where did they find women for them to marry?"[2]

After I could breathe again, I told him, "It's like in the story of Abraham and Isaac. Isaac wants to know where the beast for the sacrifice is, and his father tells him 'God will provide.' Here the same. God provided."

"How?" he asks.

I tell him, "If the Almighty could make the heavens and the earth, the sky and the seas, the plants and the animals, Adam and Khave, why couldn't He also make wives in the county next door to Gan Eydn?"

On this he thinks for a while and says "I guess He could," but from the voice and the look on his face I know he believes not a word. Still, we go on.

I wish I had a better answer. But I am a simple melamed who

gives what he can. What Allan needs is to be in the yeshive. This I told Essie and Max years ago. But Max was absolute against. He wanted to send the boy to the *folkshul*[3] from the Workmen's Circle. This Essie was absolute against. So he stayed with me. For myself I don't mind; he is a pleasure to teach. But in the yeshive he could learn much more than by me. At least he is not with those who believe nothing.

This is not the first time Allan has asked such questions. Once he wanted to know if, when the Red Sea parted, the water on each side kept running or if it was frozen. And if it kept running, where did it run to, and if it was frozen, how could that be in such a hot place.   I make a joke when something like this happens.

"Nu," I say to him, "we will have to add another book to the five, the book of Arele.[4] It begins, 'Now here are the words of Allan, son of Max.' And if not a book, we'll put you in the comments with Rashi."[5] He is amused, of course, but I believe he sometimes thinks about it.

The child is a smart one, and because he thinks, he asks the questions. If he can, he must find out. What my Khave says about a boy who looks under the ladies' skirts, is *take* true of Allan—"He wants to know from where the feet grow."

Besides seeing how his head works, I also learn a little English teaching Allan. Even a simple melamed can sometimes have a clever idea—so what if it is by accident? My books when I teach him are in Hebrew. But for him I bought Hebrew with English. We read the Hebrew and translate into Yiddish, which Allan mostly understands. But sometimes there are words he doesn't. So he looks in his English and then tries to give it back in a different Yiddish word he knows. If not, he tells me the English, and so I get for myself a new word or two.

As long as the boy is learning more than me, it will be all right. But there will always be little problems like the one today. I can imagine the kind of questions he will ask about Solomon with all his wives and women if we ever get to Kings. Better, I think, to do Proverbs.[6]

NOVEMBER 19, 1950

riday night they asked me to daven Mayriv. I foolishly agreed when I should have refused.

First of all, it is an honor. So how does someone say no? And they don't ask me so often. Weekdays—morning, afternoon, or evening—sometimes—but Shabes only once in a great while. But more than the honor itself there was vanity. Ari and Yoyne, who are never in shul during the week, would see their zeyde at the *bimc*[1] leading the entire congregation. And you could tell from their faces that they were proud of me—when I was asked, when I went up, when I came down. Even after, when we went home to make Kidesh, you could see more light in their eyes than by the Shabes candles.

But such a pride as theirs was more honest than my own. I am no *Khazn*.[2] Those who can sing would have done a better job. Does the Sabbath Queen have to be greeted by the sound of a rasp on a horseshoe? And those who can sing would have made themselves heard. If I have to do more than talk normal, I breathe these days like a bellows with a hole.

So the children I made happy for two minutes and myself miserable for two days. Not only because of my selfishness, which I hope next Yom Kippur the Lord of Mercy will forgive, but also because I had done more than the flesh could easily bear. For this reason, from Shabes until this afternoon the pills under the tongue were an appetizer to the meals and a nosh in between.

I am all right now. But if I wasn't, or if I died, the smiles on the children's faces would have been meaningless—for them, I mean. Worse, their joy in those moments might have made their grief at my death so much greater.

If they should ask me again, I will have to say "*a sheynem dank*,[3] but no." The boys will be disappointed, but maybe they will learn sooner than I that a person should know what he can do and do as much as he can, but also he should know what he cannot. The days of my life are more than the seventy years of the psalm,[4] and I have just learned this. Ari and Yoyne should only know what a slow pupil they have had for a teacher.

JANUARY 8, 1951

When I was sitting by the window this afternoon, I saw a dog using a tree. (How could I not see when it was right in front of me? Better I should not look up from the Khumesh.) But since I saw, I thought that such a sight you could see every day because a lot of the neighbors have dogs. This was not like in the old country—unless the neighbors were peasants. Jews did not have dogs. Who had property to protect? And who had extra food to feed an animal? But here these days no one is starving, and there are no peasants to offer their dogs a nosh of a Jewish leg or arm. So we are not anymore so much afraid, and besides the dogs by us are mostly small. Dogs the size of calves are not for our apartments.

But by us in the Kahn family, only Essie has a dog, little like the rest. Nu, good. But to let the animal lick her face can turn the stomach. Cats, I know, she's not so crazy about. Because once when she was a girl a grober yung threw one at her and she got scratched. Still, at a distance, she has *rakhmones*[1] on them. With the scraps she throws them from the window the cats that live in the empty lot next to her have two or three good meals every week. Of course, scraps are not exactly delicatessen. No, that kind of food is only for the pets,[2] like the black cat in Sherman's grocery store. The boy who works for him feeds it olives in little pieces he cuts away from the stone.

What Reyzl's cat ate I don't know. What I do know is that one time her cat had kittens and decided to have them in Arnie's bed. When the boy woke up to find them, it was screaming and crying and carrying on with a week of nerves even worse than usual. Her turtle was never a problem. It lived twenty years in a glass bowl, then died. *Fartik.*[3] A dog, a cat, even a bird I can understand, but the pleasure in keeping a turtle I can't figure out.

This megile, I see, began with a dog but has ended with cats, birds, and turtles. So, two days of the creation[4] taken care of. And just in time, because I hear a voice (from a different day of creation) calling "Sholem!" And if I don't go into the kitchen for supper, there will be no *sholem*[5] in this house tonight.

APRIL 16, 1951

Today I went to cut my hair by Shubin. But going and coming back I stopped maybe ten minutes by the stables on Bristol and Blake. I did not go in, only stood at the gate and watched and smelled. There were four horses altogether, the others out for the day, and some wagons that would never go out at all, missing two or three wheels or half the boards. Like me, the horses were tired and old but not too tired or old to eat. True, the hay before them was not much of a feast (by horses there is no yontif), but it was enough to keep them going even if on one of them I could see too much bone and rib. But even if they reminded me of my days in the smithy and repair shop, broken wagons and half dead horses are not exactly a joy to see.

The smells were another thing. The odors of the beasts themselves, of the hay and manure, brought me back for a minute to my old home and the days of my youth. Strong smells, fresh, geshmak, like the spring itself that has been in the air for the last week. Such smells warm the blood better than King David's virgin.[1] Better than Zipkin's snuff that I take a pinch of on a Friday night to drive the weekday stink from my nostrils—the garbage that was not picked up, the smoke of coal fires or the gasoline.

And where will I find such smells when the stables are gone? The country? Spring Valley? I haven't been for years, and Asher says it will soon be nothing but roads and houses anyway.

What stays the same? Already, Max tells me, they are talking about closing down Belmont Avenue with the stalls and pushcarts. This the A&P won't mind. Even the theft will be different. No more peddlers charging half the customers two-for-a-nickel oranges at three-for-a-dime. No, at the A&P it is absolutely one price, four-for-a-quarter.

So, why wouldn't the stables be next? Or me, for that matter, also from another time and place?

But in three or four days it is Pesakh, with eggs, salt water, and greens, a springtime of its own. And though I must eat the bread of affliction,[2] already I can smell in Rivke's kitchen the odors of redemption. So with His help and will, may all of us in this season be renewed.

Still, when I go again to Shubin in the fall, I hope the stables will be there. Maybe the skinny horse would gain an ounce. Maybe a wagon will be fixed. Most likely not. I will see yet another rib and more wheels missing. But the odors of horse, manure, and hay—these will remain. More than the scent of Zipkin's snuff that clears my head, or of Rivke's cooking that cheers my heart, these—a mix of life and sweet decay, strong and sharp—go to the marrow and touch the soul.

JUNE 12, 1951

E**ssie is pregnant. But instead of being happy, she wishes the child away and once or twice has wished herself dead. No one believes she will try to kill herself, God forbid, but we all can see her misery.

Like her mother with our Avrom, Essie must be long past forty. But she married late, had her other two late, so it will be only six or seven years between her Michael and the baby. Her surprise then is not altogether what Rivke's was, even if her unhappiness is greater.

Why so unhappy? First, Max is from time to time out of work. And, when he works, he makes enough to live on—but not so much. Still, in these times people expect more "security." My Essie expects more than enough to live on. Not the moon and the stars, but maybe an apartment with more room, a nice vacation, a meal in a restaurant besides for the birthday and anniversary—I don't know what.

Rivke and I were poor in Europe and we are poor here as well. That is the way it was and the way it is; to us it wasn't so terrible and isn't so important. But Essie is ashamed being poor—and angry. And the baby will make her poorer still and so still more angry and ashamed. This is not the way in the land of milk and honey; but it is the way in the land of gold. And if you don't have, you don't let the world know you don't have. By the butcher you buy the "steak." The children you dress like the dummies in a shop window. Until, like now, you can no longer pretend.

And maybe there is something more. For Rivke, to be a wife and mother was not only enough, it was everything. Maybe for Essie and her sisters, none of them content, it is neither. What they could want I can't imagine; I don't think they could tell you themselves. Not to go to work. Before they were married they couldn't wait to stop. Reyzl, it is true, wanted to be a singer. But Rivke and I put a stop to that risky business. And her sisters said nothing.

But between whatever she wants, and worry over money, and fear about the pregnancy itself—she had a hard birth with Allan and was sick for two years after Michael—Essie seems to be sitting shive for her own soul. I don't know what to say to her. Neither does Max or her sisters. (From Rivke we have managed to keep all this.) Only Ruven, who already came down twice, has tried to talk to her. When he is here, Essie at least weeps, for once neither raging nor staring silently ahead with empty eyes. What other good his talking does we'll wait and see.

One thought that brings Essie back to herself a little is that the child might be a girl. After the two boys, this would be something new, something maybe to look forward to. But I am afraid that it will be woe to any male child born to her if her mood doesn't change.

JUNE 25, 1951

It has been six hours now and I still can't believe it. Something as close to a murder as I have ever seen or would ever want to see. And my own grandson almost a murderer. Was there ever a Kahn or an Elbaum or a Wexler who even thought of doing such a thing? And that is the trouble—there was not thinking, just doing. Never mind Yoyne is not yet a bar mitsve.[1] Even a child knows not to chase someone with an axe.

And worse—if it could be worse—it was because of me he was doing it. One of the other children, it seems, made fun of me—the way I walk, the way I talk—who knows what. And for this Yoyne went crazy. All right, so you don't like someone to make a joke of an old man, your zeyde yet, so you talk, you yell, maybe—maybe give a smack. It should not have been done, but, after all, was I hurt by the disrespect of a foolish child with a bad upbringing?

But no, Yoyne, with a better upbringing but even more foolish, grabbed the axe by a third boy, raised it over his head, and chased the other with it up and down the block, across the street with the machines squealing and banging the horns, until the child ran into his house. Ari was there but could do nothing but shout after his cousin—whether to stop him I am not so sure.

It is a good thing for all of us that the little *mamzer*[2] was as quick to run as to mock. Once the door slammed in the face, and now out of breath, Yoyne calmed down and walked back with the axe at his side.

Right away, I grabbed him by the neck and pulled him into the house. With a glass seltzer I sat him down and for ten minutes gave him a good talking on what—according to the nodding of the head—he already knew. He knew also that Khave I would absolutely tell.

But where does such a thing come from? First, the axe. The boy it belonged to got it from the society that teaches how to live in the woods.[2] Such a kheyder I think we don't need because by us there is no woods, only empty lots. But to try to use it as Yoyne did, this comes definitely from the yeytser hore and maybe the radio (but this you don't see), the moving pictures, and the television. To the theater I don't go, but I have seen the posters and a little on television the gangsters with policemen and cowboys with Indians. Games from these the children play in the street with toy guns and knives. Wonderful playthings. Maybe, I am afraid to say, such lessons the children like and learn better than the ones from a mother and father, a zeyde, or the Toyre itself.

And maybe what happened today is not over altogether, even if there will be no more axe. Ari came in for his cousin and a glass seltzer himself. When they left, I heard him say to Yoyne in the hall, "We'll get him later." To this I shouted "No!" So they went a couple steps and Yoyne whispered "After supper." Tomorrow I will remind them that it is their bobe, not me, who is deaf.

DECEMBER 24, 1951

This afternoon Allan and Jerry gave me a "Khanike present." It was a new *Shulkhen Orekh*.[1] The book must have cost them a few dollars, what they saved from the birthdays or Rivke's donations every week or from returning the empties.[2] Money they didn't spend on the chewing gum and malteds. And it was a long shlep to Aronoff's bookstore—where else would they get it? So for all their going without and planning and trouble, the boys were excited to see if I liked the gift.

I disappointed them, I know. First, I don't get presents so often—maybe the times you could count on one hand—maybe part of the second—since I was married. So how to behave I'm not sure. And then, I am not used to someone spending what doesn't need to be spent. I have already my Shulkhen Orekh over forty years. The binding is loose, so I put a little shoemaker's glue. A page is torn, so I get from Max the tape you can see through. For the yellow I can do nothing. Books like people get old and worn out. But this one has good years left and does not yet have to be buried.[3] So foolishly I said, "If I have one, do I need two?" It was like taking their souls.

I saw the mistake right away and said again, "But maybe we will use yours to read together. A sheynem dank." That helped a little, like butter on a burn. If it heals without a scar, maybe they will forgive me in time. They are good boys the two of them.

But what also bothered me was the idea of "Khanike present." Khanike *gelt*[4] is one thing. All right, it was a kopek or two in the old country and maybe a dime or a quarter here. And with all their bobes, zeydes, aunts and uncles children can maybe get enough to go to the pictures half a year or have for other childish pleasures. But in the years since the war I think, I see the children getting not a little money but toys—a truck that goes by itself, a doll that drinks and pees, a fat glove for the baseball. And not just one— someone just on the radio last week was talking about giving them something every night of Khanike! And why? So they wouldn't be unhappy they didn't have Christmas. *Nebekh*![5]

So, like Macy's and Gimbels[6] we have a new competition. And everybody is happy. The stores are happy, the children are happy, and the mothers and fathers are happy that their children are happy. But I am not so happy. Where is the story of the Maccabees and the miracle? Where is the idea of praying freely to God and not being forced to bow to idols? It is this freedom and the joy of it that the Khanike gelt and the *dreydl*[7] playing are supposed to show. To the little money is attached a big meaning. I don't know you can have the same meaning from a doll that pees. Too big and too much makes no meaning except the big and the much.

And Khanike we must remember is only a small holiday. The story of the Maccabees is in our history but not in our Toyre or the other writings.[8] Let us keep it as it should be kept and not fatten it like we used to with a goose before yontif.

FEBRUARY 5, 1952

We have been worried about Reyzl's Nokhem ever since the army took him. Today our worry is a little less and a little different. At least they are not sending him to Korea. Korea—whoever heard of such a place before last year?[1] Only maybe the mapmakers or their neksdorikes[2]—China and Japan.[3] So Nokhem will not be where there is shooting and bombing.

He will be instead in Germany. There he will be safe from the bullets, but not from the looks and words of the murderers and their children once they find out.[4] And if not kill, looks and words can wound and damage the spirit. I would have prayed for him to be spared in battle. Now I pray for him to be spared the attacks of eyes and tongues, or, at least, with the help of the Almighty to survive them.

MARCH 9, 1952

Creating a new life on Shabes is a mitsve. But about discussing this creation on Erev Shabes I'm not so sure.

It is Max, of course, who starts the talk with a joke. Jokes, it seems, are the wisdom of salesmen—by piece goods, by dresses, and everything else. But with his joke about love-making Max gets a laugh (I can't even remember what the foolishness was) and Essie puts her two cents in. She is not shy, my daughter, or modest. Was it the same mouth that was singing "Eyli, Eyli"[1] half an hour ago?

But before my thoughts grow too dark, Max begins passing around a picture of himself, he tells us, when he was three years old and smacks Allan's and Jerry's hands when they reach for it, as if it is not fit for their eyes. Khave looks and laughs till the tears come; I laugh, I admit, once. Zelig finds it funnier and, turning it this way and that, asks which end is up. Although he disagrees with Max about most things, Asher shares his sense of humor. He laughs long and loud at the young boy above and grown man below. Asher passes it to his Leye. She studies it, then stares at Max. She examines it, then stares at Max again. A third time. "You know Max," she says at last, "it really doesn't look like you at all." This, of course, gets more laughter than the picture.

When the laughing fades away, the conversation turns, naturally I suppose, to who's "played out" and who isn't. Not exactly a topic for Shabes and not one I would talk about during the week either, but I say quietly, "I'm still able." This brings a mixture of more laughter, shock, and applause. I have even managed to embarrass my daughters. Max, who seems the most pleased by the news, shouts it to Rivke who hasn't heard. She scowls and waves a hand in disbelief, disgust or both. Maybe it isn't fitting for an old man, but is it my fault? If she has a quarrel, let her take it to Him who made me.

Almost as if he had been reading my mind, Jerry asks to sing *Adon Olom*.[2] "But not the way they do it in shul," he says, "Uncle Max's way." Uncle Max's way is lively, but he is no more a singer than I am. So it is a good thing that Essie is there to lead us. When it is over, Asher rises and says, "That sounds like the end of the service to me." It is, *take*, getting late. Nearly eleven. The others take their signal from Asher and bundle into their coats.

MAY 12, 1952

Today they sent someone to put in the telephone. Do we need it? The children think so. Maybe they are right. But somehow I managed to become an old man without ever having one.

It is true that I can't run over to Essie's or Khave's the way I used to, and Reyzl now is a few blocks too far even if I could run. With a little one, Essie, who lives closest, can't always come every time her mother needs her. So with the telephone, we can talk when we have to, and God forbid there is an emergency, I can call one of them and have them call whoever else needs to be called. A doctor for Rivke most of the time, I'm afraid. Between her aches and pains—more and worse, it seems, each day—old age, and her fear of death, my daughters will be kept busier than they bargained for.

Before the telephone man arrived and half a dozen times while he was there, Rivke nudzhed me to get him to make the bell loud enough for her to hear. This is not so easy. One reason Rivke and I will be buried together is so I can give her a poke when the shoyfer sounds to awaken the dead.[1] He must have worked fifteen minutes before she could hear the bell when she was in the room. Whether she will hear it from the kitchen will depend on what kind of day she and her arteries are having. As for me, I'm sure I could hear it from *Yekhupets*,[2] or from East New York[3] at least. Twice already it woke me from a nap. Both times I thought it was a fire alarm.

And it hasn't stopped ringing all day and night. Essie called. Reyzl called. Khave called. Then Essie called again because Michael wanted to talk to his bobe and zeyde on the telephone. Then Khave called because her Merle wanted to do the same. (I am sure Essie had called Khave to tell her about Michael.) After Merle, Leye called. And in the evening Asher and Avrom. If tomorrow is the same, it will have to go back. Not only does it disturb my nap but also my study. I may be Sholem, but not a moment's sholem[4] have I had because of it all day.

Making a call is not so bad. Last week Reyzl wrote down in a special book everyone's number, together with the doctors, the police, the fire department—even Sherman the grocer. So after each of the children called me, I called them back to let them know I could do it. What's to do? If you can read and move a finger, you can make a call. For Rivke, of course, this is a problem. The numbers maybe she can just read, even with the cataracts, but not the English letters, even without. So she dials the operator and like a wealthy woman has someone else do the work. Luckily, she can speak enough English for the operator to understand. I don't know if I could do that, but I don't have to.

With all this, I can see how the telephone can become part of you—like a tumor or a boarder you can't get rid of. The best way to use the telephone was Max's before he and Essie got one. He would give out the number of a pay telephone in the candy store. Maybe five times a year someone would call it, mostly his boss, always for something important. Wilner the candy store was not too happy, but at least when he sent a boy to call Max to the telephone, someone was not reading the magazines for free. And Max did not have his own reading or his sleep disturbed every two minutes.

Maybe everyone will soon get used to the idea that we have this tsatske, and I'll have some peace once more. If the thing is truly for emergencies, I hope I never have to use it again. I hope, but I am afraid I will be disappointed.

JUNE 1, 1952

*S*hvues[1] is over but some of Rivke's *blintses*[2] we still have. So that will be for lunch tomorrow—breakfast maybe.

Not altogether an easy holiday. To remember that the Toyre was given to us at Mt. Sinai is not a problem. This someone could do anywhere in the world. But Shvues is also a holiday for the first harvest. Nu, here in a city what can you harvest from cement? Not the grass that grows from the cracks in the sidewalk. And from the bushes and trees not one fruit a person can eat. The children, it is true, play with what falls from some of the trees and make false noses,[3] but that is altogether a different story.

Since I mention children, I will write what my Ari did on the first day of the yontif. When I and the other *koyenim*[4] went out to the foyer to have the *levi'im*[5] wash our hands before our blessing, Ari was watching us with a big smile on his face, hopping first on one foot then the other, as if he would burst with happiness. When I asked him about this later, he said that he enjoyed seeing Mr. Buchsbaum wash his zeyde's hands. Why? Because Buchsbaum is a rich man, a landlord with two apartment buildings and some smaller ones besides, while his zeyde has two cents but not more. Those who have, Ari said, should do for those who don't. At least, he went on with his *droshe*,[6] until those who don't throw off their chains.

Already I can hear Max's voice in what he says. A voice that sometimes hurts the ears.

JUNE 15, 1952

Yesterday was Ari's bar mitsve. He read very well in the shul—this is not a surprise—and the party at night was lively.

Different from most boys these days, Ari learned his portion and *haftoyre*[1] in just two or three weeks, not a year. Why? Because he has been with me since he was small and knew already the Hebrew and even some of the blessings that he has heard hundreds of times in shul. Also, I taught him the notes, so he could read from any part of the Toyre with a little work and any haftoyre with less.[2] Most of the others, even the ones I teach, must learn like a *peretz* [*sic*].[3] I say and sing, and they repeat.

So the Hebrew and the notes were perfect. His voice clear like a clarinet—already it is not anymore a flute. The whole family kveld from him, the men shook my hand, the women threw from the balcony bags with candy and nuts,[4] and Rabbi Magerman gave a short speech and a certificate. Fine. Beautiful.

But the party at night was something else. Another ceremony— with a Khazn, with Michael carrying a *talis*[5] up an aisle, with Max and Essie putting it around Ari's shoulders. And, of course, the birthday cake. For this, Rivke and I had to light a candle, and then all the aunts and uncles on both sides together with a couple cousins the same. All of this was an amusement, but what it had to do with a bar mitsve I don't know.

Finally, when all the candles were lit, the Khazn announced that the bar mitsve boy would make a speech. But no one told Ari that he must do this. So he just said: "Thank you all for coming. Let's eat." Food, of course, is never far from Ari's mind or mouth. But everyone laughed and went in to the meal.

And food there was plenty, all of it good, especially the chopped liver with fried onion mixed in. Between the dishes, three klezmorim played, so there was also plenty music and dancing. The only thing that was not plenty was the schnapps. Not that Max didn't buy but that the guests must have confused a bar mitsve with *Simkhes Toyre*.[6] So Max sent his nephew out for more bottles and in the meantime no one died of thirst. (And maybe Max's sister and another woman I didn't know could have shared the bottles they carried with them half the night.) But everyone enjoyed and Rivke even more than the others because—besides the simkhe—Freydl, her youngest sister, had come from Baltimore with her new husband.

Altogether the party was very different from Arnie's (or his brother's) years ago. That was in the house with everything cooked at home by Reyzl and the other women. The music was just Victrola records, but people talked more than danced. A good time still but more heymish. I even remember from that party a joke played by Mr. Rothstein, Max's father, on Max and Essie's friend McManus. (How a Jew comes to such a name I don't know—I think it must really be Manny.) McManus had already more than a couple drinks. This Mr. Rothstein saw and offered him another that was not refused. But quick as McManus was to take it, he was quick to spit it out. With a smile across his face, Rothstein apologized: "My mistake. In the tea I forgot to put sugar."

But heymish, I knew, was not for Essie. Not that Max doesn't like to celebrate. He always says that in life there is so much suffering you should make the most of joyful moments. Still, I'm sure that the hall, the foolish ceremony, the fancy meal, and the music were mostly Essie's idea. Maybe not so terrible if they could afford. But I don't see how they could and so the guests themselves must have paid for everything with their gifts to Ari. About the child, who enjoyed himself and the praise, and who must have kept a couple dollars, I am not worried. But Essie, how will she feel in a week or a month? Not richer, I think. Not happier. I myself am not a wise man, but I know, as she and Khave do not, to be satisfied with what little I have.

JULY 6, 1952

Between the bar mitsve and all that I have written since[1] I almost forgot to say something about the waiters. At the bar mitsve dinner there were two for the head table, both, because it was so hot, with the sleeves rolled up. Just a little, but enough to see the blue numbers by one of them and by the other a scar where the numbers once were.

I said nothing, of course, but they could see the question in the eyes and answered what I didn't ask.

Moyshe, the one with the numbers, said, "To my grave I will take it. Meanwhile, I wave it in the face of the world so they will not forget what was done."

The other, Shmuel, put a fist to his chest.

"Here," he said, "it stays forever. But I will rub out whatever trace of the beast I can."

So one put more rolls, the other a plate chicken, and finished.

After a minute I was back to enjoying the simkhe, but over the last few days, I have been chewing on what they said like a cow her cud. I think there is not a right and wrong between the two of them. We must make the world remember and also not forget ourselves—not to cry and moan—what good will that do—but to see that such a thing never happens again. For this we will need Shmuel's feeling together with Moyshe's fire. More than this, we must restore our people—with numbers and with faith. The long chapter of agony and grief must not be the end of the story.

SEPTEMBER 10, 1952

A fter Michael's lesson this afternoon, Rivke gave the boy a slice rye bread smeared over with chicken fat. "Maybe you'll put on an ounce, Mr., Pencil," she said as he closed the door. Ten minutes later, by the window, I saw the birds were having a banquet.

The child eats next to nothing and weighs almost as little. This bothers Rivke, naturally, who thinks if you can't grab a handful of flesh by someone he will be dead in a week. And because she is afraid of this, to tell the truth, she is sometimes a little unkind. If it's not Mr. Pencil, it's Mr. Stick; if not Mr. Stick, Mr. Scallion. And to make it worse, she is the opposite with his brother Allan, by who you can grab two handfuls. Allan she calls "Arele," not "Mr." anything. To Rivke, Allan is a handsome boy, a strong boy, a healthy boy. If anything is wrong with Allan, God forbid, it is not consumption.

So by his bobe Michael suffers, even if I tell her not to nudzh him. But it is worse at home. Essie yells, shakes him, gives even a smack or two. Naturally, it doesn't help. If he could eat less, he would. To me it doesn't matter fat or thin. What worries me is his quietness. He is a strange child in his silence. And at the lessons, he understands, but he learns without interest or spirit.

Sometimes I believe I am the Rabbi of Prague[1] teaching a little goylem. Yet he is not a dull child either. His writing book is filled with his drawings—a ship, a dog, an old man with a beard (me?), a hand writing in a writing book with the same pen Michael has himself. He sings too. His father calls him "canary." And in his quiet way he can make a joke. When Rivke gives him a nickel or two after Shabes, he hides the coins in the piece cake she has also given and puts the piece back in the dish. More than once I might have broken my teeth on such pieces—if the teeth were my own and not the dentist's.

But jokes or not, Michael is a solemn child who lives more in his own head than in the world. Maybe Rivke and Essie should worry more about this than whether he gains an ounce.

NOVEMBER 4, 1952

Khave has given us her old television. The truckers brought it over this morning after they delivered her new one—a "console." We put it on top of our own "console"—the old Majestic radio. True, between the size of the screen and our bad eyes, Rivke and I have to sit no more than three feet away. But for a half hour or an hour in the evening it will be an entertainment.

We both enjoy Milton Berel[1]—the "meshugener" by Rivke—she was always one for giving names—and sometimes Lucy—if the whining and crying does not sound too much like Rivke herself to be amusing. These we know from visiting Khave and since last year, when she got her television, Esther. Once in a while also there was the one who would tear apart his piano while he was singing. Rivke calls him the Milk and Honey man because at the end of the program he sounds (to her bad ears anyway) like he says goodnight to Mrs. Kholovudvash,[2] wherever she is. And I enjoy his friend the dancer, too, with the top hat and cane, who keeps asking Mr. Bailey to come home. Is it possible, I have wondered, that this Bailey and Mrs. Milk and Honey went somewhere together? But, although there is many a foolish *midrash*,[3] I should not be writing a midrash about foolishness.

Still, one thing I must confess—though it shames me to write it—best of all are the little wrestlers.[4] Of course, one should not delight in the misfortune of others. Yet there is something comical in the—how to say it—confusion? Which are they, small men or large children? And then the tumbling and the jumping and the faces they make! I confess too, that if I saw them on the street I would recite the blessing *"Meshane Habriyes."*[5] Maybe I should anyway. I will ask the rabbi for his opinion. A strange thing this box with a picture. Whatever you see seems real and not real at the same time.

Of course, having the television will mean that Rivke and I will not be going to Khave's and Essie's so often. Not that we don't see them almost every day, but a little company in the evening is not such a bad thing. Maybe others are going out a little less too. I have noticed that even in good weather people don't seem to stroll or sit on the stoop the way they used to.

We must thank Khave for the gift, of course, but I know that there was a dark side to this generosity as well. She bought the console because her sister bought one. Never mind that she herself had a television, "table model" or not, a couple years before Essie bought any at all. It used to be a blouse or a skirt with them. Now it's televisions. This, in America, is progress.

So Rivke and I now have, as they say, a "set." And we will watch it—and keep an eye on the electric. But for me, except to study by the window, the best thing is still reading the *Morning Journal* in the Morris chair after breakfast, with the Emerson radio on the table beside me tuned in to the Yiddish hour and with Rivke, still fussing in the kitchen, leaving me in peace.

JANUARY 1, 1953

Last night was New Year's Eve—not our new year of course. But for some reason my children and their friends, my Esther especially, have "parties" on this night or "go out" to a "club" or a "show" or who knows where. What exactly they are celebrating I don't know. I understand that it's the middle of a gray winter and an entertainment now and then is good for the spirit. But Khanike was here just two weeks ago. Still, if life is a struggle even in good times (better if the latest war would end and Reyzl's Norman comes back in one piece), then people will take what pleasure they can.

So last night Rivke and I were by Esther. It was almost half the neighborhood in her three rooms. Reyzl was there with Krumbein, Asher with Leye. Then Essie and Max's friends, some neighbors, a niece and a nephew and the children—maybe 30 people. There were jokes, singing, funny hats—I wore my yarmulke, thank you very much—schnapps of four or five kinds. I had one little glass and the friend McManus had one—bigger—for everyone else.

But best of all was the food. Delicatessen, naturally. Salami, corn beef, roll beef,[1] and the best pastrami, with just enough fat to make it slide down smoothly. Rye bread, of course, salads, pickles, pickled tomatoes, peppers, black olives (this they could do without), and the mustard, golden with black specks, squeezed from the paper cones. And the knishes—how could I forget—potato, of course, and liver (this could go with the olives). And the little frankfurters wrapped in dough—wonderful. I must have had six of them—all right, ten. "Pigs in blankets" Essie calls them. Such a name for kosher food even if it is *khazeray*,[2] but this is as close to eating treyf as I will ever come. Altogether tasty.

And in between you could take a handful of pretzels, potato chips, small candies. I had as many caramels as little frankfurters and some pieces out of the Barton's[3] box besides. One or two I didn't like so well, I took a bite and put back. This bothered Essie who always was a little fussy. But why waste? Maybe someone else would like the other half.

To drink, I mean besides the schnapps, were seltzer, of course, ginger ale, black cherry soda, cream soda, sesperileh [*sic*] (this I can write but can't say),[4] and finally tea, along with cookies, *mandl bread*,[5] a few sponge cakes and some seven layers. From Esther's house no one goes home hungry.

Everyone was having a good time. Even Rivke was not kvetshing, and as usual she was sneaking food when she thought no one was looking. I never knew she liked roll beef so much. Maybe every once in a while I'll bring her half a quarter.[6]

Just before twelve o'clock, Max put on the television. In Times Square, New York, thousands of foolish people were waiting in the cold for the "new year" as if for Meshiekh. A big ball started to drop from the New York Times newspaper, and when it reached the bottom a sign in lights around the top of the building flashed 1953. Everyone in the streets and in the apartment yelled "Happy New Year!" together with blowing horns and rattling noisemakers. You would think someone just called out Haman's name. Suddenly the picture changed; an orchestra was playing a song and Essie and most of the others sang along.

Some of the guests began to leave, and soon it was time for us to go too. One couple was staying over. There would be four in a bed like on the East Side. Before I left, I put six or seven caramels in my pocket and wrapped some slices of the roll beef in a paper. 1953 or no 1953, by me it was still 5713 and I had to be at morning minyen by seven o'clock.

JUNE 21, 1953

Friday, before Shabes—such respect was paid—they killed the Rosenbergs.[1] Him first. Then her. By the electric chair. Such a death is hard to imagine.

Were they guilty? Were they spies? Some say yes; some say no. Were they Jews? Of this there is no question. So definitely two Jews were killed. Not so definitely two spies.

And if they were, it was not for such an enemy either. Not in the war anyhow. Today is another thing—the Russians and America less than friends and more than competitors. So maybe what is going on now makes what they did then—if they did something— look worse. Still, before the Rosenbergs, the paper and the radio say, America never killed for spying in peacetime. So how are they different? A look at the face and the name, and you can tell.

The president did nothing. Who expected? A general, after all, will think like a soldier. Such men live by a Toyre without a Talmud.[2] But the judge, Kaufman, is altogether a tsatske. And altogether an American—a hundred percenter, if not more. To show this, he bent over not only backwards, but forwards and sideways too. Who needs more proof than the sentence?

We have seen Kaufmans before, by the Spanish, the Germans, the Russians with the rabbis chosen by the czar.[3] All of them tell us who will be our leaders and speakers. But here, this Kaufman did not have to take the case. There are other judges after all. And a gentile judge would not have needed to leap and twist and hop to show he was not doing favors. And if such a judge was not absolutely an anti-semite, justice for the Rosenbergs could have left them at least alive. But maybe someone made sure Kaufman got the case and in such a way that he couldn't refuse.

In the shul Friday night it was like a shive. Between Minkhe when they might still be alive and Mayriv when they were not, you couldn't hear a whisper. For once, Zipkin kept the snuff box in his pocket and did not go up and down the aisles offering us a pinch. We welcomed the Sabbath queen with mournful tunes, as if she were a new widow.

This afternoon, Sunday, the funeral was at I.J. Morris in the neighborhood. Zelig went. (Max, I'm surprised, didn't.) There were people by the hundreds, so many not all could get in. They stayed outside for hours, even after the bodies were taken to the cemetery. Some, I know, came just to say that they were there. But more came because so soon after the war here were two more Jews dead for no reason. Whether this is the truth is maybe not so important. But what people feel has a truth of its own. So millions have been pained by their deaths, and here Mr. Judge Kaufman is a question for the sages: Who would have suffered if they had been spared?

SEPTEMBER 20, 1953

On Rosh Hashanah our fate for the coming year was written, and yesterday, on Yom Kippur, it was sealed. So, in such a serious business what can be amusing? Can someone laugh while praying for forgiveness? *Es past nit*.[1] Still, in the world of the Kahn family such a thing is not altogether impossible.

It was late in the afternoon, the time when some of us pay more attention to how many hours till the end of the fast than to the closing of the gates.[2] This is true by the young ones more than the old since they are not so used to fasting, and in the years just past bar mitsve they can eat six meals a day if you let. Like Yoyne, who became bar mitsve not two months ago. So at the end of Minkhe and with the stomach making noises, he turns to his cousin Ari, who is fasting himself for only the second time, and says, "I could use a piece of Bobe's tokhes right now."

Mr. Rosen, who works for Asher and sits with us, hears and starts yelling at the boy: "What kind of talk is that? Fe! On yontif yet! You should be ashamed!" Some of the others have also heard Yoyne but are not upset. They know what the boy means and so laugh at Rosen, who does not. Asher and Max, with big smiles on their faces, explain. Rosen calms down but still looks at Yoyne as if he might be the angel of death.

An hour and a half later, yontif ends and we go home to break the fast. There's black bread and herring—pickled and chopped, sour cream with cucumbers and radishes, hard-boiled eggs that were cooked the day before, and cream cheese to smear on the bread. With the coffee or tea we have a honey cake and a babke. This Rivke bakes in a pot, so it is round, as it should be for the New Year,[3] but it never rises evenly. Always there is a sinking across the middle so that there are two curved halves and a separation. To Rivke, this looks like a tokhes. So "tokhes" she calls it, and so have the rest of us for years now.

Max, not one to let a joke be, asks Yoyne, who is now on his third slice, "So, Jerry, how's Bobe's tokhes this year?" Everyone laughs—by now they all know what happened earlier. Yoyne answers his uncle, but with his mouth full who can tell what he says? I think the answer is that a minute later he reaches for the fourth slice.

In truth, the tokhes was very good this year, and we'll have some left a couple days for a nosh with butter and jelly. Maybe I will take a piece across the street to Rosen, he should taste such a tokhes as this. A good deed to save for next Yom Kippur.

FEBRUARY 23, 1954

A terrible accident. Joe caught his hand in the press at work. No one knows if he'll be able to use it again. No one knows even if he'll live. There was so much blood. "Shock" too, as they call it. And his temperature fell almost six degrees.

Reyzl was at the hospital with her Marcy all afternoon and into the evening. They will probably stay all night. Not even Krumbein will say a word against this.

A good boy, Joe. He works hard, with his hands, goes fishing yet, but is no *balegole*.[1] Rosh Hashanah, Yom Kippur you see him at shul. He can find his way in the *sider*, and at Pesakh he makes a decent Kidesh. The two of them, he and Marcy, a fine couple with a kosher home. They knew each other almost since they were children. Lived on the same street. "Fell" in love — as if that also is some kind of accident. But maybe that is the way it should be here, not like with Reyzl and Krumbein.

Even after all these years that marriage still gnaws at me—and more still at Reyzl who can doubt. And if Marcy has escaped her parents' troubles, it seems one of her brothers hasn't. Arnie—nothing but nerves, always near to madness, and Iris, his wife, just as close. I am afraid for their little ones.

But at this moment I am worried most for Joe. Still, he is strong, and may the *Mishebeyrakh*[2] that I will have said for him Thursday morning add to his strength.

FEBRUARY 24, 1954

Joe will live. He is out of "shock" and out of danger even if the needle is still in his arm. He'll keep his hand too, but not all the fingers. Yet what are fingers to a life. He is alive, and in time will be able to go back to the press. When he returns from the hospital and is well enough, I will take him to shul to *bentsh Goyml*.[1]

I have been thinking that the Kahns and those close to them have not done well with fingers. On one of mine, a joint bends away from the others. An accident at the forge back in Minsk, and without workmen's insurance. I wasn't away for long, pain or no pain. And Rivke too, something worse, lost her little finger. She cut herself in the kitchen, which led to a tsore with the blood, which led to taking it off.[2] No penicillin back then. And Henry, my Asher's Leye's nephew, right across the street, came back from the war with one knuckle missing.

And one other I almost forgot—Rivke's sister Hinde's a grandson. Just after the war, his hand was run over by a streetcar. Four operations he has had already and maybe will have more. But even if not perfect, the hand has been saved.

And now Joe's *umglik*,[3] worse than all the others. But he is with us still. Borukh Hashem!

AUGUST 16, 1954

Again this morning I called Essie and Khave to save their mother who was in terrible pain all night. Her head (this time) and almost fainting when she got up from bed. The doctor (Horowitz this time) came in the afternoon. He examined her as he always does, said something about the pressure and hardening of arteries as he always does, then gave her a pill to make her sleep and a new prescription as, of course, he always does. One thing new he told us—to use an electric fan in such a heat that we are now having.

Essie and Khave stayed until their mother was asleep. Maybe Horowitz should have taken their pressure too, they were so worried and nervous—as they always are. But when Rivke carries on like today there is nothing I can do for her myself, and she carries on this way more and more often. Sometimes it is hard to believe she is suffering so, but who can say that she is not feeling what she says she feels? Rivke was never altogether a strong woman. Even before Avrom was born she had problems with her digestion, and the headaches were already starting. After Avrom things got worse. A little one was hard for a woman her age even with the others helping. And, of course, little one or not, there was what happens with the years anyway.

But Rivke is also a complainer. If she sticks herself with a needle, it becomes a knife in the heart. If she finds a bump on her arm where she banged into an open door, it is to her a tumor absolutely. Somehow, she never could see that pinches, splinters, bruises, coughs, sneezes, and creaking bones are part of life, not omens of death—except that life itself is such an omen. But no, for her the slightest ache must become a drama. Maybe it was from her mother that Reyzl so long ago got the idea to go on the stage.

Take, at times like this morning, a crisis, there is nothing to make a joke about. But through the years, sometimes Rivke's usual kvetshing has been amusing. First of all, there is the list of doctors—never less than ten names, not counting four or five "professors." Even this morning, Khave and Essie had to decide between Horowitz and some others, and he was the second choice because Krasner was on vacation. When she's not so bad, Rivke herself decides: "My leg hurts, so call Weiner. My throat is sore; get me Wasserman or Smolinsky, whoever will come quicker. I have a temperature. It's too high for Lustig; I need Braverman." And it's no good to call Lustig if Braverman can't come. Because even if we get Lustig and the temperature goes down, she will have Braverman anyhow.

The "professors" she doesn't use so often. First, they won't come to the house, except once after the operation for her digestion, Simonson (may he rest in peace) came to check her. Second, Rivke doesn't like to travel these days. Twice a summer maybe she will let Asher drive us to the ocean to sniff the air for an hour. Otherwise, she's home. So if she wants a "professor," we know that there is something out of the ordinary, at least something the rest of us would maybe go to a regular doctor for. But even in such a case there are choices.

"Sholem," she will call, "I need to go to Elkin."

I answer, "Elkin the eyes, or Elkin the heart?"

"Elkin," she calls again.

"Which Elkin?" I try once more.

"Yes, Elkin, Elkin. That's what I said."

Though it hurts me that she grows deafer by the day, I sometimes lose patience: "What you need is Ingerman the ears."

With Greenwald the stomach and Rossman the rashes there is no problem. But for the feet again we must be careful—Teplitsky for the bunions, Lewitas for the corns.

But today was not amusing at all. What can be amusing about suffering—or even the fear of suffering? So Horowitz came. And Rivke is now asleep four hours. Essie called a few minutes ago to say Max will bring a fan. When I put down the telephone, I laid a wet a cloth on Rivke's forehead.

Now I am sitting across the room as she sleeps, writing by the last daylight. (If I put on the electric, it might wake her up.) She is peaceful and breathes softly. The shadows seem to fill the folds and wrinkles of her skin. For a moment I see her as she was in youth, and I remember some verses of the Song of Songs.

SEPTEMBER 2, 1954

T sipora left today to go back home to Israel. It is a miracle that I can write such a thing even after six years. I wish I could go as well. But that miracle will *take* have to wait until Meshiekh comes.

Altogether, the week Tsipora was here was more bitter than sweet. Naturally, everyone was happy to see her. A relative, after all, and the only one we know who survived. The granddaughter of my eldest brother, Naftali, who was dead even before the Nazis. But because she was the only one who lived, she reminded us of all the others who did not. We asked about this one, about that one, almost as if we did not believe what she had told us in her letters. She only shook her head. Soon we stopped asking.

About herself almost the same. Living, as they called it, in the ghetto; watching the young men marched off by thousands; hearing the engines of machines with poison gas or screams of the dying as they were shot over open pits. And the little ones, thrown into other pits and buried alive. It was after that she escaped. To the woods, to the partisans. For more than a year hiding herself, being hidden by others. Until the Nazis pulled back and she could hope, if not to live, at least not to die.[1]

She showed us the inside of her arms. "Clear," she said. "No numbers. But, one way or the other, they have marked me forever."

"One way or the other," Max answered, quietly for a change, "they have marked us all."

Better to talk then about Israel. How she kissed the ground when she arrived. How she learned to speak Hebrew. How she lived six months on the kibbutz. How she was now in Tel Aviv with her husband—a sabra, an electrician—and two children, with a life and a future. Still, that future had also a dark side. Everyone was afraid of another war with the Arabs. And meanwhile, with high prices and little money, life was hard.

It was to make things a little easier that she had come to see us. America, after all, was the golden land, and we would have some of the gold to give her. She was as disappointed now as I and millions of others had been fifty years ago. How is it that such foolishness lives on while wisdom perishes among the people? Max and Arnie would say "capitalist propaganda," but a person has to want to believe. Tsipora did not go away with empty hands, but not with full pockets either. Maybe with a few dollars more than the fare.

So Tsipora learned that in America there are poor people too. From her we learned with our heads what we already knew in our hearts—that except for her there was no one left.

But another thing I learned was altogether a surprise. The Yiddish I thought I spoke had somehow changed in fifty years. Hers I could understand, but it was so deep, so formal, and with words sometimes I had stopped using long ago. "Potatoes," *take*, were "kartofln," or "bulbes" and a "window" was a "fenster," but for us in America they had been "pateytes" and "vinde" for so long it seemed forever. And with "supper" and "chicken" and a dozen other words the same. And even the sentences more and more only like the English—"He goes to shul every morning," not so much "To shul goes he every morning." If I live much longer, I will be speaking like an American altogether.[2]

Of course, I will still write to Tsipora, as I have now for three years, and she will answer my letters. We will never see each other again. But to see her once reminded me that the old country had not been a dream but a reality that—cruel and fearful in the end—had surely passed. All our hope now was in America and especially Israel—in our children's children and those to come after. As in time, after a terrible fire, the forest is reborn.

SEPTEMBER 30, 1954

Yesterday, the second day of Rosh Hashanah, my grandsons Ari and Yoyne for five dollars bought me *Koyen*.[1] I have two thoughts.

The shul needs the money. It has just a few members, and the holiday tickets pay only for the Khazn and some small bills. Also, it was not so different in the old country, and the rabbis tell us that sometimes a custom is just like a law. But, to me, an honor should be given and accepted for its own sake. It is not a bottle milk or a box sugar to be bought and sold.

Still, when I was called up, my eyes filled with tears, and, choking them back, I just managed to recite the blessings. That the boys should think of doing such a thing was the true honor. And what have I ever done for them? And how much time is left me?

JANUARY 23, 1955

This afternoon four of them—all but Reyzl and Avrom—sat down in the kitchen for a meeting. Rivke went unaware from one to the other with tea and cake. Myself, as soon as it started, I went into the front room. Who likes to be talked about? Who likes to hear himself talked about? I didn't hear everything. But I heard enough.

What they were talking was how to keep their mother and me alive. The old age pension is not enough. The lessons I give buy a khale for Shabes, a few quarts milk, but not much more. The children must help.

This I am sorry to say, sorry I have no more in my old age, sorry to need the children so. But I am not ashamed. Since a boy I worked, until Sussman told me to stop for my heart. From horseshoes to pushcarts, to piecework, to the farm, to a factory—with overtime near the end. Rivke and I went sometimes without eating; the children never. If I didn't have, I borrowed from a brother, a cousin, a lantsman, twice the free loan society.[1] And no one went naked in the street. But such a borrowing was not a business, a "deal."

Nobody owes me. Still, there are commandments they must keep and mitsves they must do—feeding the hungry, clothing the naked, honoring parents. My children are willing to do this—and more, see that they have to, but can't agree how. The sons want everyone to "chip in" the same. Fine for them to say; they have more than the others. My daughters want everyone to give what they are able. Of course, they are not so able themselves. Yet, they are right. I have said the same in my will, written years ago now. But that was about how they should care for their mother when I am gone. It is not fitting for me to say something now. That, *take* would make me ashamed.

But to have them quarrel about me while I could hear whatever in the next room, I felt dead already. Growing old is not just to lose the sharpness of the eyes or the strength of the arms. This one expects. But it is also to lose the power to decide. Sitting there this afternoon, what choice, after all, did I have? And however much you lose, this is how much you stop being a person. That is why the four of them could talk about me like I was a table or a lamp. Sholem Kahn, a piece furniture. Already no more human being.

The meeting went on for an hour and a half. By the end, they were filled with Rivke's tea and cake but not with wisdom. For this I opened the bookcase. If I could find a sentence or two, good; and if not, even the search itself would be worthwhile. There were some words that described, *take*, how I felt:

But I am as a deaf man, I hear not;

And I am as a dumb man that openeth not his mouth.

Yea, I am become as a man that heareth not,

And in whose mouth are no arguments[2]

But between the spinning head and fumbling fingers I could find nothing useful.

JULY 12, 1955

Today my grandson Dovid, Ruven's boy, came to visit. He is home from medical school for the summer. His cousins Ari and Yoyne were here too. Which was a good thing because soon we didn't have what to talk about. After all, how well do I know Dovid? He is maybe 24 years old and maybe I've seen him 24 times, but I don't think so. It's hard when people live so far away.

It's been hard for him too. What kind of life is it with your father at home only every other Shabes and your mother spending her life caring for your crippled brother? And in her spare time trying to make a little extra money with speech lessons. I don't think in the Bronx she has so many customers.

Not that Golda ignores him. He is her pride just as Nathan is her pain. And maybe she wants him to be a doctor even more than he does himself. But she must give her time to Nathan, so he has been on his own more than a little. Maybe that explains what my Khave once told me—she, of course, knows Golda better than anyone else in the family—about the cats. I can't believe he would kill them. He must have found them dead. Every day I see them in the street after a car has hit them. At least, I hope he found them.

But I do believe that he would cut them up—to study them. This is not the studying I know, and it can turn your stomach, but he was a child then with a child's sense.

And now he is a young man with a good "future," as they say, who seems normal, with a sense of humor (more in this like his father than his mother). He spoke Yiddish with me and English with the boys. But once, when he got excited, he suddenly changed to Spanish and no one understood a word. From this we all laughed.

Except he used it, the Spanish is not such a surprise. It has been two years that he left America for medical school. Of course, I don't understand this language, but it seems to me that Dovid has done better with it in two years than I have done with English in fifty.

When he left, Rivke gave him a package of apple cake for Nathan then pressed a couple dollars into his hand and, in whatever language, would not hear of refusing.

NOVEMBER 8, 1955

The doctor was here today. For me, for a change. They all insisted, so Max called the one he uses—a Doctor Lazlow. Why? Because I am having a little trouble walking these days more than maybe a mile. Younger men I know couldn't take more than two or three blocks. From the house to the elevated, that's it.

Until the last year or so, even my grandsons, Allan and Jerry, had a hard time keeping up with me. We would come home together from shul and I'd call to them over my shoulder, *"Gikher! Gikher!"*[1] They were amused that their zeyde could still outwalk them.

But I must have complained lately once too often—maybe just once was too often—complaining after all isn't in my nature—and Rivke is in charge of complaints in this house anyway (not altogether without reason). So the doctor was here.

First, he wants to know how old I am. I shrug the shoulders.

He figures it out: "You were born the year the red cow had the white calf."

He laughs. Max, who is also in the room, laughs. I laugh. It's true, no one had a birth paper in the old country. Who needed one? You came into the world, and *mazl tov*![2] Maybe the Russians wanted to know your age to draft you into the czar's army, but whenever they came for you, you were always old enough for them. And, to tell the truth, they were much more interested in a Jew's death than in his birth.

Meanwhile, the doctor is examining. And giving orders: "Breathe in. Breathe out. Don't breathe."

"Your lungs are clear," he says. "The heart and blood pressure so-so but not too bad." And he puts his tools away.

"So, what's wrong with him," Max asks when all the poking and pressing is done.

This time Lazlow shrugs.

So I tell him the answer: "Old feet."

The doctor laughs and nods. Max pays him. He packs his bag, wishes me good health, and says goodbye to Rivke on the way out.

"He seems like a fine man," I say to Max. "He speaks a good Yiddish too. But if you were paying for an opinion, you should have given me the five dollars."

When Max left and Rivke slept a while, I took a walk. If my feet hurt I will complain only to the Master of the Universe. His is a large and willing ear, and besides only He can do anything about it.

JUNE 17,1956

L ate this afternoon, Ari walked past on the other side of the street. He did not look across at me sitting by the window as usual. Dressed up he was with the hair just so. A *meydl*[1] he must have somewhere. And most likely he was going to the bus stop—hours before Shabes ended. Why didn't he go around the block the other way? He must want me to know.

I know. He was not in shul this morning. These days he doesn't come so often. Not like when he was little or even through the year after bar mitsve. It hurts me, but I can do nothing. Essie can do nothing. True, he is not yet a man, but he is not a child either.

I cannot believe he does this to hurt me. Maybe, though not a child, he has not yet learned to pretend or lie or hide to spare someone's feelings. I could wish he wasn't so honest. Yet he is a good boy, even a good Jew—if not as frum as he should be. But if Ari, the most gentle, the brightest, maybe my best pupil—then what can you expect from the others?

They are still killing the Jews. Hitler's way was only one way. Amerike. Amerike. A blessing and a curse.

NOVEMBER 20, 1956

K have grows worse. She gets out of bed only to feed the children, and not even then sometimes. Her sisters make sure that there is something for Yoyne and Malke's supper and for Zelig when he comes from the job.

Zelig is a hard worker, but a plain man, a simple man, and he is beginning to lose patience. But yelling doesn't help. To be honest, Reyzl and Essie have done their share as well. Khave just turns her face to the wall.

I don't know what to do except pray for her recovery. I have not given up hope, but the prayers seem to do me more good than her. It is the same for Zelig, I think, who goes to shul morning and evening if his work lets him.

It is hardest on the children. Yoyne is becoming nervous. He can't sit still more than a minute. Malke doesn't stop eating. All I can do is ask them how they are and about their mother's health. Their aunts give what comfort they can. Of all this, Rivke knows nothing. But because Khave has come over so little in the past few weeks, we have told her mother that she is having trouble with veins in a leg and the doctor says she should stay off her feet for a while.

But it isn't a doctor for the veins or the feet she gets dragged to. It is a doctor for the nerves. Whatever he tells her and whatever pills he gives her don't help either. Soon, if there's no change, they will give her a special treatment with a machine maybe—who knows—or maybe put her in a hospital, also special.

In all the misery of the last two months, there has been one good thing—how Essie cares for her sister. For now, at least, it doesn't matter who has how much or who has more or better. Essie does a little shopping for Khave, a little cooking, shleps her to the doctor whether she wants to go or not. This is as it should be, a fine thing. Yet there is something to be said for old quarreling. At least then Khave was herself.

APRIL 11, 1957

As usual in the afternoon, I sit at the front window, reading. Today it is not the portion for the week, but since it will be Pesakh next week, the story of our people in Egypt. It is not so warm, but there is sun, so I open the window a few inches for a little air.

Outside, the women gather on the stoop, talking for a while between taking care of the children after school and before making supper. They speak about the shvartses[1] moving in—a favorite subject these days.

"Friedman," someone says, "is the latest to sell to them."

So that starts it.

"Where will it end?"

"Who needs them, with their wild music and parties till all hours!"

"And such language!"

"Better hide whatever jewelry and the little money, buy extra locks, and sleep with one eye open."

With such a noise I cannot read. So I lift my head and see across the street a new neighbor with some of the smaller children gathered around her. I raise the window a few inches more.

"It's so terrible," I say, "that Mrs. Kimball—I think is her name—reads a story to the little ones?"

Then comes a murmur like against Moyshe Rabeynu—not to compare.

So I say again, "They are people too."

Soon it is quiet enough. I close the window to keep out the chill and go back to the book. Not that I need to find out how the chapter ends. Haven't I read it maybe a thousand times before? With His help and our own strength we will once again manage to leave Egypt in spite of Pharaoh's nine no's and half a yes. I read it not so much to remember, but more I should not forget.

OCTOBER 20, 1957

Today it was lively in the house. Asher and Leye came, together with their Elke and her husband and the boy, Ira. I have seen him already five or six times. A pretty child. Essie and Khave were also there and Allan with Jerry for a while. With Avrom, Ruth, and their Sheldon the house was *take* full. Krumbein was not there, and not Max to argue with Asher, so I thought there would be peace. But no.

The two boys, Ira and Sheldon, they are about the same age, were playing checkers—not such a bad game. Mr. Geller from across the street plays all the time on his stoop. A quiet game. Except, first of all, Sheldon is not quiet. He is not like his father or his cousin Arnie, walking up and down and talking without a stop. No, he yells and runs and jumps—from the bed to the table, from the table to the chair—if you let. And his mother lets. When he came today, I was sitting in the window, and saw that before Avrom stopped the car he already jumped out to Allan and Jerry on the sidewalk. But instead of making him quiet, the two of them put him in a tree where he went swinging in the branches until Avrom pulled him down by a leg. So he was wild already before he came inside.

The checkers were supposed to calm him down. And if the boys played by themselves maybe it would have. But each of them, thank God, has a father. And the fathers, each one bragging how smart his son is, made from a game a battle. If a child moved a checker to not such a good place, the father would howl "oy!" If the other jumped over only one when he should have jumped over two, this father would shout "gevalt!" Between the two of them, Avrom and Neil made more noise than a dozen Sheldons. Worse yet, to the yelling they added a "dope" and a "dummy"—you wouldn't know ten minutes ago they both had geniuses—and finally a poke and smack to the head like a melamed in a bad kheyder. By the time they stopped—they never finished the game—both children were crying and the bigger children, their fathers, were sweating and red in the face.

All this noise even Rivke heard, so she sent the little ones out for a half hour to play in front of the house. Avrom and Neil did not go, but watched them from the window, once in a while shaking a head or making a face, about what I didn't want to know.

I am not such a one for playing. I don't even play checkers like Geller. And cards altogether I don't know. But a child must sometimes play, and like a child, not like a grown person. How many did I see ruined in the sweatshops, not just by the misery of the work but because such work did not leave time and strength for the head and neshome to prosper, and not even the flesh itself. With God's help, I was mostly able to spare my own.

But with Avrom and Neil they were more interested in the winning than the playing. The winning is fine, good. But there is more than this in the playing and more in the living too. But go tell this to my son the property salesman or almost anyone else. It is not such a popular idea in this country where everything, even in peacetime, is a war—Democrats with Republicans, workers with bosses, tenants with landlords. There is a reason Macy's doesn't tell Gimbels,[1] but what would be so terrible if they did?

I do not live in another world altogether. I understand something about the competition and the "getting ahead." I also understand that to be a mentsh a person cannot give his whole life to such things. Once, when Ruven was in college, he showed me in a book a sentence, "The child is the father of the man."[2] This, I thought was *gut gezogt*[3] because, after all, how does one become a man without being a child first, and because what the child will learn the man will know. But what a child and a man should know (beside from the books) must be how to get along with another person, how to have a little amusement sometimes, and not how to grab right away for the throat.

OCTOBER 16, 1958

It seems I have taught my last pupil. Essie's Cheryl will go to the kheyder beginning next week.

Not that I didn't teach her anything. The alef-beyz she knows and the sounds[1] and can read a little in the *sider*. But sometimes in the middle of the half hour lesson I have fallen asleep, once or twice lost my place so the child couldn't understand. Who can learn like this? And it's not so good for the child to see her zeyde look helpless and foolish. Not so good for the zeyde either.

At kheyder she will do well. The rabbi's wife is good with the children and Cheryl is a bright child. Smart enough to ride a bicycle behind Essie's back, even if Essie tells her "No, you can get hurt." But children must play, and what isn't dangerous? She could maybe cut her hand on the creases and pleats of every blouse and dress, her mother puts so much starch.

Sheyndele[2] is my last pupil and I think my youngest grandchild. Sheldon Avrom's is about the same age—they are months apart— but him I see just three or four times a year. And after Allan and Jerry there was only Essie's Michael, who had his bar mitsve just when I started with Cheryl. Sheldon's sister—Dina—Diana—was also a-once-in-a-whiler, and Khave's Merle went to the yeshive for girls. From the neighborhood for the last few years I had maybe five or six and not all at the same time. Their fifty cents or dollar a week maybe paid for the leather soles I wore out going from house to house. But it was something good to do—except for the little money almost a mitsve.

It is a strange thing, but over the twenty-five years I don't remember many of them well. Those who lived on the street or around the corner, yes, especially if they come back to visit their bobes and zeydes. But of the others only two. One of them, the Schoenfeld boy, serious, the mind of a scholar. Together with Allan my best pupil. Maybe better than Allan. How can a grandfather judge between his own and a stranger? The other, Daniel Birnbaum, not such a good student, but dead not more than a year past bar mitsve. An accident. Playing ball. His father, a foot doctor, almost lost the practice from grief. And Mrs. Birnbaum was never the same, hardly spoke a word to anyone after, but sometimes talked to herself staring straight ahead as she walked.

From such a tsore I know. My Reyzl lost a baby. Asher's Leye the same. And a lifetime ago, Rivke and I lost our eldest, little Gitl, two years old.[3] Now, it doesn't hurt so much--only when it happens again to someone else, or if I see a little one that reminds me, the scar on the heart seems to throb by itself. But in our family, the women were young and had other small ones or could have. By Mrs. Birnbaum, the boy was her youngest, the only son, and there would be no others.

But I was writing about Sheyndele. Where does Mrs. Birnbaum come into it? Maybe this is why the child is going to kheyder. An old man forgets—what he's doing, where he's going, what he's saying. These days if I go to the druggist for aspirin and magnesia, I'm sure to come home with only one. The same in the bakery. The rolls I remember but not the sponge cake. So more and more

I hear Rivke's blessing: "Forgot? May you forget to breathe!" Well, that will not be so long either.

But again I've lost my place. Sheyndele. When she was maybe two, I picked her up, such a little *kneydl*[4] that she was, and kissed her. The child made a face and a noise and shook her head from side to side. When Max asked her what was the matter, she looked straight at me, touched my beard, and said "Feathers." Even Rivke laughed.

So now at four in the afternoon there will be nothing to interrupt my nap except for Rivke kvetshing. If I doze as I sit by the window studying, or as I listen to the radio with the newspaper in my hand, I can sleep on until it is time for shul—if I wake up and remember—or, if not, practice, I tell myself, for the great sleep to come. After all, I wouldn't want to do it badly.

NOVEMBER 3, 1958

Reyzl is moving away. To Flatbush somewhere. Who can blame her? After they took away her Gitl,[1] for three years she lived in the projects. In the beginning it was fine. New. Clean. But soon it was with writing on the walls, in the halls urine, and worse. The delicatessen went out. To find a kosher butcher was five or six blocks. And not so safe. Breaking into the apartments. Stealing the pocket books by the women. Got tsu danken, not by her. Already for a year she did not go out at night.

Rivke and I have missed her Erev Shabes when the whole family in the neighborhood is here. Of course, to tell the truth, lately not everyone comes. Khave misses one week, Asher or Essie another. Not like it used to be. But we are not yet alone altogether.

Still, when Reyzl moves, how often will we see her at all? Shabes afternoon she comes and two or three times during the week. But after? Maybe on a Sunday, and maybe not every Sunday. So she'll say hello on the telephone for two minutes—more Krumbein won't let her and Rivke can hardly hear—but a voice from a machine is not a person.

Rivke and I have been lucky to have all our lives most of our children nearby. The four of them in the neighborhood and Avrom now just twenty minutes from us with the car. Only Ruven is far away. And Gitl. I look across the street and see Mr. and Mrs. Kaplan who get a visit maybe once a month from the Long Island daughters, maybe twice a year from the son in Philadelphia (more often Rivke's sisters used to come from Baltimore), once in two years from his brother, the professor, in California. Why not, already, in *yenem velt*?[2] Mr. Dashevsky even worse. From his son, a doctor, he has nakhes. Also postal cards—from Eastern Parkway.[3] When his father is sick, he makes a house call.

So Rivke and I should not complain. We are not happy that Reyzl is moving—Rivke, in fact, has been moaning for two days. But for Reyzl it is the best thing. Still, I wonder which of them will leave next. To know that everything changes you don't need to be King Solomon; to make peace with changes and survive—for this you need strength to be wise.

FEBRUARY 7, 1959[1]

Yesterday . . . this morning, maybe . . . I went across from the shul because the milk. Rivke was sick so she had to have. I went by Sherman after the car horns were too loud. A quart Sheffield I told him. After all, a sick woman. But he didn't and said I should wait and sit on the box. But then he came. . . My Essie's husband . . . Motke? Meyer? A son-in-law, yes? Max. So he said, "Papa, why are you in the grocery on Shabes?"

I told him, "So, what's wrong with that?" And he said, "Papa, it's Shabes. You never go into a store on Shabes. You always go to shul."

I told him, "Your mother needs a quart milk, so I went to daven by Sherman. Across the street in the shul they don't have Sheffield's."

He walked home with me. Rivke was making Postum from the kettle she leaves on the asbestos once a week. She was putting milk and sugar. "You see, Mordke,"[2] I said, "Sherman delivered already. And sugar I didn't even know we were out."

I found my writing book and went in to hear the news on the radio. Rivke and the boy remained in the kitchen. He was telling her about the shopping. I couldn't hear exactly—except for Rivke's "oy" and "oy" once again. What was the matter this time? Didn't she have her milk—and the sugar into the bargain? But a sick woman will complain. You must be patient.

When the radio warmed up, there was no hum or whistle, the sound altogether clear.

APRIL 26, 1959

For the first time since Rivke came to America we have not had our own Seder. Neither of us had the strength. She hardly cooks as it is, hardly gets out of bed most days. And I? It's four or five years since I made my own wine—let Schapiro[1] do it. And if my legs would let me run all over to find the best horseradish, my hand and arm would not let me grate it. It is time to let go a little, to let others begin to take over. It is time, to tell the truth, to die.

Foolishly, I said this out loud a while ago. Did I hear it then! What are you saying! There are things to look forward to! You'll have nakhes from the grandchildren! So, I agreed with them—for the sake of peace. But I was—I am—right.

I have lived my life. I have seen my children married, have seen grandchildren--and some of them married—have seen even great-grandchildren. I have worked, I have studied, I have taught, I have prayed; I have suffered, I have known joy. I have witnessed the destruction of our people and the hope for our renewal in Israel. I have had the great adventure of crossing the ocean. What is there to keep me? Another bris, another funeral—do I need to go to any more than my own?

My health fails. I grow forgetful. I will not improve, and if the common destiny approaches, let it rather be swift than slow. But as the saying goes, it is as hard to die as to be born.

So this year the Seders were at Khave's. Her Zelig, of course, insisted I should lead them. When I recited the Kidesh, my hand trembled, and with the notes caught in my throat it sounded more like a moan than a blessing. Later, still not in the yontif spirit, I mentioned that I probably wouldn't be here next year. "Taking a trip?" Allan asked. At this we all laughed. That and the singing changed my mood—but not altogether.

There were not so many at the table this year—with Asher gone to the mountains and Reyzl moved away. But Allan brought his girlfriend—maybe his intended? She is a tall girl and has the look of a *sfard*.[2] Judith? Judith, I think her name is, seems respectful, seemed to enjoy, but except for *omeyn*[3] I didn't hear a Jewish word. Nu? Ari Will have to teach her. Maybe I will last till their wedding. And whether or not, maybe they will have a son to give my name.

OCTOBER 12, 1960[1]

It smells here different. From there . . . with the urine. Not soap exactly. Maybe floor soap. Like a hospital. Years ago I went to see Borukh in Montefiore. And so white. She. . . my. . . my. . . is here too. Somewhere. With the women. Far away. Who can see her? The wall is white. A young woman . . . Essie . . . brought me French toast. Last week. In the summer. The bed is white. My glasses. I don't know where. My teeth. The sheet is white. Soon those people are coming. A small village near Minsk. They wash the shame of my bowels. Leave me naked. White . . . White. . . my shroud.

JULY 25, 1996

We lie here quietly, my Rivke and I. Done . . . all breathing, all falling away of flesh. Bones only . . . and a new, clear vision. Above us, of us, in truth, a low shrub, dark green, trimmed to the edge of our footstones. Sometimes a child—a grandchild—comes, says prayers for our souls, reads maybe a psalm, talks to us even (such a foolishness), and puts a pebble on the stones.[1] Rivke does not complain about a tumult. A changed woman altogether.

Quietly, but not at peace. A grave, after all, is not Eden. There, I have seen the face of God. But here, the memory of my brothers left behind and our millions murdered churns forever through this endless sleep. And who knows how or whether Israel will live on? Grandchildren—some childless themselves—some gone to strangers, my generations soon end, the blood running thin through an alien land.

APPENDIX A

THE ETHICAL WILL OF SOLOMON KAHN

I, your father, wish you many good, long years of life, and together with your mother, wish that we could still live on and be with you. But no one lives forever. We all must leave this foolish world—and even those we love. And so I come to write, dear children, hoping that you all may live more than a hundred years[1] and bring to the new world the light of your souls and the good deeds of your hearts, and heads, and hands.

For myself and for your mother, who has helped me throughout my life, I thank God that we have been together until old age, and I pray that we may not be parted for as long as we live. When God wills that we have both lived out our years, I believe it is best that we travel on together. But everything is in His hand, and whatever He does will be good.

So, my dear children, in case I go first, I ask that you do not abandon your mother, but make her happy always and do all for her that must be done. Remember that a sickly person is always easily upset.

You should not worry about what I write here,[2] for a person does not know what may happen to him. One is not certain until death. But something may still be said to those who live on, and it is best that what I think of saying be written down.

First, you will find a bank book here in the envelope, with money in a New York bank.[3] This you will have for a monument. You should know to give in my memory a few dollars to the Shames and ten to the shul, and to the yeshive[4] where Ruven studied according to your understanding.

And I ask, children, that you live in peace all of your life, and ask again that when you accompany me for the last time,[5] you do not quarrel about money, whether this one should give or that. But whoever has more should give more.

I ask you also to give my clothes away to the poor and to sell none of them. Remember that the shul must provide a minyen for a whole week. I owe no dues up to now, except for one quarter, and when I pay for that quarter I will owe nothing. According to the rules, *Mishnayes*[6] must be studied. I have a book of the rules that you will find in the drawer with the receipts. My books should be given to a yeshive, but those that you need and can use you may take for yourselves.

And so, of such things I will write nothing more. In the meantime, let us all be well, and all will be for the best.

Yet, be sure to walk in the well-trodden way of our Toyre. Your God will give you long life, and you will live to have great-grandchildren, as I have.[7] For I have not strayed from the Toyre or from the commandments of God. And I am very happy with my life and with all that I have done. God has helped me live to see what I have asked of Him, and I hope that in the future He will also hear me and answer my plea. Therefore, dear children, obey me: If you would live long, walk the road I have walked.

I thank you very much for all the honor you have given me, and your mother thanks you the same. But if you also honor God you will make us very happy.[8] May I live still to see you righteous Jews before God and men. From me, your father, who wishes you long life and happiness.

Sholem Kahn

To this your mother says omeyn.

Rivke Kahn[9]

16 Sh'vat 5696[10]

APPENDIX B

THE KAHN FAMILY: NAMES AND RELATIONSHIPS

The entries below are arranged in generational sequence and include, primarily, those people mentioned by name in the text. If both English and Hebrew (or Yiddish) personal names appear in the journal, they occur here as well, separated by a virgule. Names that are known but not found in the text, all but one in a second language, appear in brackets, as do question marks indicating that names are unknown.

Information regarding bracketed names has been gleaned from diverse sources. These range from interviews with the late Claire Wexler, the late Abraham Kahn, and the surviving grandchildren of Solomon Kahn to perusal of documents such as preserved invitation lists for weddings and bar mitzvahs.

Arrangement of items in section III reflects birth order. Although some of the family bore or bear middle names, particularly in the third generation, they are omitted here as inessential for purposes of identification in the text. In three instances, the names of the husbands of Rivke Kahn's sisters, so far as they are known, have been provided to complete the "family portrait."

I. Ancestral Generation

Esther Elbaum. Mother of Rivke Kahn.

II. Generation of Solomon/Sholem Kahn— Rivke Elbaum Kahn

A. Solomon Kahn's Brothers and Their Spouses[1]

Borukh Kahn—Dina [?]

Eliezer Kahn—Sorke [?]

Khaim Kahn—Tsaytl/Therese Elbaum

Menakhem Mendl Kagan— [marital status unknown]

Naftali Kagan [spouse's name unknown]

Yisroel Kahn—Miriam [Futterman]

Zalmen Kagan—Gitl [?]

B. Rivke Kahn's Sisters and Their Spouses

Brayne Elbaum—Velvl Weinstock

Freydl/[Frieda] Elbaum—[Morris Bienenfeld][2]

Hinde Elbaum [Motl Gorelik]

Rokhl Elbaum—[Benjamin/Binyomen ?][3]

Tsaytl/Therese Elbaum—Khaim Kahn

C. Cousin

Big Reyzl [?], cousin of Rivke Kahn[4]

III. Children of Solomon and Rivke Kahn with Their Spouses and Offspring

Gitl Kahn. d. in infancy or early childhood

Reyzl/Rose Kahn—[Gershon] Krumbein

Arnie [Arnold/Alter] Krumbein—Iris [Nadler]

Marcy/Mindl Krumbein—Joe/[Yosel Lapinsky]

unnamed female child

unnamed male child (stillborn)

Norman/Nokhem Krumbein

Asher Kahn—Leye [Leah] Blank

Ellen/Elke Kahn—Neil/Nokhem [Shechter]

Ira /[Yakov] [Shechter]

Phyllis/[Feyge] Kahn

unnamed male child (d. shortly after birth)

Ruven /[Reuben] Kahn—Golda [Hirshkovitz]

Dovid/[David] Kahn

Nathan/[Naftali] Kahn

Esther (Essie) Kahn—Max [Moyshe] Rothstein

Allan/Ari [Arye Leyb] Rothstein

Michael/[Menakhem Mendl] Rothstein

Cheryl/Sheyndel(e)[5] Rothstein

Khave/Claire Kahn—Zelig Wexler

Jerry [Jerome]/Yoyne Wexler

Merle/Malke Wexler

Avrom/[Abraham] Kahn—Ruth [Chernoff]

Diana/[Dina] Kahn

Sheldon/[Shmuel] Kahn

IV. Additional Relative

Tsipora [?][6], Solomon Kahn's grandniece, granddaughter of his eldest brother, Naftali.

GLOSSARY

A sheynem dank. Thank you very much.

Alef-beyz. The Hebrew and Yiddish alphabet.

Allrightnik. One who has achieved material success, especially a formerly poor Jewish immigrant.

Azoy. So; in this manner. Often used as an exclamation expressing attitudes as varied as disbelief and disapproval.

Baleboste. Housewife; literally, mistress of the house.

Bris. Circumcision.

Bobe(s). Grandmother(s).

Daven. Pray.

Daytsher. Germans; German (adj.). In Kahn's usage, the term refers to German Jews.

Erev Shabes. Sabbath eve.

Farputsen. To decorate; ornament; deck (oneself) out (probably to excess).

Fe. Ugh! Yuck! Fie! An expression of disgust or disapproval.

Freser. A glutton.

Frum/e (adv. and adj.). Devout; pious; observant.

Gan Eydn. the Garden of Eden; paradise.

Geshmak. Tasty; delicious.

Gevalt (interj.). An expression (often preceded by *oy*) that indicates reactions ranging from surprise to shock to dismay to horror, depending on circumstances.

Goy(im). Gentile(s).

Goylem. In Jewish lore, a clay figure created and given (servile) life; particularly, the golem reputedly created by Rabbi Loew of Prague in the sixteenth century.

Haman's name. The name of Haman, thwarted enemy of the Jews, is customarily drowned out by noisemakers, the stomping of feet, etc., during the public reading of the Book of Esther on the festival of Purim.

Hatikvah. The Zionist anthem; now, the national anthem of Israel.

Heymish/e. Homey; down to earth; homespun.

Kadish. The prayer affirming faith recited by mourners, Also, metaphorically, a son (i. e., one who will eventually say the Kadish).

Khale. A braided bread served on the Sabbath and major holidays.

Khazn. Cantor.

Kheyder. School, particularly a Hebrew religious school.

Khumesh. The five books of Moses collectively; a volume containing these books.

Kidesh. The blessings of sanctification recited over wine.

Kugl. A pudding made, most typically, of potatoes or noodles.

Kvel[ing]. Swell[ing] with joy, delight, or pride.

Kvetsh (v. and n.) Complain; complaint

Lantsman. Countryman; a person from one's place of origin.

Latke(s). Pancake(s).

Mayriv. The evening service.

Machine. Automobile (in cases where the word does not bear its usual meaning).

Mameloshn. Mother tongue; often a synonym for Yiddish specifically.

Matse. Unleavened bread required to be eaten during Passover but available year-round.

Melamed. A teacher of Hebrew and Jewish studies, especially one in a Hebrew religious school.

Mentsh. Human being; person. (Used honorifically as well as descriptively.)

Mentshlikhkayt. Humanity; humane behavior.

Meshiekh. Messiah.

Meshugas. Literally and figuratively, madness; foible(s).

Meshugener. Literally and figuratively, an insane person.

Minkhe. The afternoon service.

Minyen. Quorum of ten required to hold a communal service; the congregation so constituted.

Mitsve. Good deed; one of the 613 commandments that Jews are obliged to fulfill.

Mizrakhi. Organization of religious Zionists.

Monday and Thursday. Proverbial for regularity, since these are days on which the Torah is always read.

Moyshe Rabeynu. Our teacher Moses.

Nakhes. Joy; delight; parental pride.

Neshome. Soul; spirit.

Nu. Well; so.

Nuhdzh (n.). Prod.

Nuhdzhen (v.). Prod; pester; urge repeatedly to the point of annoyance.

Omeyn. Amen.

Patsh. Slap; smack.

Pesakh. Passover.

Postum. Trade name for a cereal product made to be mixed with hot water and served as a coffee substitute.

Purimshpil. A Purim play.

Pushke(s). Charity box(es).

Reb. Mister.

Seder. The home service for Passover; literally, order.

Shabes. Sabbath.

Shames. Beadle; sexton.

Shande. Shame; disgrace; embarrassment.

Shive. Seven-day period of mourning immediately following interment.

Shlep (v.). To drag; (n.) a long, tedious, difficult journey.

Shoymer Shabes. Guardian of the Sabbath; Sabbath observant.

Shul. Synagogue.

Sider. Prayer book.

Simkhe. Joyous occasion; celebration.

Take. Really; truly; in fact.

Taleyner. (contracted form of *Italyeyner*). Italian (n.).

Tokhes. Buttocks; behind.

Toyre. Torah.

Treyf/Treyfe (adj.) Not kosher; ritually impure.

Tsatske. Bauble; plaything; nicknack. Also used in sarcastic deprecation of people.

Tsholent. A thick stew made of meat, potatoes, beans and other vegetables, usually slow-cooked over many hours.

Tsimes. A fruit or vegetable stew. Metaphorically, a fuss or row.

Tsore(s). Trouble(s); woe(s); problem(s).

Yarmulke. Skull cap.

Yeshive. A school devoted to Jewish education. The term may be applied to everything from an orthodox elementary day school to a rabbinical or Talmudic academy. At lower levels, secular subjects are also taught.

Yeytser hore. Evil inclination.

Yid(den). Jew(s).

Yontif (pl. yontoyvim). Holiday; literally, a Jewish holy day but sometimes used less restrictively and humorously by SK.

Yortsayt. Anniversary of death.

Zeyde. Grandfather.

NOTES

Preface

[1]*Mentshlikhkayt*. Humanity; humane behavior.

[2]*Essie, for his daughter Esther, might be another, perhaps influenced by English usage.* It is clear from the entry for October 16, 1906 that the unborn child, if a girl, would be named Esther, and so she is referred to in several entries, especially early on. But far more often SK uses "Essie," which is itself possible as a Jewish given name.

November 8, 1904

[1]*Battery Park*. Terminus for the Ellis Island ferry. Those meeting new-comers might have done so on the island itself. Why SK had not exercised this option is not clear.

[2]*Tule, oy Tate*. Papa, oh, Papa.

[3]*Machines*. Automobiles. In later entries SK uses both this word and the transliterated "car."

[4]*By the streetcars . . . horse car*. Manhattan had various forms of surface transportation at this time. The Kahn family seems startled by a street railway run by electricity from a third rail. As SK states, the cars from the Battery to the Lower East Side were still horse drawn.

[5]Kahn uses the Yiddish word *klozet*, as in "water closet." Whether Rivke would have recognized the term, however, is problematic since indoor plumbing was a rarity in Russia at this early date. It is quite possible that SK himself learned the word (and became familiar with its referent) only after his own arrival in the United States.

[6]The Kahn's apartment appears to be in a dumbbell tenement, so called because of its shape since such buildings, all constructed after 1879, were narrowed in their middles to allow for air shafts. Typically, apartments

consisted of three rooms each, four units to a floor of a structure that might be as many as seven stories high. However, some of these tenements were apparently built with four-room apartments at the front of the building and three-room apartments at the rear. Facing the street, the four-room would have received more light than the three, particularly since existing law required only ten feet of open space at the back of a building. Apartment size ranged from 300 to 400 square feet.

Dumbbells were hazardous. Staircases and fire escapes were flimsy, the latter often blocked by items stored there by tenants. In addition, garbage and other debris tossed down the air shafts became breeding grounds for vermin and disease. And absent these, the air was fetid in any case.

Structures of this type were an intermediate (if unsuccessful) alternative to still older tenements, in which living conditions were even more primitive—no indoor plumbing, for example—and "new law" tenements, built after 1901, in which such improvements as private toilets were mandated. Under the new law, however, older buildings were required to undergo a number of improvements, but compliance and enforcement were uneven at best. The Kahn apartment, for example, has running water for washing and cooking but shares a hall toilet with other tenants.

(For floor plans of dumbbell tenements and a more extensive description see Moses Rischin, *The Promised City: New York's Jews 1875-1914*. Rev. ed. Cambridge: Harvard University Press, 1977, 81-83ff.) Floor plans are also available online.

On the whole, the Kahn family seems better off at this time than many other Lower East Side residents who might have had more people living in the same amount of space. Crowding for the Kahns increased, however, as the family grew.

[7]*When they need to paint . . . move*. In times when the housing supply exceeded demand, this became, in fact, a convenient and, therefore, common practice. It was far less common, however, in SK's densely populated Lower East Side than (somewhat later) in developing neighborhoods of the outer boroughs.

October 16, 1906

[1]*Kadish*. The prayer affirming faith recited by mourners during the eleven months following burial; also, colloquially, a son (i.e., one who will

eventually say the Kadish). In orthodox tradition, reciting the prayer is an obligation of specific adult male relatives only. In the absence of suitable male relatives, a man would be hired by the family (or might volunteer) to say the prayer during the period of mourning. The late Esther Elbaum had only daughters in America. Her husband is presumably dead, her son, either dead or in Europe and beyond immediate reach.

[2]*Shive*. Seven-day period of mourning immediately following interment.

[3]*Shul*. Synagogue.

[4]*Bobe*. Grandmother.

[5]*Low stool*. Mourners are traditionally required to forego all creature comfort during the shiva period and therefore sit on low stools or benches. SK's dispensation is in accord with approved practice of abrogating rules and commandments in order to preserve life or health.

[6]Ashkenazi Jews traditionally name newborns after deceased relatives.

April 4, 1910

[1]*Policemen*. These, very likely, were the local sheriff and/or his deputies. At this early date, at least, SK is not aware of distinctions among law enforcement officials.

[2]*Society*. During the great wave of immigration, several organizations attempted to settle Jews on the land, either in cooperatives or (while providing some financial assistance) on individually owned farms. SK's situation appears to have been the latter.

[3]*Ha-Novi*. The prophet.

[4]*Shlep*. A long (difficult) distance; a long haul.

[5]*Davening on Shabes*. Praying (davening) on the Sabbath (Shabes [Heb. Shabat]). As an orthodox Jew, SK would have regarded a mile's walk as a violation of the Sabbath and on that day, therefore, would have prayed at home. Nevertheless, his complaint and subsequent remark concerning study imply his recognition of the communal nature of Jewish religious life.

Davening is an example of words in the translated text that conflate a Yiddish word with English *ing*. As noted in the Preface, such constructions were common among bilingual English/Yiddish speakers in the generation following SK's. (Kahn's text, however, consistently uses the appropriate Yiddish word, *davnen* in this instance.) Cf. *kveling* in the entry for June 29, 1930 and *farputsing* in the entry for June 19, 1933. The text occasionally includes other hybrid forms as well,

[6]*Minyen*. Quorum of ten required to hold a communal service; the congregation so constituted. Orthodoxy requires that the ten be male.

March 27, 1911

[1]*Cloud of the Lord*. A reference to the cloud concealing God that hovered over the tent of meeting during the period of Israel's desert wandering. See Exodus 40:34-38.

[2]*So many ways to die*. In this and subsequent paragraphs, SK's account of the Triangle Waist Company fire of March 25, 1911 is generally accurate. Ultimately, the fire claimed 146 victims, overwhelmingly women and girls, as described. Firefighting equipment of the day was inadequate to deal with fires so far above street level. The company occupied space on the eighth, ninth, and tenth floors of the Asch building, just off Washington Square.

The disaster prompted a great public outcry that led, eventually, to reform both of regulations and their administration. Triangle had, in fact, been in substantial compliance with the weak fire and safety codes of the day. However, that a door leading to one of two staircases was inappropriately locked at the time of the fire is a near certainty. More than a year earlier, organized workers had won from manufacturers safety code concessions that would have saved lives had Triangle subscribed to them.

David van Drehle provides an excellent account of the event and its aftermath in *Triangle: The Fire that Changed America* (New York: Atlantic Monthly Press, 2003). An earlier work that incorporates a number of interviews with survivors, is Leon Stein's, *The Triangle Fire* (Philadelphia: Lippincott, 1962).

[3]*Rivke. . . from Monroe*. Rivke Kahn's information seems to be accurate. *The New York Times* of March 27 reported the deaths of Esther Goldstein and Annie Novobritsky, giving their address as 143 Madison Street. The casualty list for that date also includes Fannie Lansner of 78 Forsythe Street and Ethel Schneider of 95 Monroe Street. Victims living at higher

numbered addresses on Monroe, Madison, and Henry Streets are also included. However, given that word of mouth information is likely to remain quite local in the short run, it is probable that Rivke Kahn's informants lived rather close to the four victims SK mentions. Given this assumption, it is possible to approximate SK's address at the time. He was likely living in an area bounded by East Broadway, and Catherine, South, and Pike Streets in the shadow of the Manhattan Bridge. Kahn's late daughter, Claire Wexler, informed Professor Redstone that the family once lived on Monroe Street. A toddler at the time, however, she could not provide the precise address.

Examination of census records for 1910 suggest that the family was missed in the count that began on April 15 and lasted up to thirty days in populous towns and cities. Having moved to Newark only days before the count began, their omission from the Newark census is understandable. And, as is likely, if they did not move to New York until after May15, they would have been omitted from the New York count as well. It is evident, however, that the Kahns' stay in Newark (see entry for April 4, 1910) had been brief.

[4]*Lantsman*. Countryman; a person from one's place of origin. The reference to Brooklyn underscores the fact that the Lower East Side was not the only neighborhood affected. Little Italy, immediately to the west, and points in Manhattan further north also shared the woeful burden.

[5]*Strength . . . in the gates*. SK quotes from Proverbs 31:25, 31. Although the sentiments might seem less than absolutely appropriate at first glance, they are taken from a passage (Proverbs 31:19-31) usually titled "A Woman of Valor" or "A Woman of Worth," one often recited in honor of wives during the home service on Sabbath eve. It serves as well as a generic eulogy for women, hence, perhaps, its association for SK here.

It must be noted that SK makes no reference to Jewish victims having broken the Sabbath by their labor. Generally speaking, his orthodoxy is humane rather than legalistic.

August 24, 1911

[1]*Nu* (interj.). Well; so.

[2]*Oy* (interj.). A flexible term that might indicate anything from surprise to pain, weariness, grief, dismay, and resignation among other possibilities determined by context. Here, Kahn is most likely referring to pain, weariness, and grief, particularly since the journal later shows that Rivke is not generally a well woman and who, at this time, is responsible for homemaking and caring for a family that includes five children.

[3]*At the hospital . . . healing.* The entry sketches the medical care locally available. There is a free clinic in the area (popularly known as the Essex Street Dispensary) and, at the time, Beth Israel Hospital. Although SK appears to use the words for clinic and hospital interchangeably, his reference to Essex Street strongly suggests that the clinic is where the diagnosis and surgery were done. The visiting nurse mentioned might well have been one of the corps established at the Henry Street Settlement by Lillian Wald.

January 30, 1912

[1]*After . . . all the same.* The suggestion is that except for some minimal, cognate vocabulary, speakers of Yiddish and German have no linguistic advantage over other students.

[2]*Mameloshn.* (The) mother tongue. Often a synonym for Yiddish specifically.

[3]*Kheyder.* School, particularly a Hebrew religious school.

[4]*Shande.* Shame; disgrace; embarrassment.

[5]*Kvetsh* (v. and n.). Complain; complaint.

[6]*But for others . . . the writer.* This passage clearly lends credence to the historical basis for such comedies of error as Leonard Q. Ross's (pseud. Leo Rosten) *The Education of Hyman Kaplan.*

April 17, 1912

[1]SK elaborates on this occurrence in the entry for March 6, 1947.

[2]SK alludes to Psalms 90:10: "The days of our years are threescore years

and ten, or even by reason of strength fourscore years; yet is their pride but travail and vanity; for it is speedily gone and we fly away."

[3]*As Koheles. . . striving after wind*. SK quotes from Ecclesiastes. He will later refer to the book in the entries for January 22, 1935 and March 2, 1947. In the earlier of these, he reports reading from it frequently.

A number of sermons given in the aftermath of the event decried at least the materialism that the Titanic symbolized to some, if not the hubris that SK suggests here.

[4]*Another ship . . . life boats*. The Carpathia arrived in New York the following day (the evening of April 18) with more than seven hundred survivors. SK's initial estimate of a thousand deaths was far too low; more than two thirds of the 2,228 aboard had been lost.

[5]*The dead are. . . than from the rich*. At least one eyewitness reports that during the catastrophe there was no preferential treatment given to passengers on the basis of class. Nevertheless, according to figures printed in *The New York Times* on April 19, it is clear that among passengers those in steerage suffered the greatest losses, whether measured in percentages or absolute numbers. Survival rates for first and second-class passengers exceeded sixty percent and forty percent, respectively. The rate for third class (steerage) passengers was approximately twenty-five percent. Only the staff and crew fared slightly worse.

[6]The level of sarcastic skepticism in this entry is puzzling, especially as it is atypical of the journal as a whole.

[7]The name of the ship in Kahn's manuscript is illegible. None of the surviving family knows the name, and researches into Kahn's passage have, to this point, been futile.

May 3, 1914

[1]That payday for SK was a Friday is significant. At the time, a six-day workweek was the rule, making payday Saturday. But in the entry for October 10, 1918 Kahn claims never to have worked on the Sabbath, so either Goldstein is Sabbath observant as well, a rare, but not unheard of, possibility among employers of the day, or that SK has some special arrangement with him that allows for Saturdays off.

[2]*Made Shabes*. Prepared for the Sabbath.

[3]*Pushkes* (sing. *pushke*). Charity boxes.

[4]*On this . . . would agree*. The Torah as well. Lev.19:13 and, more emphatically, Deut. 24:14-15 explicitly forbid employers to withhold payment beyond the completion of the day's work.

[5]*Tsores* (sing. *tsore*). Troubles; woes; problems.

[6]*Mentsh*. Human being; person. (Used honorifically as well as descriptively.)

[7]*Neshome*. Soul; spirit.

September 8, 1914

[1]*Khavele*. Diminuitive of *Khave*, the base form of the name that is used throughout the rest of the entry and the journal as a whole. A diminuitive form also occurs in later entries with regard to Kahn's daughter Gitl, grandson Allan, and granddaughter Cheryl.

[2]While Jewish boys are named at their circumcisions, girls in orthodox Ashkenazic communities are traditionally named in the synagogue shortly after birth, their fathers having first been called to the Torah.

[3]*Toyre*. Torah.

[4]*Changed . . . a veyz to a beyz*. Changed the medial sound from *v* to *b*, rendering in English the name *Reuben*. SK ignores the additional *e* because it does not affect pronunciation. As he invariably does, Kahn spells the Hebrew original correctly; however, pronunciation of the final syllable varies from the *en* used here, to *eyn* and syllabic *n*. Although SK fails to mention it, this name, like *Asher* and *Esther*, is also biblical. All but two of SK's offspring bear biblical names. The exceptions are Reyzl and Gitl (see entry for February 4, 1931) whose names are Yiddish.

[5]*They should. . .either*. Rather surprisingly, SK seems aware that the name Esther is derived from foreign sources. (It has, in fact, Persian and, perhaps, Babylonian origins.) His specific recognition of correspondences between the Torah and the Christian Bible is, at least, equally surprising.

[6]*So from Kagan . . . gentile ears*. Despite appearances and contemporary English pronunciation of the two names, the difference between them

to European ears would have been comparatively slight. In addition, at points of departure, overwhelmingly from northern European seaports, passenger information for the ship's manifest was taken orally by vessel employees who wrote down what they heard, not always accurately, In addition, for various reasons, passengers sometimes took this opportunity to choose new names. See note 7 below for further comment.

[7]SK's statement regarding name changes at Ellis Island is inaccurate. A primary task of Ellis Island officials was to match the names immigrants gave with those on the manifest. That names were changed by immigration officials on arrival is essentially a myth, albeit a popular and often amusing one. Once admitted to the United States, however, immigrants were free to alter their names in the ways Kahn mentions and of which he disapproves, as they connote assimilation, a process he consistently resists.

For a brief account of the name change question that includes references to more elaborate discussion, see Philip Sutton, "Why Your Family Name Was Not Changed at Ellis Island (and One That Was)" available on the New York Public Library website (https://www.nypl.org/blog/2013/07/02/name-changes-ellis-island).

[8]*Daytsher* (n. pl. and adj.). Germans; German. In SK's usage, the noun refers to German Jews.

[9]*One day . . . would also faint.* According to the *Encyclopedia Judaica*, August Belmont senior (1816-1890) had abandoned Judaism by 1872. The reference here is probably to the younger August Belmont (1853-1924). Of course, the family was a prominent one, and Kahn might have easily read or heard about it. Kahn, however, seems unaware of what he would have perceived as the original apostasy but appears to treat whichever Belmont simply as a Jew who changed his name. The *Judaica* adds that the elder Belmont's enemies, accused him, like SK, of having changed his name from "Schoenberg," a reasonably common name among Jews, and of which "Belmont" is an exact French translation.

Research suggests that Benjamin Blumenthal, father of the co-founders of Bloomingdale's department store, had changed his name from Blumenthal to Bloomingdale upon his arrival in the United States in 1838 or shortly thereafter. His eldest son Lyman, one of the store's co-founders, was born in New York in 1841. By 1914, however, Lyman Bloomingdale, sole proprietor since his brother's retirement, had been dead for nearly a decade, having left the business to his sons. But unlike August Belmont, Lyman had been involved with Jewish life, as a member of B'nai B'rith, Jewish fraternal organizations ("lodges"), and treasurer of Temple Beth-El, a congregation that later merged with Temple Emanu-El.

In regard to the name change of these two men and of the practice generally, it is assimilation and, as Kahn sees it, the consequent erosion of faith and tradition, to which he objects.

October 23, 1917

[1]*Goyim* (sing. *goy*). Gentiles.

[2]*Klezmer* (pl. *klezmorim*). Musician.

October 10, 1918

[1]*Freser.* Glutton. SK's metaphor is appropriate since, as the text later asserts, the influenza pandemic of 1918-19 took far more lives than World War I with estimates ranging from half again to nearly three times as many. However, contrary to Kahn's suggestion, those in their prime were more likely to succumb to the disease than the elderly or very young.

[2]*Blood on the doors*. A reference to the lamb's blood smeared on the doorposts of the Israelites in Egypt, just prior to the Exodus, as a sign that their houses were to be passed over and their inhabitants spared from the tenth plague, the death of the firstborn.

[3]*I would tell him . . . have to eat.* SK and Weinstock are engaged in word play. The Jewish surnames *Halber* and *Ganz* (often *Gans)* mean *half* and *goose*, respectively. However, a third term, transliterated as *gants*, and implicit here, means *whole*. Although SK's spelling omits the consonant that would produce the sound of *t*, the context clearly suggests that Weinstock expects SK to recognize the verbal ambiguity since changing one's name to *Goose* is not an appropriate response to the charge of being "a proper Jew" only half the time.

(N.B.: Modern Yiddish spelling of the word for goose would render *gandz* in English transliteration. However, Alexander Harkavy's *English-Yiddish Dictionary* of 1891 gives the same Yiddish spelling as Kahn's.

Although, oddly, his *Yiddish-English Dictionary* of 1889 omits the word, it does translate *gander* in a spelling that transliterates as *genzer* which, while altering the stressed vowel, still does not include either the voiced consonant for *d* or for the unvoiced *t* that is implicit in Kahn's and Weinstock's banter.)

[4]*Bar mitsve*. Literally, "son of the commandment," the term implies the point (age 13) at which a Jewish boy assumes full religious responsibilities. *Bat mitsve* is the equivalent for Jewish girls who might assume such obligations at age 12. The terms for both sexes also refer to the ceremony that marks the rite of passage and the attendant celebration.

[5]*Twelve of us in four rooms will not be easy*. The Kahns have apparently moved from the apartment described in the first entry of the journal. Whether they are in the same tenement, however, is uncertain. While such buildings usually contained three-room apartments exclusively, some had both three-room and four-room units. In any case, the extra room would certainly have meant added expense. (For a more complete description of dumbbell tenement design and living conditions see the entry for November 8, 1904, note 6.)

But poor though they were, the Kahns were not the poorest of the poor. Nowhere in the journal, for example, is there a reference to piece work done at home, whether by adults or young children, as was common in other families, particularly in slightly earlier times. With the aid of an occasional loan, and later with the addition of small contributions from offspring who had entered the work force, the Kahn family scrapes by with SK as its primary provider.

[6]*Sit with the body . . . Psalms*. Traditionally, the deceased is guarded from the time of death until burial to prevent desecration of the corpse. Psalms are recited during the watch to comfort the soul of the departed. If the watch is kept by prospective mourners—official mourning begins with burial—the recitation serves as an affirmation of faith in light of their loss and as a source of comfort to them.

February 28, 1920

[1]*Alte moyd*. Old maid. Women were expected to marry early. But Kahn's daughters remained single into their mid to late twenties.

[2]*Shadkhen*. Marriage broker.

[3]Family survivors attest generally to Reyzl's political activity, reporting that she bore signs, distributed literature, and spoke on street corners for a variety of causes. But the one specific bit of information that they provide is that she was active in Women's American ORT, a Jewish labor and educational organization. This group, however, was not established until 1927. Apparently Reyzl Kahn continued her activity after her marriage, to someone other than Murray Farbstein. See the entry for January 14, 1923.

[4]*Israel*. Here, Kahn refers to the beliefs and practices of the Jewish people collectively, not to the prospective nation state.

[5]*Shoymer Shabes*. Literally, guardian of the Sabbath; i.e., Sabbath observant.

January 14, 1923

[1]*We have. . . would shame us*. SK refers to *tenaim*, a contract specifying conditions for a forthcoming marriage, including such things as the wedding date and financial arrangements, In modern times, the marriage contract was (and is) signed immediately prior to the wedding ceremony, in part to minimize the possibility of either party's refusal to fulfill it.

Marriages, however, can be arranged but not forced. Apparently, Reyzl Kahn did not protest vigorously enough or was simply persuaded to go through with the match. Breaching the contract would have been embarrassing, of course, shameful, as SK sees it. But, on the whole, the generations following his would not have shared his view.

Whether Reyzl is still in love with Murray Farbstein, as noted in the entry for February 28, 1920, is not clear.

[2]SK seems somewhat imprecise in stating his daughter's age. According to the entry for February 28, 1920, she is either twenty-one or twenty-two. Here, three years later, she is past twenty-five. Such imprecision is not unusual, as Reyzl had been born in Russia at a time when record keeping of this sort was likely to have been erratic and of little importance to Jews of SK's class.

Kahn is similarly uncertain about Khave's age in the entry for May 3, 1920, and as the entry for November 8, 1955 shows, he does not know his own birth date.

August 12, 1923

[1]*Erev Shabes*. Sabbath eve.

[2]*Zemires*. Songs, particularly religious hymns sung at home after Sabbath and holiday meals.

[3]*Taleyner*. Italian (n. sing. and pl.). SK regularly uses this contracted form of *Italyeyner*. The word is capitalized throughout the translation to conform to English usage. There are no case distinctions in the Hebrew alphabet with which Yiddish is written.

[4]*Yeytser hore*. Evil inclination.

June 29, 1925

[1]*Monday and Thursday*. Proverbial for regularity, since these are days on which the Torah is always read.

[2]*Frieda Baron*. Apparently, SK's rendering of "Theda Bara," star of silent films but at this point past the peak of her career.

The reference nevertheless illustrates SK's awareness of American popular culture, however imprecise, but particularly as a threat to his values.

[3]*Painted knees*. Applying rouge to the newly exposed knee was a fashion fad of the day.

[4]*Shaytl*. Wig.

[5]*Gemore*. The second portion of the Talmud, consisting primarily of commentary upon rabbinic interpretation of Jewish law as set forth in the first portion or Mishnah.

April 23, 1926

[1]*Shmuts*. Dirt; filth.

[2]*Keap Street*. The Kahns are now living in the Williamsburg section of Brooklyn, immediately across the East River from the Lower East Side. Their stay here appears to have been fairly brief. Street names in subsequent entries together with some descriptions of the neighborhood indicate that the family had moved to Brownsville by the late 1920's.

[3]Although none of Kahn's extant entries deals directly with World War I, this passage clearly suggests that he followed events closely enough to have acquired some of its vocabulary.

October 14, 1926

[1]*Heymishe*. Homey; down to earth.

[2]*Eggplant*. SK's Yiddish text attempts a phonetic spelling of this English word that would be transliterated as *egplent*, suggesting that his unfamiliarity with the food perhaps extends even to his being unaware of the Yiddish word for it, *patlezhan*.

[3]*Posternak*. Parsnip.

[4]*Latkes* (sing. *latke*). Pancakes; specifically, in this instance, potato pancakes.

[5]*Khanike*. Chanukah, the Festival of Lights.

[6]*Forshpays*. Appetizer. SK is describing an eggplant salad or "caviar," common to many Mediterranean and Middle Eastern cuisines.

[7]*Geshmak*. Tasty; delicious. SK's assessment of the adoption of foods by Jews in the Diaspora is essentially accurate.

This entry is one of several that reveal SK's interest in food. Hardly an epicure, he nevertheless experiences eating as a sensual pleasure, especially when consuming something other than his usual diet.

February 27, 1928

[1]*Ikh vel geyn . . . tsuzamen zayn*. I will go through every street, shouting "Doing laundry" [i. e., perform even the most menial labor], as long as I can be with you. The lyrics are SK's take on lines in "Her Nor Du Sheyn Meydele" ("Just Listen, Pretty Girl").

[2]In three entries (August 30, 1922, August 23, 1942, and February 24, 1954), SK refers to Minsk as his place of origin, but Reyzl's reference to "a shtetl near Minsk" in the entry for February 28, 1920 suggests that he came from outside the city proper. In addition, the entry for October 12, 1960, written by Professor Redstone, mentions "a village near Minsk," indicating that the belief that SK did not hail from Minsk itself had some

currency in the Kahn family. And in the present entry, Kahn himself refers to a village, which might not or might be his own.

August 5, 1928

[1]*Shames*. Beadle; sexton.

[2]*Reb Yid*. Literally, "Mister Jew," but best translated as "sir" or "mister." The form is typically used as polite address for a Jewish male whose name is not known. The relative formality of the phrase is at comic odds with Brayne's gestures.

[3]*Beys din*. Rabbinical court.

[4]*A hot woman lies here.* The proposed sign is hardly a concession since, as in its English translation, Brayne's Yiddish sentence is a double entendre.

[5]*But at the evening minyen . . . prayer for rain.* The sentence "Thou causest the wind to blow and the rain to fall" is included in all services between the festivals of Succoth and Passover, which occur in autumn and spring, respectively. SK's use of it in the heat of August attests to his rather comical desperation.

July 11, 1929

[1]Spring Valley. A town (and its vicinity) in Rockland County, New York. Although Jewish resorts in the Catskill "Borsht Belt" were far more famous and numerous, they were also found in counties of the lower Hudson River Valley. In a 1944 study, Saxby Vouler Penfold describes Spring Valley as leading "all other villages in Rockland County in the acquisition of temporary summer population" (*The First Hundred Years of Spring Valley* 23).

[2]*Kokhaleyn*. (Literally, "cook[ing] alone"). A vacation residence at which guests prepared their own meals. Kokhalayns were either units in bungalow colonies or boarding house rentals, with cooking in the latter especially, done in communal kitchens. After World War I, such establishments began to evolve into hotels proper. However, it is clear from SK's account that Lowenstein's transformation was somewhat uneven and incomplete.

[3]*Pesakh*. Passover.

[4]*Shvitsing*. Sweating; perspiring.

[5]*Khumesh* [Heb. Khumash]. The five books of Moses collectively; a volume containing these books.

[6]*Vos makht a yid*. An idiomatic greeting between two Jews roughly equivalent to "How's it going?" or "How are you [doing]?"

[7]*Rabbi Shimon bar Yokhai and his students*. According to legend, Rabbi Shimon bar Yokhai (2nd century C. E.) defied the Roman prohibition against teaching the Torah by disguising his disciples as archers and going off with them to study in the woods.

[8]*Klezmorim* (sing. *klezmer*). Musicians.

[9]*Fe*. Ugh! Yuck! Fie! An expression of disgust or disapproval.

September 2, 1929

[1]*Got tsu danken*. Thank God.

[2]*Eastern Parkway*. A main Brooklyn thoroughfare, one segment of which skirts Brownsville, but home largely to the middle and upper middle classes.

[3]The late Claire Wexler and Abraham Kahn, recalled that their mother used a tablecloth only on holidays and that it was not to protect the kitchen table, which was made of metal, copper colored, and trimmed with a design in black. Professor Redstone confirms their recollection, adding that when the extended family gathered on Passover and the breaking of the fast after Yom Kippur, meals were served in the apartment's front room on two or three long wooden tables covered with either butcher paper or cardboard and bed sheets.

[4]*Yontif*. Holiday; more specifically, a Jewish holy day but sometimes used less restrictively and humorously by SK.

[5]*Neshome*. Soul.

May 4, 1930

[1]*Fomferd*. Hemmed and hawed; stammered; mumbled.

[2]*Grandmother whose name you carry*. Rivke Kahn's mother. See entry for October 16, 1906.

[3]*Take*. Really; truly; in fact.

[4]*Mikve*. Ritual bath.

May 7, 1930

[1]*Yidishkayt*. Jewishness; the essence or spirit of Jews and Judaism.

June 29, 1930

[1]No such entry is to be found among the journal's extant pages.

[2]*Kveling*. Swelling with joy, delight, pride.

[3]A Kahn family story suggests that Reuben Kahn was denied a scholarship because the family could not produce his birth certificate. Such a scholarship, however, would not have involved tuition since none was charged at CCNY (or other New York City municipal colleges) before 1976. Whether the purported scholarship was one offered by the institution or other sources to cover supplemental expenses, such as those for books, is not clear.

[4]*A special child—even at the ceremony . . ."* There is some question about where Reuben Kahn received his ordination. His survivors all maintain that it was at the Jewish Theological Seminary. There is no evidence of this, however, in the seminary records. A Benjamin Kahn was graduated in 1938, but he is clearly another person. Still, the report of a ceremony and students singing (there was a glee club) are consistent with seminary practices. On the other hand, SK's ethical will (see Appendix A) describes the place as a yeshiva (although it is conceivable that SK would use the word to embrace *seminary*). The seeming inconsistency between SK's orthodoxy and his tacit approval of Ruven's attending JTS, is perhaps mitigated by the fact that in the 1930s JTS, still evolving, had not yet fully become the bastion of Judaism's Conservative movement.

[5]*A gentle boy, who would run from the house when his mother took the live fish from the tub.* In days when refrigeration was limited and often unreliable, fish were sometimes kept alive as described. This was especially true at holiday times, when gefilte fish was on the menu. Preparation, of course, would involve killing the fish, a process that prompts Ruven's flight.

[6]*Baltimore.* SK's comments about Baltimore, here and elsewhere, is an unexplained prejudice. The city, in fact, had a significant Jewish presence and reputable Jewish institutions. Kahn's negative view is more fully expressed in the entry for May 30, 1949.

[7]SK's history is a bit rusty. Lincoln was born in Kentucky. However, he later moved with his family to Indiana and then to Illinois.

[8]*New York.* Like many, perhaps most, of his contemporaries who lived in the other boroughs, SK uses the designation to refer to Manhattan.

February 4, 1931

[1]*Bris.* Circumcision and the attendant ceremony. SK's comment about the ritual is at odds with orthodox practice of performing a graveside circumcision and naming of boys who die before they are eight days old. Historically, however, the practice has been controversial, and local customs might differ. SK's remarks suggest either that he was not familiar with the practice or perhaps disapproved although his questioning prevailing rabbinical authority would have been unusual to the point of aberration. (N.B.: Girls who die in early infancy are also named.)

[2]*Arnie.* In more than a dozen entries throughout the journal, and multiple times in some of them, SK uses the familiar form of his eldest grandchild's English name exclusively. For all other grandchildren who live in the neighborhood, he uses an English name in some instances, Hebrew or Yiddish in others. This curious difference is perhaps explained by Arnie's Jewish name, Alter.

Alter, meaning "old", is an amuletic name typically given in one of two instances: to replace a name previously given to a child who has become so seriously ill that its life is endangered, or to a child born after a sibling has died young. In both situations the name expresses the hope (or belief) that the child bearing it will be long-lived. Occasionally, the name is given in the absence of either condition, and perhaps without regard to the Ashkenazi custom of naming children after dead relatives. There is, however, no record of Arnie's having been so seriously ill as to provoke a name change, nor of a birth in the Krumbein family prior to his.

Although Kahn typically confronts life and death squarely, in this instance the absence of "Alter" in the journal text suggests a rare possibility of superstitious avoidance.

[3]*Gitele*. Kahn uses the diminutive of Gitl here, an expression of tenderness sensitive to the solemnity of this entry.

May 10, 1933

[1]*La Guardia*. Fiorello H. La Guardia (1882-1947). At this time a former congressman, he would soon become mayor of New York City. The sentiment attributed to him, however, was actually that of another speaker, Rev. John Haynes Holmes of the Community Church. The misattribution is likely a consequence of SK's having not heard all the speakers and his limited understanding of English, both of which are openly admitted later in the entry.

[2]*Jewish Congress*. The American Jewish Congress organized the march. Its chief rival, the American Jewish Committee, preferred the *sotto voce* approach of which Rev. Holmes, as observed in note 1 above, was critical.

[3]A little more than two years earlier, the name of Rutgers Square on the Lower East Side had been changed to Straus Square in honor of department store magnate and philanthropist Nathan Straus (of Macy's and other retail fame) who had died in January of 1931. SK uses the older and undoubtedly more familiar name.

[4]*Old soldiers*. Jewish veterans' groups and the American Legion were participants.

[5]*Priests*. SK would have used the term to refer to any Christian clergyman.

[6]*A brother to the mayor*. The grand marshal was Major General John F. O'Ryan, the mayor John P. O'Brien. SK fails to distinguish between the two surnames.

[7]*Azoy*. So; in this manner. Often used as an exclamation expressing attitudes as varied as disbelief and disapproval.

[8]*Books. . . burning*. On the night of May 10th book burnings, as previously scheduled, were conducted throughout Germany. The march was specifically conceived as a protest against this cultural atrocity. Nevertheless, its general condemnation of Nazism was unmistakable. SK, in fact, focuses on the broader issue throughout this entry.

[9]*Ploughshares . . . swords*. Apparently, an inversion of a familiar biblical reference, usually cited to Isaiah 2:4 although it appears in Micah 4:3 as well. However, SK's sentiment appears as he states it in Joel 4:9, a passage urging preparation for war.

SK seems rather prescient here (as he seems overly optimistic elsewhere in the entry). However, despite Hitler's having come to power only recently, his ideology was by now very much a known quantity.

[10]*Hatikvah*. The Zionist anthem; now, the national anthem of Israel.

[11]*Spangled*. SK leaves a space between "Star" and "Banner" as if he could not recall the word or recall it accurately.

June 19, 1933

[1]*Farputsing*. Decking oneself out (probably to excess). The word is a hybrid form, with English "ing" grafted onto the base of the Yiddish verb *farputsen*. Cf. entry for April 4, 1910, note 5.

[2]*Grober yung*. A crude or coarse fellow; a boor.

July 25, 1933

[1]*Patsh in tokhes*. Smack (*patsh*) on the behind (*tokhes*).

[2]*When we were in the desert . . . if there was no son*. A reference to Numbers 27:1-8, in which the daughters of Zelophehad petition Moses to receive the estate of their father, who had died without male issue. Their appeal is granted and the order of succession institutionalized, so that daughters inherit before all male relatives but sons. The judgment is modified somewhat in Numbers 36 when daughters who inherit are restricted to marriages within their father's tribe in order to preserve its wealth.

[3]Still . . . answer. Regardless of whether Asher was survived by a son, the obligation to recite the Kadish would fall as well to his father and

brothers if they survived him. As previously noted, in the absence of male survivors, a man might be hired to say the prayer or might simply assume the responsibility, as SK does upon the death of his mother-in-law. (See also entry for October 16, 1906, note 1.)

[4]*And . . .woman.* The Talmudic opinion SK cites is, in fact, the prevailing one. He is perhaps more adventurous in his own interpretation of the point at issue here than he is in matters of faith generally.

January 22, 1935

[1]*Allrightnik.* One who has achieved material success, especially a formerly poor Jewish immigrant. But the word might also suggest those negative qualities attributed to the nouveau riche. SK's usage here, however, distinguishing an allrightnik from a millionaire, suggests he is applying the term to one who has made it to the middle class.

[2]*Old age pension.* It is extremely unlikely that SK received a pension from any source. He seems not to have distinguished between a pension and public assistance to the destitute and elderly of which, in fact, he was a recipient.

[3]*Cloak and suit operator.* In the entry for June 7, 1926, SK describes himself as working on women's dresses. The change in occupation, then, took place at some unspecified time after that. He had undoubtedly been working for Fassbinder, his current employer, prior to May 10, 1933. Since the techniques for each type of sewing overlap only in part, the move attests to SK's versatility and probably to his skill.

[4]*Melamed.* A teacher, especially in a Hebrew religious school. Or, as SK perceives himself, a tutor presenting an equivalent curriculum.

[5]*Baleboste.* Housewife; homemaker; literally, mistress of the house.

November 10, 1935

[1]Kahn describes a version of an Ashkenazi custom reserved originally for the marriage of the family's last daughter. As it evolved, the ritual in some places was associated with the marriage of the last child regardless of gender. Here, Essie Kahn is the Kahns' last daughter to marry (although not the youngest, as SK notes) but not their last child to do so. The older tradition also reserved the crown SK mentions for the mother.

[2]*Nakhes*. Joy; delight; parental pride.

[3]*Yeshive bokher*. a male student at a yeshiva, an academy devoted to Jewish religious education.

[4]*Frume Yidn* Devout Jews.

[5]*Like me*. Nearly a year after his retirement, Kahn still identifies himself by his former occupation. That his loss of employment continues to rankle is evident in the next entry (March 24, 1936) in which he becomes so irate at the prosperous Eisenberg turning beggar that he needs to take a pill (probably nitroglycerin) to calm down.

[6]*King Lehrman*. The Rothstein family often spoke of their matriarch having read Shakespeare in Yiddish, *King Lear* in particular. Although Shakespeare's plays, translated and allegedly improved, had been produced in Yiddish theaters, whether printed versions were generally available is uncertain. It is most likely, however, that Max Rothstein's mother read Jacob Gordin's *The Jewish King Lear*, a comedy in Yiddish first produced in 1892. (Professor Redstone concurs in this opinion.) From Shakespeare, Gordin borrowed the plot device of a father dividing his wealth among his three daughters but little else.

[7]*Mitsve*. Good deed; one of the 613 commandments that Jews are obliged to fulfill. But here SK uses the word sarcastically.

[8]*Meyer Lansky*. One of the leading figures in the American underworld during the twentieth century, Lansky had gambling and other illegal interests across the United States and in the Caribbean.

[9]SK's tacit acceptance of Rothstein's working on the Sabbath is a far cry from his insistence on strict Sabbath observance in regard to his daughter Reyzl's marriage more than a decade earlier (See entries for February 28, 1920 and January 14, 1923.) In the interval he might well have come to realize, however reluctantly, that the religious practices of others were beyond his control. In a later entry, October 30, 1938, he notes (ruefully) not only the infrequency of Rothstein's going to synagogue but his son Asher's as well.

[10]*Lewis and Dubinsky*. John L. Lewis and David Dubinsky were, respectively, the presidents of the United Mine Workers and the International Ladies Garment Workers Union.

March 24, 1936

[1]Almost immediately after taking office on March 4, 1933, President Franklin Delano Roosevelt declared a four-day "bank holiday" (March 6-9) in order for new banking legislation to be enacted and to restore public confidence in the banking system.

[2]*For a minute . . . kvetsh of Rivke's*. A rare display of pique, but as the succeeding paragraph indicates, SK's motives are as much ethical as personal.

April 21, 1937

[1]*Shmates*. Rags. As here, the word is also applied to items of clothing, often with a touch of deprecating humor.

[2]*Gevalt* (interj.). An expression that indicates reactions ranging from surprise to shock to dismay to horror, depending on circumstances. However, as the columnist Philologus observes: "'Oy, gevalt!'" (or just plain 'Gevalt!') has the sense of 'Oh, my God!' or 'Good grief!' as uttered when something unfortunate has happened — when you have just discovered, say, that you have locked your car keys in the car, or when your dinner partner has spilled wine all over you." ("Oy, gevalt!" (http://forward.com/articles/4093/oy-gevalt/) *Forward*. December 31, 2004.) Such is the case with Rivke's reaction to the hubbub here.

[3]*Ganif*. Thief.

[4]*Daven alone in the house*. When possible, Jews pray communally, hence the quorum of ten required for a group service. See also entry for April 4, 1910, note 5.

[5]*Dairy for supper*. As an orthodox Jew, Kahn would have waited several hours after eating meat before consuming dairy products. (The exact number varies according to rabbinical judgments.)

[6]Ahashueres. King of Persia. A leading figure in the Book of Esther, which is read on the festival of Purim (Lots). The allusion is to the process by which Esther is chosen queen (Esther 2:1-17).

[7]*Nudzh* (n.). Prod; poke. In other contexts, the word might mean *pest*. Forms of the related verb, *nudzhen* (prod; pester), are found in the entries

for May 30, 1948; May 7, 1950; May 12, 1952; and September 10, 1952. In three of these instances, the verb form, in translation, takes the English endings *–ed* or *–ing*, typical of the sometimes-blended usage of Kahn's offspring.

However, both the noun and the verb have a particularly American cast in SK's original, the one approximate to English *nudge*, the other with meaning seemingly derived from the noun rather than reflecting earlier definitions: to bore, nauseate, or disgust. Such vocabulary tends to confirm what SK observes elsewhere about how his Yiddish has changed since his arrival in the United States. See entry for September 2, 1954.

[8]*Meshiekh*. Messiah.

July 12, 1937

[1]*For maybe ten years*. The entry for July 11, 1929 records SK's visit to Spring Valley eight years earlier. His use of so large a number as "ten" is strong evidence that no other visit had been made in the interim.

[2]*Megile*. A long, often complicated story; literally, a scroll, especially the one in which the Book of Esther is inscribed.

[3]*Hit a rock . . .stick*. An allusion to Moses striking a rock with his staff to bring forth water instead of speaking to it as commanded. For this disobedience he is barred from entry to the Promised Land. See Numbers 20:1-12.

[4]*Alef-beyz*. The Hebrew alphabet (and the respective names of its first two letters).

August 11, 1937

[1]*WEVD*. A radio station founded by the Socialist Party of America that in its heyday was devoted to broadcasting in Yiddish. The call letters include the initials of socialist and labor leader Eugene V. Debs.

[2]*My Morning Journal . . . believe*. *The Morning Journal* [Morgen Zhurnal] was a socially conservative and religiously orthodox Yiddish newspaper. SK would certainly have trusted it far more than the rival sources of information mentioned. Although the *Journal* had not been laggard in reporting Nazi atrocities, Kahn might be recalling that, early on, it had

been more optimistic about the Nazi threat than most of the Yiddish press. [I am indebted to Charles Cutter's doctoral dissertation, "The American Yiddish Daily Press Reaction to the Rise of Nazism, 1930-1933" (Ohio State University, 1979) for much of the information in this note.]

[3]Cutter (see note 2 above) states that "The Morning Journal at times posited the view that the tragedy that befell German Jewry was the will of God. Jews must pray, give charity, and repent; hopefully matters would then improve" (279). SK does not seem to subscribe to this view, or, at the very least, distinguishes between divine will and divine retribution. Typically, his response to the burgeoning Holocaust is moral and compassionate rather than theological.

[4]*Nineveh*. The city whose doom Jonah was to declare but which was spared upon its repentance. (See Jonah 1-4.) The reference to "hands" just above is an allusion to the book's final verse: "And should not I care about Nineveh, that great city, in which there are more than a hundred and twenty thousand persons who do not yet know their right hand from their left, and many beasts as well!"

March 17, 1938

[1]*Purim*. Holiday commemorating the triumphant survival of the Jews in the face of a genocidal plot against them as recounted in the Book of Esther, which is read on this day.

[2]*We must be so drunk that we can't tell Haman's name from Mordecai's.* Such prescribed drinking recalls the celebrations recounted in chapter 9 of the Book of Esther. Rabbinical opinions, however, differ on what degree of drunkenness is acceptable.

Haman, having plotted to kill all the Jews, is the genocidal villain of the piece, his name customarily drowned out in public readings of the Book of Esther by noisemakers, the stomping of feet, etc. Mordecai and his cousin, Queen Esther, are the book's protagonists.

[3]Purimshpil. A Purim play.

[4]*Grager*. A ratcheted noisemaker used on the festival of Purim as described in note 2 above.

July 7, 1938

[1]*Minkhe*. Afternoon service.

[2]*Banditn* (sing. *bandit*). Rascals (often used affectionately); literally, bandits. (Stress in both singular and plural is on the second syllable.)

[3]*One game . . . pillow*. The game is Johnny-on-the-pony, in which one team leaps on the backs of another, whose members are bent over in a straight line with arms and legs interlocked, and tries to collapse them by sheer weight. The human "pillow," usually backed against a wall, braces the player at the head of the line. The other games mentioned in the passage are stickball, kick the can, "packs," hit the penny, and jump rope. The last of these needs no explanation.

Stickball is essentially a game derived from baseball that uses a firm, hollow rubber ball and that requires no running. Balls caught on the fly are outs as are those grounders caught before reaching a predetermined marker. The value of hits—singles, doubles, triples, home runs—for balls not caught as described depends on the distance traveled before striking the ground. Imagined runners advance according to the value of subsequent hits. A "runner" on first base would go to second on a single, to third on a double, etc.

Kick the can, also modeled on baseball, includes running but substitutes a kicked can for a bat and ball.

"Packs" is a game played with rubber heels, as Kahn states, or with decks of cards fastened (typically with rubber bands) so that the cards do not separate. The object of the game is to land on a specified pavement crack and then to cover the "packs" of rivals with one's own by placing it on top of them from one's own fixed position. Usually, gambling is involved, rather for comic books or baseball cards than for money.

Hit the penny (or any other coin) takes two forms. In one, a single penny is placed on a sidewalk crack and two players, each a cement square away, attempt to strike it with a rubber ball. Whoever reaches a predetermined number of hits (e.g., 11 or 21) wins. The second form involves a number of coins placed on the crack, typically five, the object here being to knock all of them into the opponent's square.

October 30, 1938

[1]Because strict Sabbath observance forbids the lighting of fires and most food preparation, one burner of the gas range was left on a low flame from before sundown Friday evening till after dark on Saturday. An asbestos disc with a handle attached was typically placed over the flame in order to control the heating of pots or pans and their contents.

[2]*Rogelakh.* Small rolled pastries with assorted fillings.

[3]*Frumkayt.* Devotion; religiosity.

[4]*Mazl.* Luck.

[5]*Yosele Rosenblatts.* Born in the Ukraine, Josef (Yosele) Rosenblatt (1882-1933) was arguably the foremost cantor in America after his arrival in 1912, his fame extending beyond the Jewish community. In 1927, Rosenblatt made an enduring contribution to popular culture by recording the liturgical music for the sound track of <u>The Jazz Singer</u>, the first film to use sound throughout.

November 12, 1938

[1]Early in 1938 Germany had annexed Austria and that part of Czechoslovakia known as the Sudetenland, which had in earlier days been Austrian territory. The event is known as the "Anschluss" (union).

[2]*Before this . . . Jewish businesses.* Kahn refers to earlier actions designed to prevent Jewish participation in German life. These restricted, removed, or barred Jews from the civil service, educational institutions, and professions such as law and medicine. The "Nuremberg Laws" of 1935 deprived Jews of citizenship and forbade them from either marrying or having sexual contact with non-Jews.

[3]The events that are central to this entry are referred to as "Kristallnacht" or the "Night of Broken Glass." As Kahn fears, they mark a transition to greater use of violence against Jews. This development ultimately results in the Holocaust, already signaled in the reference to "camps," which prompts Kahn's gallows humor.

[4]*If the letters survive . . .at least for now.* This is perhaps the journal's strongest affirmation of SK's faith. Despite his grief, he sees at least the possibility of salvation. As he does in the entry for August 11, 1937,

Kahn lays blame for the atrocities on the oppressors rather than on their victims.

March 6, 1940

[1]*Shpilkes*. Nervous energy; ants in the pants; impatience.

[2]Eliezer is identified as SK's youngest brother in the entry for May 30, 1948.

[3]*Meshugas*. Literally and figuratively, madness; foible(s).

[4]*Their worth as numbers*. Each letter of the Hebrew alphabet has a numerical value. Although the Khumesh in question might have used Arabic numerals for page numbers, all elements of the text itself, including chapter numbers, would have been in Hebrew.

[5]*Accountants' shul*. SK jests. His reference is to synagogues that are established for the needs of those engaged in a particular occupation in areas where the business, trade or profession is concentrated, as in New York's garment center and diamond district.

June 27, 1940

[1]There are several puzzling aspects to this paragraph. First, Kahn does not specifically name any of the charities involved. Second, what he calls "boxes" (i.e., pushkes) might not have been those provided by these charities, which would have had at least their names printed on them. The receptacles, in fact, might well have been empty jars or tin cans that the Kahns provided and labelled themselves. Third, it is quite surprising that so staunch a Zionist as SK does not mention a box to prepare and provide for Jewish settlement in the Holy Land (namely for the Jewish National Fund), perhaps the one most likely to have been kept at this time.

Nevertheless, one may make reasonable assumptions for identities of two of the charities. The "orphans" are very likely residents of the Pride of Judea Children's Home, located in East New York, an area of Brooklyn bordering Kahn's Brownsville. Pride of Judea changed its name from "Orphan Home" to "Children's Home" in the 1930's since few of the residents by that time were orphans. Ultimately, it became a mental health center associated with the Jewish Board of Children and Family

Services, accepting clients regardless of background. Renamed Pride of Judea Community Services, the organization serves part of the borough of Queens, removed now by more than a century from its Brooklyn origins.

The home for rabbis and scholars is almost certainly the Home for the Sages of Israel, located in Kahn's former Lower East Side neighborhood. This institution seems to have been unique.

On the other hand, yeshivahs at both home and abroad were too numerous even to speculate about identity. Although less plentiful, several hospitals in Manhattan, Brooklyn, and the Bronx had Jewish origins and/or bore Jewish names. Among them were Mt. Sinai, Beth Israel, Brooklyn Jewish, and Montefiore, but Kahn appears to have had no particular connection with either any of these or with a local hospital, Beth El, only blocks away.

Still, whether the charities have provided Kahn's boxes or not, they obviously know that he is a client. [This editor has discovered neither written nor graphic evidence of their having made such provision.]

[2]*Twenty times khai*. The letters of the Hebrew word *khai*, meaning life, have the numerical value of eighteen. Because of its association with life, the number eighteen and its multiples are considered good omens. Charitable donations (and even personal gifts of cash) are often made in *khai* units. In this case, twenty times eighteen (*khai*) equals $3.60.

[3]*Crackers*. Kahn uses the words for *cracker* and *cookie* interchangeably, but, as in this instance, *cookie* is what he always means.

[4]*Postum*. Trade name for a cereal product made to be mixed with hot water and served as a coffee substitute.

[5]*Goylems*. (Anglicized pl. of *goylem*; SK's text, however, gives the standard Yiddish pl. *goylomim*). In Jewish lore, clay figures created and given (servile) life; particularly, the figure reputedly created by Rabbi Loew (Yehuda Leyb ben Bezulel) of Prague in the sixteenth century. Cf. entry for September 10, 1952, note 1.

[6]*Bobishke*. Babushka. However, Jerome Wexler recalled his grandmother wearing it like a turban rather than tied like a kerchief under the chin.

February 12, 1941

[1]*Figs and dates for the holiday.* On Tu Bishvat (the fifteenth day of the month of Shevat), roughly the equivalent of Arbor Day, it is customary to eat the fruit of trees native to the Holy Land. Although figs and dates are appropriate, carob is particularly associated with this day. That SK does not include it in his gift is somewhat surprising, unless, perhaps, it was not readily available.

[2]*Teamster.* An epithet because of its connotation of crude ignorance. Cf. entry for February 23, 1954, note 1.

[3]*Yoyne.* Yiddish pronunciation of Hebrew Yonah, equivalent to English Jonah. As in the case of both Jerry and Allan, English names do not necessarily correspond to Hebrew or Yiddish names beyond an approximate initial sound, if at all.

[4]*Bas.* Daughter of. The word here reflects Kahn's Ashkenazic pronunciation of Hebrew *bat.*

[5]See entry for July 11, 1929, note 7.

December 2, 1941

[1]Louis "Lepke" Buchalter was, in fact, sentenced to death the following day.

[2]*A shande far yidn.* An embarrassment or disgrace for Jews.

[3]*Rothstein.* Arnold Rothstein, a leading underworld figure of the early twentieth century, supposedly responsible for fixing the 1919 World Series, a charge that he denied and that was never substantiated.

[4]*Borukh Hashem.* Blessed be the (Holy) Name, i.e., Thank God.

[5]*Bulvan.* A boor, brute, or dolt, particularly a muscular one.

[6]*Rambam, the Vilna Gaon, this magid or that. Rambam* is an acronym for "Rabbi Moses ben Maimon," i.e., Maimonides (1135-1204), the great medieval scholar and philosopher. The Vilna Gaon, i. e., the Sage of Vilna, was Elijah ben Solomon Zalmen (1720-1797). As used here, "gaon" is an honorific title indicating great knowledge. A "magid" was a religious preacher, often itinerant, and not necessarily as learned as SK implies.

[7]*Prize fighters*. Like most impoverished groups before and since, Jews provided their share of boxers for the ring in the earlier part of the twentieth century. Perhaps most notable among them were Benny Leonard (b. Benjamin Leiner, 1896-1947) and Barney Ross (b. Dov-Ber Rosofsky, 1909-1967). Leonard held the lightweight championship from 1917-1925; Ross was champion in three weight divisions during the 1930's. Given the dates of their prowess and fame, it is likely that SK, obviously no lover of the sport, knew of these two fighters at least.

The popularity of boxing in the Jewish community, generally, may be attested to by the existence of the Eastern Parkway Arena, which, located at the edge of Brownsville, continued as a boxing venue until 1955. It resumed activity briefly in 1958 then closed for good. In addition, Professor Redstone reports that a childhood neighbor of his (and, hence, of his grandfather's) had been a professional fighter, but whether SK was aware of this is not known.

August 23, 1942

[1]SK would not have kept the journal during the initial seven-day period of mourning (shiva). It is somewhat surprising that he permitted himself this activity before the second stage of mourning, the thirty-day period (sheloshim), had been completed.

[2]SK again alludes to Psalms 90:10. See entry for April 17, 1912, note 2.

[3]One would have expected to find an entry regarding Khaim's death in light of SK's frequent recording of such events as already seen in entries regarding his mother-in-law, brother-in-law, and two infant grandchildren. He will later write of the death of Mickey Aaronson, a neighbor's son lost during World War II. (See entry for August 16, 1945.) Khaim's absence from the journal except for this and one other passing reference provides further evidence that the surviving text is incomplete.

[4]*But from . . . almost a year*. The German army had entered Minsk in June, 1941.

[5]*Yortsayt candle*. A memorial candle lit on the anniversary (yortsayt) of the death of parents, siblings, spouses, or children. A large version of such a candle also burns throughout the first seven days of mourning. SK's final statement likely refers not only to his brothers left in Europe but to Jews collectively since *Yisroel* translates as *Israel*.

May 17, 1943

[1]*Sider*. Prayer book.

[2]*Sh'ma*. The fundamental affirmation of Judaism: "Hear, Oh Israel, the Lord our God, the Lord is one."

August 22, 1943

[1]*Mr. Kahn*. SK regards the English mode of address as more respectful, a rare (if unconscious) instance of assimilation that is reinforced by his quotation from the Rabbi's speech at the end of the paragraph.

[2]*Daven Minkhe*. To lead the afternoon service.

[3]*Mayriv* [Heb. Ma'ariv]. The evening service.

[4]*Kidesh [Heb*. Kidush]. The blessings of sanctification recited over wine.

[5]*Tsimes*. Fruit or vegetable stew; also, metaphorically, a fuss or row.

[6]*Gan Eydn*. The Garden of Eden; paradise.

[7]*Gehinem*. A place of temporary abode for souls as yet unfit for paradise; essentially, the Jewish approximation of purgatory rather than of hell.

For further elaboration on the subject (and of the topic of afterlife in Jewish thought as well) see the following: (https://www.myjewishilearning.com/article/life-after Death) and (https://www.chabad.orgww/library/article_cdo/aid/ 1594422/jewish/Do-Jews-Believe-in-Hell.htm)

November 3, 1943

[1]*Meyvin*. Authority; expert.

[2]*Treyf* (adj.). Not kosher; ritually impure. (n.)

[3]*Flanken*. A cut of beef taken from the short ribs; here, a stew or pot roast made from that cut.

[4]*Kashe varnishke*s. A dish comprised chiefly of buckwheat groats and noodles.

[5]*Sauce*. SK's text reads *zup* (soup). He is describing a Spanish omelet.

[6]Rationing of meat and fish, among other foods, had been instituted in

March, 1943. But, with the exception of SK's allusion to the scarcity of lox, the Kahn family seems (at this point at least) not to have been seriously affected by the restrictions. Similarly, references later in the entry to pie, ice cream, and drinks requiring syrup, indicate that sugar, the first food to have been rationed, was more readily available to enterprises in food production and service than to individual consumers. SK's mention of "real eggs" refers to his suggestion that his son might have been fed powdered eggs by the army, rather than to rationing, since eggs were never rationed.

[7]*Egg cream.* A soda fountain drink consisting of chocolate syrup, milk, and carbonated water. Whether the concoction ever included either an egg or cream is a much-vexed question. Some latter-day revisionists substitute vanilla syrup for chocolate.

August 15, 1945

[1]*Makher.* Bigshot; a mover and shaker.

August 16, 1945

[1]*Kibits.* A jest.

April 14, 1946

[1]*Erev Pesakh.* Passover eve, i.e, the evening on which the holiday begins. The Jewish day begins at sunset in accordance with the passage describing the creation: "And there was evening and there was morning, one day" (Genesis 1:5).

[2]*The dishes have been changed.* Orthodox practice requires that dishes, along with cooking and eating utensils, as well as appliances, be purified through various processes to avoid all possible contamination by forbidden foods during Passover. Many find it simpler to keep separate sets of dishes, utensils, and even appliances for Passover use exclusively.

[3]*Khomets.* Leavened bread, various grains and grain products, or other foods forbidden to be eaten during Passover. Part of the preparation for the holiday traditionally involves a ritual search for leaven on the evening

prior to the festival and burning what is gathered early the next morning.

[4]*Kharoyses*. A mixture of wine, chopped apples, and chopped nuts, eaten at the Passover Seder and symbolic of the mortar used by the Hebrews in the labors of their Egyptian enslavement.

[5]*Seders*. The two home services for Passover conducted on successive evenings. Traditionally, Jews in the diaspora hold two seders because of ancient confusion about when the holiday should begin. Although such confusion no longer exists, the custom persists. However, Jews in Israel and many liberal Jews in the diaspora hold only one.

[6]*Yarmulke*. Skull cap.

[7]*Kitl*. White robe worn by the person conducting the Seder as a symbol of purity. It signals as well a limit to what might otherwise be unbridled joy in the celebration of freedom since the garment is also used as a shroud. Additional uses include its being worn during Yom Kippur services and by a bridegroom. In the latter case, the color additionally suggests his union with the bride, who is also in white.

[8]*Afikoymen*. The portion of unleavened bread set aside at the Passover Seder and used after the meal as "dessert." Traditionally, the portion is hidden early in the proceedings to be sought out by children and returned when needed in exchange for a (usually) small reward offered by the leader of the service. An alternative tradition, referred to here, requires that the children "steal" the afikoymen and hold it for ransom.

[8]*Elijah's cup*. A cup of wine set ceremonially for Elijah during the Passover Seder service in the belief and hope that Elijah will return and presage the coming of the Messiah.

[9]*Matse* [Heb./Eng. matzah/matzo]. The unleavened bread with which the Israelites fled from their enslavement in Egypt. Although the cracker-like "loaves" may be eaten year-round, they are mandated to be eaten during Passover and are essential to Seder services. Matzah balls are dumplings made of ground matzah known as matzah meal.

[10]*Kugl*. A pudding made, most typically, of potatoes or noodles. Since pasta products are essentially forbidden during Passover, SK's would have been a potato kugl.

April 18, 1946

[1]In his entries for Passover, SK repeatedly refers to Allan's absence from the first Seder. At one level, as indicated in the first of the entries, he is disturbed by the child's violating the holiday by travelling, although it is Max, his father, who is culpable both for the travel and paying the fare. But Kahn seems more disturbed by the absence per se since the rest of the family available—and even a prospective in-law—are in attendance. For him, without Allan and even the antagonistic Max, the family circle seems incomplete.

[2]*Zisn Pesakh*. Sweet Passover. The succeeding wish for a good year is appropriate because the month of Nisan, during which Passover occurs, begins the biblical or religious year and is designated as the first month in Exodus 12:1-2. Rosh Hashanah, falling on the first day of the seventh month (Tishri) begins a new calendrical year, i.e., the transition from year x to year $x+1$. To complicate matters further, Judaism has two other "new years" as well. See the *Encyclopedia Judaica* or online sources such as *My Jewish Learning* and *learnreligions.com* for additional explanation.

[3]The Japanese surrender was announced on August 14, 1945 and the surrender document signed on September 2, officially bringing the war to a close. But American soldiers in Europe had been discharged in great numbers beginning with Germany's surrender in early May of 1945. One possible reason for Avrom's not having been discharged more than a year later is that having served as an MP in the European theater he was particularly useful to the American army of occupation. Japan's surrender might not have greatly affected the return of soldiers still stationed in Germany.

At the time, demobilization was supposed to take place within three months after the end of the war. This was changed to six months in January of 1946, which meant that Avrom should have been discharged no later than March of 1946, in time for Passover that year. His serving several months beyond that date might easily be attributed to bureaucratic error.

[4]*But more . . . for my son*. At a fixed point in the Seder service, the front door (or apartment door) is opened to allow the prophet Elijah to enter. See also note 8 of the previous entry (April 14, 1946).

July 23, 1946

[1]*Seventy years of the psalm.* The journal's third and final reference to Psalms 90:10. See note 2 in entries for April 17, 1912 and August 23, 1942.

[2]*Because cupping. . . dead one.* SK alludes to a Yiddish proverb applied to a useless remedy for a hopeless situation, namely, that it will help as much as cupping will help someone who has died.

Cupping is a therapeutic process of drawing blood to the surface of the skin, typically by using small glass cups and suction in order to increase blood flow and reduce muscle tension and pain. The process has enjoyed some increasing popularity in recent years as a "natural" therapy. Traditional medicine, however, remains skeptical about its efficacy.

October 2, 1946

[1]*Shoyfer* [Heb. Shofar]. Ram's horn. Except on the Sabbath, the shofar is blown in a series of ritual notes during the month preceding Rosh Hashanah (the New Year) and on Rosh Hashanah itself. It is also sounded at the conclusion of Yom Kippur (the Day of Atonement).

[2]SK refers to the tale that David knew that he was destined to die on the Sabbath, but that he nevertheless steeped himself in Torah study on this day because it was believed no one could succumb while so engaged. At the appointed time, however, the Angel of Death distracted David from his devotion and so carried him off (See Louis Ginzberg, *Legends of the Bible* 550).

[3]*Yontoyvim* (sing. *yontif*). Holidays.

[4]*Tayglekh.* Cookies made of small dough balls boiled in a sugar/honey syrup in which they are sometimes served. Tayglekh are traditionally prepared for the Jewish New Year.

February 1, 1947

[1]*Plotkin, our landlord now.* In the entry for October 30, 1938 SK refers to his landlord as Shenkman. There are two possibilities. The first is that SK moved twice after leaving Orloff's building or that Shenkman and Plotkin owned the building where SK is currently living at different

times. Professor Redstone and SK's other surviving descendants recall only Plotkin. The chronology is such that the Kahns and Rothsteins could have lived in Orloff's building simultaneously for only a short time.

[2]*Shmitshik*. Doohickey; whatchamacallit; in this case, the term refers to a thermostat.

[3]*Tsholent*. A thick stew made of meat, potatoes, beans and other vegetables, usually slow-cooked over many hours.

[4]*Moyshe Rabeynu*. Our teacher Moses.

[5]*Khokhme*. Wise saying.

March 2, 1947

[1]*A year and a Wednesday*. Literal translation of a Yiddish idiom that implies an extremely (or excessively) long time.

[2]*Mizrakhi*. Organization of religious Zionists of which SK was a member.

March 6, 1947

[1]Dachau was liberated on April 29, 1945. Dead bodies in various stages of decomposition, both within the camp and in rail cars just beyond it, numbered in the thousands. Citizens of the town of Dachau were compelled to bury the corpses.

July 16, 1947

[1]*Gantsermakher. . . Kleynermakher*. These two names are SK's coinages. The first, meaning a prodigious mover and shaker, is a conflation of the two words *gantser* (complete, total) and *makher* (big shot) that occur together idiomatically. The second is more completely original, with *kleyner* (smaller) implying moving and shaking to a lesser degree.

[2]*Shabes goy*. A gentile hired to perform chores on the Sabbath and major holidays that are forbidden to Jews on those days. Typically, these might include lighting fires and turning electric lights on and off. The advent of timing devices has all but eliminated the need for such services even in the orthodox community, which had been their principal consumer.

August 6, 1947

[1]*The last Indians.* The Kahns are visiting Canarsie, a Brooklyn neighborhood bordering the Atlantic. Although the Canarsie tribe for whom the area is named had all but disappeared from the region before 1800, it is conceivable that a few scattered descendants remained even as late as the mid-twentieth century. (*Note: Such descriptors as "Native American," largely created and popularized in the late 20th century, were unknown to SK and, at this date, to his immediate descendants. The editor maintains, therefore, that their use here would be inappropriate for the present text.*)

[2]*. . . Hoffman's, so it was all right.* This editor has not been able to discover whether the product was certified kosher at the time. If it were, one would have expected SK to have mentioned the imprimatur of the certifying agency on the label to determine whether the soda might be drunk. Instead, he seems to have relied on the product's reputation, the list of acceptable ingredients (if present), and the name *Hoffman*, a reasonably common one among Jews.

[3]*Shoykhet* [Heb. Shokhet]. Ritual slaughterer. Although fish are not subject to ritual slaughter, SK suggests that even when taking the life of a fish one must proceed conscientiously.

[4]*Maykhl.* A delicacy. It is clear that SK's desire to sample eggplant expressed in the entry for October 14, 1926 has been fulfilled at least once. However, why he refers to it as an American delicacy is puzzling, since in the entry for October 14,1926 he identifies it as Romanian.

May 14, 1948

[1]*Six months . . . being.* The United Nations had decided to allow the British mandate over Palestine to lapse. It expired at midnight, May 14. Earlier that day, the document declaring the State of Israel had been prepared and signed in semi-secrecy at Tel-Aviv.

[2]*We. . . right arm remains strong.* An allusion to Psalms 137:5:

If I forget thee, O Jerusalem,
Let my right hand forget her cunning.

[3]*Maybe. . . all their power.* Hostilities had intensified during the waning days of British authority. With the British gone, Arab states immediately launched an all-out attack on several fronts.

[4]*Eretz Yisroel*. The land of Israel.

[5]*Ani Ma'amin*. Title of a hymn expressing absolute faith in the coming of the Messiah despite all delay. Since it was sometimes sung by Jews on their way to death in the Nazi concentration camps, SK's allusion to it in the present context is especially poignant.

[6]*. . . to set a table for us though we are surrounded by enemies*. An allusion to Psalms 23:5— "Thou preparest a table before me in the presence of mine enemies."

May 30, 1948

[1]*Shabes Shire*. The Sabbath of Song, which invariably occurs during the winter. SK's marrying on Tuesday is of some significance. According to myjewishlearning.com, "For much of Jewish history, the third day of the week (Tuesday) was considered an especially auspicious day for a wedding. This was so because, in regard to the account of the third day of creation, the phrase '... and God saw that it was good' (Genesis 1:10 and 1:12) appears twice. Therefore, Tuesday is a doubly good day for a wedding."

[2]*Khale*. A braided bread served on the Sabbath, certain holidays, and at life cycle celebrations.

[3]*Koshered*. Meat ritually prepared for cooking by soaking and salting. The process tends to drain the meat of blood, the consuming of which is forbidden in Leviticus 17:13-14.

[4]*Mashgiekh* [Heb.Mashgiakh]. One who oversees that the rules regarding kosher food and its preparation are followed.

[5]*Kishke*. A dish made of seasoned mashed or ground vegetables that are mixed with fat and stuffed into beef intestine, cooked, and served sliced. These days, the intestine (kishke) has generally been replaced by vegetable casings.

[6]*Shmalts*. Fat, especially rendered chicken fat.

[7]*Gribenes*. Cracklings (typically with fried onions).

[8]*Drank a l'khaim*. Made a toast to life.

[9]*Parev* (also *pareve*). Containing neither meat nor dairy products and therefore fit to be eaten with any meal.

[10]*Kazatske*. A vigorous Russian dance.

July 14, 1948

[1]*Bilha(h) and Zilpa(h)*. Servants, respectively, of Rachel and Leah; as Jacob's concubines, the one bore Dan and Naftali, the other Gad and Asher. (See Genesis 30:1-13.)

[2]*Zeyde*. Grandfather.

[3]*Apikoyres*. Skeptic; unbeliever; heretic.

September 12, 1948

[1]*It's only a petition . . . the five-cent fare*. On July 1, 1948, fare for the New York City subways rose from five cents to ten. Heading unsuccessful drives first to preserve the older fare and then to restore it, was Vito Marcantonio (1902-1954), long-time Congressman from East Harlem and by that time leader of the socialist American Labor Party. The ensuing comments of Essie and SK reflect the climate of fear then developing in the context of the burgeoning "cold war" with the Soviet Union and of congressional inquiries (often characterized as "witch hunts") into the political activity of American citizens. The House Committee on Un-American Activities had already investigated communism in the entertainment world, particularly in its focus on the "Hollywood Ten," and the semi-secret "Lee list" of purported communists among State Department employees (past, present, and prospective) had been compiled.

[2]*Mamelige*. A Romanian corn meal porridge that in some preparations can be sliced like a bread or cake.

[3]*Meshugener*. Literally and figuratively, someone who is insane; SK indicates elsewhere (see entry for November 4, 1952) that this was Rivke Kahn's pet name for comedian Milton Berle.

November 2, 1948

[1]Henry Wallace, who had been FDR's vice-president during his third term, was running for president on the American Labor Party ticket. Thomas E. Dewey, was the Republican nominee and sitting governor of New York. Dewey was so strongly favored to win that the *Chicago Tribune* infamously ran the headline "Dewey Defeats Truman." When all the votes were counted, however, it was Truman who had been elected.

[2]SK here cites some of the several difficulties that faced Truman in the 1948 campaign: post-war inflation and housing shortages; objections on the parts of some taxpayers and isolationists to the nascent Marshall Plan for European recovery; backlash against his civil rights agenda (the Southern Democrats, "Dixiecrats," were running a candidate of their own—Strom Thurmond). Given Truman's overall record and recent (overridden) veto of the hated Taft-Hartley Act, his labor backing was strong but still qualified by memory of his aggressive actions to end or prevent major industrial strikes in 1946.

[3]SK might be engaged in a bit of wishful thinking here. In fact, two years later, Thomas E. Dewey was re-elected to his third four-year term as governor of New York.

December 19, 1948

[1]*Alte zeyde*. Great-grandfather; literally, old grandfather.

March 14, 1949

[1]*Simkhe*. Joyous occasion; celebration.

[2]*Sits . . . Shabes*. See entry for October 30, 1938 note 1.

[3]*The flounder [filets]· the vegetable [cutlets], the salmon krikets [sic]*. SK has transliterated the Anglo-French as *fil hays*, two Yiddish words meaning "very hot." He has similarly rendered "cutlets," the next item listed, as *cutlers*, perhaps confusing the unfamiliar English word with a reasonably common Jewish surname. There is little doubt that the third item, left here as transliterated in SK's text, is his version of *croquettes*.

[4]*Kishkes*. Guts; digestive track. More specifically, intestines. Cf. note 5 of the entry for May 30, 1948.

May 30, 1949

[1]*Tishe Bov* [Heb. Tishe B'Av]. Literally, the ninth day of the month of Av; the fast day which marks the destruction of the Temple at Jerusalem on that date, first by Babylon in 586 B.C.E. and then by Rome in 70 C.E.

[2]*Lamentations*. The book of Lamentations is read on Tishe B'Av.

[3]*Mt. Sinai*. SK errs slightly. It would have been the Sinai hospital in Baltimore.

[4]Seyfer Toyre. Book of the Law; the Torah scroll.

July 5, 1949

[1]*Fleyshik*. Having the qualities of or being prepared with meat; in this case, SK proposes declaring by fiat that the rides are such.

[2]*An hour after dairy*. In SK's practice, the minimum time permitted between the consumption of dairy foods and the consumption of meat, provided that the former were eaten first. Cf. entry for April 21, 1937, note 5.

October 31, 1949

[1]*Goyishe* (adj.). Gentile.

[2]*Halloween*. SK's unfamiliarity with this word is reflected in his two differing transliterations, *helevin* and *heyligvin*, the latter an unwitting near use of the Yiddish word *heylig* (holy) that is cognate with *hallow*.

[3]*Tsatske*. Bauble; plaything; nicknack. Used as well in sarcastic deprecation of people.

December 10, 1949

[1]*Shtup*. Press upon; indulge. Literally, push, shove. (The [vulgar] slang definition—to engage in sexual intercourse—is irrelevant here.)

[2]*Khazeyrim* (sing. *khazer*). Pigs.

[3]*Havdole*. The ceremony performed at the end of the Sabbath to emphasize the separation of that day from the six others.

February 14, 1950

[1]*Horowitz-Margareten*. A manufacturer of kosher foods.

[2]*Vilmans and the medzhik o*. Probably SK's misperception of the names [Ted] Williams and [Joe] DiMaggio.

May 7, 1950

[1]The home is almost certainly the Pride of Judea, as suggested in note 1 of the entry for June 27, 1940. Here, however, SK's description of the child as not having been orphaned reflects the change of status among the institution's residents as described in that note.

[2]*Dveyre*. Yiddish version of D'vorah, which translates to Deborah in English. Although undoubtedly aware of the Hebrew original, SK accepts the more familiar Yiddish variant as equivalent.

[3]*And if . . . saved the world*. SK invokes one of the best-known Talmudic precepts that saving a life is equivalent to saving the world.

May 24, 1950

[1]*Mishpokhe*. Family

[2]SK's account of extended families and inter-family connections describes situations that were not unusual but were by no means universal.

[3]SK's sense of the neighborhood is cultural rather than geographic, a state of mind and lifestyle that ignores the rigidly exclusive boundaries of postal zones and police precincts.

[4]SK's conclusion is unduly optimistic. Jewish Brownsville would be all but gone a decade later. His own children would leave, whether before or after his death. (See entries for April 11, 1957 and November 3, 1958.) And like many of their contemporaries, his grandchildren would scatter upon marriage to other parts of the borough, to the Long Island suburbs, and even to southern New Jersey.

October 26, 1950

[1]*Bereyshis* [Heb. Bereshit]. The book of Genesis and its first chapter.

[2]Genesis reports marriages for only Cain and Seth. Abel, presumably, was slain before taking a wife.

[3]*Folkshul*. A secular Jewish school, dedicated to preserve and perpetuate Jewish culture in a non-religious context. Schools of this sort were established by the Workmen's Circle, a Jewish socialist labor organization. In

recent times, the organization's name has been changed to The Workers Circle, which continues to operate schools and advocate for social justice.

[4]*Arele*. Affectionate diminutive of Ari, itself a shortened form of Aryeh.

[5]*Rashi*. Acronym of Shlomo Yitskhaki (Solomon ben Isaac, (1040-1105), among the foremost of biblical commentators. His commentary and the Aramaic interpretive translation of Onkelos were routinely printed in Hebrew biblical texts such as those owned by SK.

[6]Aside from the general moral and ethical implications of Proverbs (especially as contrasted with Solomon's amorous proclivities), SK might have had in mind, specifically, Proverbs 1:4, which presents the book as offering "to the young man knowledge and discretion."

November 19, 1950

[1]*Bime*. A central raised platform in traditional congregations that holds a table or desk on which the Torah is placed to be read.

[2]*Khazn* [Heb. Khazan]. Cantor.

[3]*A sheynem dank*. Thank you very much.

[4]*Seventy years of the psalm*. Psalm 90:10.

The days of our years are threescore years and ten,
Or even by reason of strength fourscore years;
Yet is their pride but travail and vanity;
For it is speedily gone, and we fly away.

January 8, 1951

[1]*Rakhmones*. Pity.

[2]*Pets*. SK appears to transliterate the English word here, seemingly oblivious to the fact that in Yiddish it is frequently a vulgarism for penises (sing. *pots*). For the most part, other of SK's forays into English in the manuscript have been dealt with silently.

[3]*Fartik*. Finished.

[4]*Days of the creation*. According to Genesis, the creatures SK mentions were created on days 5 and 6.

[5]*Sholem*. Peace. SK engages in a bit of word play here on his name and its meaning.

April 16, 1951

[1]*King David's virgin*. A virgin was brought to David in his old age in order to rejuvenate him. See I Kings 1:1-4.

[2]*The bread of affliction*. That is, matzah. This phrase is the standard translation of an early passage in the Haggadah, the text used for the home service at the Passover Seder. SK quotes the Aramaic original (Ha lakhma anya) directly. The "affliction," of course, is the Egyptian enslavement. But matzah is also the bread of "redemption" since the Israelites escaped to freedom with their bread baked before the dough could rise.

June 25, 1951

[1]*Yoyne is not yet a bar mitsve*. Younger than thirteen, Yoyne has not yet assumed his religious obligations as a "son of the commandment." But as his grandfather states, even a child knows better than to attack someone with an axe.

[2]*Mamzer*. Bastard. This is the sole instance of intemperate language in the journal, probably an indication of the intensity of SK's distress.

[3]*Society . . . woods*. The Boy Scouts. (The axe was apparently a hatchet.)

December 24, 1951

[1]*Shulkhen Orekh* [Heb. Shulkhan Arukh]. Literally, "The Prepared Table." A synoptic codification of Jewish law composed by Joseph Caro (1488-1575) and first published in Venice, 1564-65.

[2]*Returning the empties*. Beverages such as milk and soda were sold in deposit bottles, the deposit refunded on their return.

[3]*Buried*. Religious texts and Torah scrolls that are no longer serviceable are either buried or stored in a secure space called a genizah to prevent their desecration or destruction.

[4]*Gelt*. Money.

[5]*Nebekh*. Poor things (here used sarcastically).

[6]*Macy's and Gimbels*. For most of the twentieth century, Macy's and Gimbels department stores were arch rivals.

[7]*Dreydl*. A four-sided top, each bearing the first letter of a word in the Hebrew sentence translated as "A great miracle happened there," or, in Israel, "A great miracle happened here." The statements refer to the story of the Maccabees, in which a day's worth of the Temple's holy oil burned for eight. The top is used at Khanike in a penny-ante gambling game, the initials (this time, in the diaspora, standing for words in Yiddish) directing the course of play. SK implies that such sport is possible only in the security of freedom.

[8]*Other writings*. Canonical books other than those comprising the Torah. The books of Maccabees are not part of the Jewish canon. In Christianity, their canonicity varies among the multiple denominations.

February 5, 1952

[1]SK's dating is inexact. The Korean War began on June 25, 1950 with the North Korean Army's invasion of South Korea.

[2]*Nexdorikes*. Next-door neighbors. (The word conflates elements of English and Yiddish.)

[3]SK has learned something about Korean geography. His chief sources would undoubtedly have been Yiddish radio and newspaper reports.

[4]SK makes several broad assumptions: that Norman Krumbein's Jewish identity would be discovered by the German populace, that the discovery would provoke hostility, and that Germans were collectively murderous or guilty where Jews were concerned. Regardless of the historical accuracy of the last, especially, SK's beliefs and fears regarding these matters are understandable, given that WWII had ended only seven years earlier.

SK would have been astonished and then appalled to learn that Norman Krumbein was later sufficiently taken with one German girl to consider marrying her. According to Professor Redstone, that action was staved off through exchanges of letters between Norman and his mother, Reyzl, and between him and the Rothsteins.

March 9, 1952

[1]*Eyli, Eyli.* "My God, My God," a popular solemn song of Jewish suffering and religious affirmation originally included in an 1896 operetta with the intriguing title *The Hero and Bracha or the Jewish King of Poland for a Night.* See the *Encyclopedia Judaica* article about composer Jacob Koppel Sandler for additional information and commentary.

SK would likely have been familiar with the song, despite its secular origins, through recordings (often cantorial) broadcast on WEVD. He would have been in total sympathy with its sentiments in any case.

[2]*Adon Olom.* Hymn that typically concludes Sabbath morning services. Its first words, by which the piece is known, translate as "Lord of the world"; hence, SK's transition and Asher's subsequent remark.

May 12, 1952

[1]*When the shoyfer sounds to awaken the dead.* An event to occur at the coming of the Messiah and the subsequent return of living exiles and those revivified to Israel.

[2]*Yekhupets.* The Yiddish equivalent of "Timbuktu." Replying in the *Forward* (March 17, 2010) to a correspondent's query about the use of *Yah-Chupetz-Ville* as a reference "to places that were hard to find or get to," Philologus identifies Yehupetz [sic] as "the fictional name given by the great Yiddish writer [Sholem Aleichem] to the Ukrainian capital of Kiev [now Kyiv], then part of czarist Russia." How the name took on the meaning that the correspondent's parents, SK, and others attribute to it is unclear.

[3]*East New York.* A Brooklyn neighborhood similar to SK's Brownsville and bordering it on the east.

[4]Sholem. Not above repeating himself, SK again plays on the meaning of his name, peace. Cf. entry for January 8, 1951.

June 1, 1952

[1]*Shvues* [Heb. Shevuot]. A two-day festival that falls precisely seven weeks from the second day of Passover. As SK states, it is a holiday that commemorates the giving of the Law and marks the harvest of first fruits.

[2]*Blintses*. Filled crepes, with soft white cheese undoubtedly the filling here, as dairy foods are traditionally eaten on the holiday in question.

[3]*False noses*. Children often made "pug noses" of seed pods fallen from trees. The pod was split at the thick end and, sometimes with the aid of saliva, stuck to the nose in an upward curving arc.

[4]*Koyenim* (sing. *Koyen* [Heb. Kohanim/Kohen]). Priests.

[5]*Levi'im* (sing. *Levi*). Levites.

Traditional Judaism recognizes three classes of Jews: Priests, Levites, and Israelites. The status is inherited patrilineally. Orthodox and some Conservative congregations still recognize the distinctions, which have mainly ritual rather than social significance. In Temple days, Levites (members of the tribe of Levi as were the priests themselves) assisted and served the descendants of Aaron who comprised the priesthood. The washing of hands SK describes is a principal vestige of that ancient service. Such ablutions are performed in preparation for the priestly blessing recited on major holidays in traditional Ashkenazi congregations in the Diaspora. Studies of DNA markers have provided some biological evidence of priestly descent and continuity.

[6]*Droshe*. Sermon.

June 15, 1952

[1]*Ari learned his portion and haftoyre* [Heb. haftorah]. Ari's portion would most likely have been the final passage of the prescribed Torah reading for the week, Numbers 12:14-16. His haftorah, a prescribed selection from other canonical writings that follow weekly Torah readings, was, in this instance, Zechariah 2:14-4:7.

[2]*Also . . . with less*. SK taught Ari the cantillations for reading both the Torah and Haftorot. Therefore, Ari, did not have to rely entirely on rote memory when chanting. The added difficulty in preparing a Torah reading arises from the fact that the Torah scroll is written without vowel markings. Inexperienced readers must learn their portions by using a marked, printed version and/or recording. In Ari's case, successful reading would have been the result of both memory and word recognition.

[3]*Peretz*. Obviously, *parrots*, one of SK's misguided forays into English.

That *Peretz* is a Jewish personal name and surname, as in that of a renowned (secular) Yiddish writer to boot, might have contributed to his confusion.

[4]*Women threw . . . nuts*. Traditionally, sweets are tossed at a prospective groom called to the Torah before his wedding to signify a wish for a sweet married life. This custom has been extended to the bar mitzvah boy to enhance the celebration and perhaps to underscore the sweetness of the obligations he has now assumed as a member of the adult community. Here, the candies are bagged so as to be easily retrieved, primarily by younger boys, and thrown from the women's gallery. In egalitarian congregations, the practice is extended to prospective brides and to girls at their bat mitzvahs.

[5]*Talis* (Heb.Talit). Prayer shawl.

[6]*Simkhes Toyre* [Heb. Simkhat Torah]. Festival of rejoicing in the Law, observed at the end of the annual cycle of Torah readings; one of the few celebrations during which drinking to excess is permitted.

July 6,1952

[1]*All that I have written since*. The phrase implies the existence of entries other than the one concerning Ari's bar mitzvah, a clear indication that SK's journal was more extensive than the version extant.

September 10, 1952

[1]*Rabbi of Prague*. Yehuda Leyb ben Bezulel, sixteenth-century rabbi. His supposed creation and subsequent destruction of a golem is the best known of golem legends. Cf. entry for, June 27, 1940, note 5.

November 4, 1952

[1]*Milton Berel*. i.e., Milton Berle. SK's misspelling of the surname is possibly influenced by *Berel*'s being a fairly common Yiddish name for males. Cf. entry for September 12, 1948, note 3.

[2]*Kholovudvash* (Heb. khalav u'dvash). Milk and honey. "Mrs.

Kholovudvash" is Rivke Kahn's misconstruction of "Mrs. Calabash" to whom Jimmy Durante regularly bade goodnight at his program's end. If "Kholovudvash" seems a bit remote from "Calabash," one must take Rivke's hearing impairment into account and perhaps some familiarity with the Hebrew pronunciation as well. SK refers to her loss of hearing in the entries for February 14, 1950, June 25, 1951, and August 9, 1954 and to its progression in the first and third of these.

That Rivke Kahn is familiar with the phrase "milk and honey" is not especially surprising even if she is unlikely to have been literate in Hebrew, for the description of the land of Israel as one flowing with milk and honey is a commonplace, appearing in nine biblical books and sometimes more than once. SK uses the phrase himself in the entry for June 12, 1951.

The dancer SK mentions was Eddie Jackson, with whom Durante had teamed in vaudeville; the song is "Bill Bailey Won't You Please Come Home."

[3]*Midrash*. A scriptural commentary often grounded in parable and legend; more generically, a story.

[4]*Little wrestlers*. Kahn is referring to what was then known as "midget wrestling." His English-speaking contemporaries would have instantly recognized the phrase, not least because it was used in marketing and broadcasting the matches. At the time, the word "midget" was not generally considered offensive.

It is possible that SK, whose English was admittedly limited, did not understand the word, if it registered with him at all. He was certainly unlikely to have seen it in any of the Yiddish publications he might have read. On the other hand, as is evident from his reference to the prayer (see note 5 below), he recognizes these wrestlers' deviation from the norm.

[5]*Meshane Habriyes* [Heb. Meshane Habriyot]. The name and final words of the Hebrew blessing that praises God for the variety of His creation.

January 1, 1953

[1]*Corn beef, roll beef*. Standard spelling adds *ed* to *corn* and *roll*, but local pronunciation regularly dropped the *ed* ending. Roll beef, now difficult to find, was in fact rolled; its seasoning was similar to pastrami's.

[2]*Khazeray.* Junk; junk food; food (or other matter) fit for pigs.

[3]*Barton's.* A chocolatier that operated its own retail shops in New York City and elsewhere. It was especially popular in the Jewish community because of its line of kosher for Passover products. The brand still exists although the stores are long gone.

[4]*Sesperileh [sic] (this I can write but can't say).* SK's spelling of the word *sarsaparilla* reflects its pronunciation rather than its orthography. Why he might have had difficulty saying the word is a puzzle. However, since he was likely aware of its English spelling, the word (as written) might have appeared to be something of a tongue twister, as it would have to English speakers as well. Merriam-Webster provides a pronunciation that, like Kahn's, omits the first "r" and second "a", reducing the syllables from five to four.

[5]*Mandl bread.* A cookie containing almonds or other nuts that is sliced from baked loaves.

[6]*Half a quarter.* Two ounces, i.e., half of a quarter pound.

June 21, 1953

[1]Julius and Ethel Rosenberg were convicted of conspiracy to commit espionage. Their trial, appeals, and ultimate execution were an international cause celebre.

Except for conceding the possibility of wrongdoing, SK generally expresses the sentiments of the vast majority of Jews (and many others) at the time. They perceived the trial as essentially political and tinged with anti-Semitism. That the defendants, the prosecution and defense teams, and the presiding judge (but no jurors) were all Jews, introduced a fratricidal element as well.

According to attorney Louis Nizer, Judge Kaufman conducted himself appropriately. However, even he suggests that the judge might have been guilty of the kind of "reverse chauvinism" that SK implies here (*The Implosion Conspiracy* 31). In addition, Kaufman's statements at sentencing, including the claim that the defendants were responsible for the deaths of 50, 000 American troops in Korea, were certainly intemperate. Whether, as some have charged, Kaufman was a government puppet, controlled by J. Edgar Hoover and the F.B.I. in particular, he was clearly the "court Jew" in the eyes of the Jewish masses.

Support for the Rosenbergs went well beyond that of their co-religionists and the political left wing to include internationally known scientists of diverse backgrounds, heads of state, and the Pope.

Disclosures long after the fact tend to confirm Julius Rosenberg's espionage and either to absolve Ethel Rosenberg of the conspiracy for which both were tried and convicted or to qualify her culpability. However, the manner in which the trial was conducted and the underlying motives for that conduct are still controversial. For a brief introduction to the disclosures and their significance see the following articles:

Roberts, Sam. "Rosenberg Son Says Father Was Guilty of Spy Charge." *New York Times*. April 6, 2011. (http://cityroom.blogs.nytimes.com/2011/04/06/rosenberg-son-says-father-was-guilty-of-spy-charge/)

Roberts, Sam. "Figure in Rosenberg Case Admits to Soviet Spying." *New York Times*. September 11, 2008. (http://www.nytimes.com/2008/09/12/nyregion/12spy.html?pagewanted=all& r=0)

Kramer, Mark. "Why Ethel Rosenberg Should Not Be Exonerated." WBUR *Cognoscenti*. January 5, 2017. (https://www.wbur.org/cognoscenti/2017/01/05/julius-rosenberg-soviet-spying-mark-kramer)

As of this writing, attempts to pardon or exonerate Ethel Rosenberg are still ongoing.

[2]*Toyre without a Talmud*. Since the Torah is the law and the Talmud commentary upon it, Kahn implies that, in regard to the Rosenbergs, President Eisenhower took an untempered, legalistic, by the book approach.

[3]*We. . . chosen by the czar*. In the case of Spain and Germany, SK refers to court Jews. In nineteenth-century Russia, however, the government literally appointed official "rabbinical" spokesmen for Jewish communities. Such appointees had indifferent qualifications for their posts and were generally held in contempt by the populace they purported to represent.

September 20, 1953

[1]*Es past nit*. It is unfitting/unseemly/inappropriate.

[2]*The closing of the gates*. The final service for Yom Kippur is called *Neilah*, which means closing of the gates. SK's reference is to the phrase's metaphorical meaning, the last opportunity to repent and be forgiven.

[3]*Round . . . for the New Year*. Although the New Year begins with Rosh Hashanah, the sense of that beginning extends at least through Yom Kippur ten days later and arguably through the holidays of Succoth and Simchat Torah nearly two weeks after that. Because Rosh Hashanah also marks the anniversary of humanity's creation and the continuity of the life cycle, challah loaves for this holiday and the others that soon follow are round rather than long and braided. Similarly, although apples are eaten (with honey) on Rosh Hashanah primarily in accordance with the tradition of eating first fruits of the season, they too are round and so secondarily share the symbolism of the loaves. Rivke Kahn has apparently seen fit to endow her babke with similar symbolic qualities, the vagaries of her oven or preparation notwithstanding.

February 23, 1954

[1]*Balegole*. Ruffian; tough guy, with implications of crudeness and brawn without brains. Literally, a teamster.

[2]*Mishebeyrakh*. Conflation of two Hebrew words (mi shebeyrakh) that begin the prayer for recovery from illness and, hence, the name by which the prayer is known. When recited at the synagogue, it would have included Joe's Jewish name specifically.

SK is writing on a Tuesday. The prayer would be said on Thursday because it is traditionally offered on days when the Torah is read.

February 24, 1954

[1]*Bentsh Goyml*. Recite the blessing for escape from peril. The prayer is known in Hebrew as Birkat Hagomel. Here, contrary to his usual practice in dealing with Hebrew words of religious significance, SK writes the abbreviated form of "Hagomel" as pronounced in Yiddish.

[2]For a more elaborate account of Rivke Kahn's infection and surgery see the entry for August 24, 1911.

[3]*Umglik*. Misfortune.

September 2, 1954

[1]*About herself. . .not to die*. The Jewish population of Minsk was reduced to a few thousands, essentially on site, by the means described here. Only a small number were sent to their deaths at Sobibor. Gassing vans, mobile prototypes of the notorious gas chambers, had been used experimentally as early as December, 1941. During the period of Nazi occupation, ghetto security was sufficiently lax and resistance sufficiently well organized to have permitted a significant number of escapes (*Encyclopedia Judaica*; Exhibit, United States Holocaust Memorial Museum).

[2]*Speaking like an American*. SK suggests that his Yiddish sentences tend to be increasingly in the subject-verb-object pattern typical of English. As his first sample sentence demonstrates, that order is also possible in Yiddish. But there are other possibilities, for although the verbs of main clauses in Yiddish must be the second sentence element, other elements are not restricted. Even Kahn's simple example shows what is impossible—or at least unidiomatic—in English, as the subject in his second sample sentence follows the verb. Another possible English variant, "Every morning to shul he goes," is equally unacceptable.

September 30, 1954

[1]*Koyen*. Priest. (See entry for June 1, 1952, note 4.) Here, the right reserved to members of the priestly caste to be called up for the reading of the first Torah portion. SK describes and discusses the practice of auctioning off such honors as a means of fundraising. Typically, these honors centered on being called to the Torah and on opening and closing the Torah ark at various points in the service.

January 23, 1955

[1]*Free loan society*. Established in 1892, the Hebrew Free Loan Society continues its work today on a nonsectarian basis but still attends to the needs of impoverished Jews. One iteration of its web pages described how the organization might have functioned in the lives of SK and his contemporaries: ". . . A loan from the Hebrew Free Loan Society helped establish a pushcart venture that was a family's way out of poverty. For others, our loans helped avert eviction or bought essential medical care."

[2]*But I am . . . in whose mouth are no arguments*. Psalms 38:14-15. SK seems less concerned about his feelings than about suggestions for coping with his situation. The latter would have been "useful."

November 8, 1955

[1]*Gikher*. Faster

[2]*Mazl tov*. Good luck.

June 17,1956

[1]*Meydl*. Girl.

April 11, 1957

[1]*Shvartses*. Blacks. The word is used either descriptively or, more often, pejoratively, as in the instance of SK's neighbors here.

October 20, 1957

[1]SK's comment is a take on the rhetorical question "Does Macy's tell Gimbels?" with its implication of the obvious need for corporate (or other) secrecy. See also December 24, 1951, note 6.

[2]*The child . . .man*. A slight misquotation of "The child is father of the man" from Wordsworth's "My heart leaps up when I behold." Read independently, the line's aphoristic wisdom undoubtedly appealed to SK, although his unexpected citation of it remains startling, if not astounding.

[3]*Gut gezogt*. Well said.

October 16, 1958

[1]*Sounds*. SK refers to diacritical marks representing vowel sounds (especially) since the Hebrew alphabet itself lacks such indicators.

[2]*Sheyndele*. The diminutive of *Sheyndel,* which is itself a diminutive *of Sheyne*.

[3]*And a lifetime ago . . . two years old*. Elsewhere, in the entry for March 3, 1930, SK gives Gitl's age at death as less than a year. The discrepancy here possibly indicates a lapse in memory.

[4]*Kneydl*. Matzah ball; dumpling.

November 3, 1958

[1]SK confuses Reyzl's foster child, Dveyre (see entry for May 7, 1950), with his long dead infant daughter. His second reference to Gitl, below, treats her as a surviving child. Such slips hint at SK's mental decline that is seen full blown in the entry immediately following. Again fully lucid in the entry after that, Kahn is aware that he is failing both physically and mentally.

[2]*Yenem velt*. The next world.

[3]Eastern Parkway. Dashevsky's son was undoubtedly practicing (and probably living) in the section of this street known as "Doctor's Row" some miles to the west of Brownsville.

February 7, 1959

[1]Date. This is the sole entry written on the Sabbath. Its content makes the reason for such breaches of SK's religious practice abundantly clear.

[2]SK's inaccurate attempts at his son-in-law's Jewish name compound the confusion here. The name was, in fact, *Moyshe*.

April 26, 1959

[1]*Schapiro*. A bottler of kosher wines based in New York's Lower East Side. It boasted wine so thick "you can almost cut it with a knife."

²*Sfard*. A Sephardic Jew.

³*Omeyn*. Amen.

October 12, 1960

¹This entry and the one that follows are obviously not the work of SK. They were written by his grandson, Allan Redstone. For further explanation, see the Foreword.

July 25, 1996

¹Placing a small stone or pebble on the grave or tombstone is a Jewish custom whose origins remain obscure, but today the act is frequently regarded as a sign of having visited and therefore of having remembered the deceased.

Appendix A. The Ethical Will of Solomon Kahn

¹*A hundred years*. The conventional wish (or blessing) for someone's longevity is 120 years, the life span of Moses. Since the passage is replete with references to long life, SK might simply have used 100 as marking a prodigious span. However, he might also have been prompted by the following from Isaiah 65:20:

There shall be no more thence an infant of days, nor an old man,
That hath not filled his days;
For the youngest shall die a hundred years old . . . .

²*You should not worry about what I write here*. Here and elsewhere in the document, SK writes as if communicating with his offspring in the present. The emotion involved in composing the will might easily account for some irregularities in both chronological focus and structure.

³*Bank*. According to the late Jerome Wexler, when the bankbook was found, its funds had been withdrawn and the account closed. It had never held more than $43. At the time SK dated the will, the balance was $27.14. Regrettably, the document itself no longer survives.

⁴*Yeshive*. SK perhaps uses this word for *seminary*, the Yiddish *seminar* being far less familiar if known to him at all.

[5]*And I ask . . .whoever has more should give more.* SK appears to look beyond his death to his children's possible support for Rivke, assuming that he will predecease her. In light of the entry for January 23, 1955, which records their squabbling over financial support for their parents, his message to them here is clearly warranted.

[6]*Mishnayes.*Selectons from the Mishnah, a topical compilation of the oral (rabbinic) law composed by Rabbi Judah the Prince about 200 CE. For the connection between mourning and Mishnaic study see "Study in the House of Mourning." *Jewish Funeral Guide*: http://www.jewish-funeral-guide.com/tradition/study.htm.

[7]*You will live to have great-grandchildren as I have.* Since SK's first grandchild was born on December 19, 1948 (see entry for that date), Kahn appears to have revisited this document after having composed the bulk of it more than a decade earlier but without changing the original date.

[8]*But if. . . make us very happy.* SK seems to suggest that the level of his offspring's devotion is not where he would have it be. Professor Redstone can recall no significant falling away of which his grandfather would have been aware, save that Asher Kahn operated his business on the Sabbath and all but the high holidays of Rosh Hashanah and Yom Kippur. The sentiment of this sentence and the one that follows accord well with Proverbs 23:24-25, a possible source:

The father of the righteous will greatly rejoice;
And he that begetteth a wise child will have joy of him.
Let thy father and thy mother be glad,
And let her that bore thee rejoice.

[9]*Rivke Kahn.* SK has affixed his wife's name and has written on her behalf throughout. However, there is little reason to believe that she was at all aware of the document.

[10]*16 Sh'vat 5696.* The date corresponds to February 9,1936. That this is shortly after the first anniversary of SK's retirement is perhaps significant, the event itself having possibly prompted him to write the will in the face of diminished health and increasing age. One may speculate that SK's spirits might have been buoyed by his daughters' marriages in 1935 but also that their departure from the Kahn nest later compounded any underlying depression. The entry for March 24, 1936 clearly indicates that retirement was still a sensitive issue for SK.

Appendix B. The Kahn Family: Names and Relationships

[1]In the entry for September 8, 1914, SK reports that prior to emigrating his family name had been Kagan. It is assumed that those of his brothers who remained in Europe retained that name. SK's survivors confirm that his brothers in the United States all bore the Kahn surname.

No information about the spouses of Menakhem Mendl and Naftali Kagan is available. Whether Menakhem Mendl married is unknown; however, Naftali's marriage is established by his granddaughter Tsipora's appearance late in the journal.

[2] Morris Bienenfeld was Freydl Elbaum's third husband. The names of the other two are unknown.

[3]Both Claire Wexler and Abraham Kahn confirmed that Rokhl Elbaum had been married, but neither they nor Solomon Kahn's grandchildren could recall her husband's last name.

[4]Like her married surname, whether Big Reyzl was an Elbaum is unknown. The kinship might well have been matrilineal.

[5]SK uses only the expanded diminutive form of Cheryl Rothstein's Jewish name.

[6]Tsipora would have been a Kagan at birth. (See note 1 above.) Since SK corresponded with Tsipora after her marriage, he must have known her married name, but no written record or memory of it remains.